S0-ARG-697

AN OFFICIAL KILLING

Molly Sutton Mysteries 7

NELL GODDIN

Beignet Books

Copyright © 2017 by Nell Goddin

ISBN: 978-1-949841-07-7

All rights reserved.

No part of this book may be reproduced in any form or by any electronic or mechanical means, including information storage and retrieval systems, without written permission from the author, except for the use of brief quotations in a book review.

To Nancy Kelley, editor extraordinaire.

CONTENTS

❄ I ❄

2005

Josette approached the house on rue Malbec with jangly nerves. She was eighteen and no stranger to work, but her new job as house-maid for Monsieur Coulon was entirely different from the farm chores she was used to. Monsieur Coulon was the mayor of Castillac, the *most famous person* she had ever met, which made her hands feel clammy whenever she thought of it.

She stood on the street for a moment before ringing the bell, trying to gather her confidence. The house was built of the warm golden limestone that the Dordogne is famous for, and it was four full floors, the tallest building she had ever entered. She looked up and saw that the blue shutters were still closed and wondered if opening all of them each morning would be one of her tasks. Counting, she saw twelve pairs just on the street side of the building.

Josette reached to ring the bell but then paused. She smoothed the apron she had put on over her blue jeans while a sudden panic swept through her that she'd chosen the wrong

3

thing to wear. What if Monsieur, no—*Mayor* Coulon wished her to wear something more proper, even a dress?

As the young woman stood on the sidewalk unable to summon the courage to ring the bell, the front door of the mayor's house opened and the mayor himself appeared.

"Ah, bonjour, Josette!" he said, his voice booming as though he were making a speech to a crowd. He was balding, and his strategy for bucking this trend was to call in the classic comb-over, which Josette stared at before forcing herself to look away. The mayor was something of a gourmand, as his large belly indicated, but despite the belly and the comb-over he was not an unattractive man, at least that was what he told himself when he faced the mirror each morning.

Josette dipped a small curtsy, as her mother had taught her that morning, and mumbled a greeting, though she could not quite meet Coulon's eye, feeling afraid that he might not approve of her.

"Come in, come in," he said, making a sweeping gesture. "And please, call me Maxime. I must check the mail for something I should have received yesterday. Wait in the foyer and I will be right with you." He walked to the mailbox, his eyes on Josette, congratulating himself on finding such a very pretty house-maid. She had enviable curves, not the stick-straight boyish figure that seemed to be in fashion lately, and her hair fell in soft chestnut waves around her pleasing face.

Josette stepped into the house, marveling at the high ceilings and the small chandelier in the foyer. It was so bright compared to the dark farmhouse where she lived, and she squinted at the broad staircase curving up to the next floor and at the red carpet that unspooled down the center of it.

When the mayor came back in, he showed Josette all around the four floors of the house, as well as the small backyard where the clothesline was, along with a neat vegetable garden that he tended on the weekends. He described her duties thoroughly and made it clear that if she had any questions, she had only to ask. She would be responsible for dusting, vacuuming, polishing furniture and silver, as well as laundry. As Coulon described each job, Josette nodded. He admired her reticence, much preferring the sound of his own voice to anyone else's, and even more he admired her substantial backside as she went up the stairs ahead of him.

Those blue jeans, however...they were too modern, too casual, he thought. It was nearly an insult for her to be wearing them as a member of his staff, even if the staff was comprised only of Josette.

She was a country girl who had never been to a big city, and even Bergerac only rarely. Her life on the farm had been isolated, and she knew little about, well, anything but raising chickens and how to grow lettuce. The Barbeaus had no computer and the reception on their ancient television was poor. She had paid little attention in school and all she knew of the wide world was what her mother, Madame Barbeau, told her, along with stray tidbits from her younger brother, who went to the market in Bergerac twice a week to sell their poultry and produce.

But as of that beautiful July day she had left the farm behind, and with Madame Barbeau's urging, Josette intended to make the most of the opportunity at 1 rue Malbec.

ॐ

PROMPTLY AT FOUR O'CLOCK, Josette's younger brother Julien pulled up in front of the mayor's house in a beat-up truck. It was Wednesday, a smaller market day in Bergerac than Saturday's but still quite lucrative; he had sold out of chicken in a matter of hours now that it was June and tourists were beginning to appear at the markets, swelling the pool of potential customers. For several months he had been skimming a little off the day's take instead of turning it all over to his mother, and on that Wednesday, since he had to pick up his sister later in the afternoon, Julien had gone to a bar to treat himself to lunch.

Madame Barbeau believed that restaurant meals were hell on earth, or perhaps even that Satan himself worked in restaurant kitchens, spitting in all the dishes; Julien did not know the precise details of his mother's objections because he had learned to tune her out years ago when she got started on one of her Subjects. In any case, he enjoyed the meal even more knowing its mere occurrence would be appalling to his mother, and availed himself of one more beer than he should have, arriving at rue Malbec rather worse for wear.

"Joseeehhh-tuh!" he called, singsong, leaning against the hood of the truck. When she did not immediately appear, he shook a Gitane out of a crumpled pack and lit up. Julien didn't mind waiting. There was nothing to hurry home to except for a barn cat he was friendly with. And the barn cat was a biter.

He was halfway through his second cigarette when Josette let herself out of the front door, carefully closed it, and ran to the car.

"So?" asked Julien. "How was it?"

"Awesome," said Josette.

"Really. Cleaning some guy's house is awesome? You *are* simple-minded."

"Not that part, you lunk. I'm talking about the house. You see it's four whole floors? And each floor is *huge*, Julien. Room after room. Like for a king."

"You didn't do well in history if you think that a king would have spent even one night in a dinky house like that."

"It's not dinky!"

Julien laughed, pleased at having gotten under his sister's skin so easily. The farm was a forty-five minute drive from Castillac and they drove the rest of the way without talking, Julien daydreaming about the voluptuous waitress who had just served his lunch, and Josette imagining each room of the mayor's house in turn, trying to remember the details, both for her own pleasure and because she knew her mother would have a pile of questions about all of it.

They pulled up to the farmhouse just as a drizzle started. Dark clouds loomed up behind the barn and Josette saw that the chickens had all roosted, preparing for a storm.

"Hey, what time do I need to take you in tomorrow?" Julien asked. "If you would just learn how to drive, you could take the truck yourself."

Josette shook her head. "Nine o'clock, and I can't be late," she said, running to the front door, anxious to tell her mother about the day before she forgot anything.

Madame Barbeau sat by the fireplace in the kitchen. The farmhouse was very old, and the fireplace immense, big enough to roast a deer. Three hundred years' worth of soot blackened the mantel and ceiling. The windows were small and infrequent, the room dark and dingy.

"Sit," said Madame Barbeau to her daughter. "Julien? Where are you going with that envelope?"

Julien stopped on his way through and reluctantly gave his mother the rest of the day's take. "Sold everything early on," he said. "On Saturday, give me more whole birds."

Madame Barbeau nodded, thumbing through the bills with satisfaction. "So, Josette? Speak up."

Josette opened a package of cookies and sat down, chewing. "It was awesome, Maman."

"You say everything is awesome. I don't even know what the word means anymore, and you certainly don't either."

Josette ate another cookie.

"First tell me about the mayor. Is he a good boss? Clear with his instructions? Not too harsh? Of course, you won't really know until you make a mistake. That's the test. You didn't happen to make a mistake on your first day?"

"No, Maman," said Josette.

"All right. Good. Come on, girl, speak up. What is the inside of the house like? Does he have paintings? They can be very valuable, you know. How about silver?"

"I polish the silver, on Tuesdays. This was Wednesday." Josette saw her mother was waiting for more, so she added, "It's Wednesday so I didn't do anything with the silver. I didn't even see any, apart from some candlesticks in the dining room. I dusted the whole house, with rags and a big stick with feathers on the end of it. Big puffy feathers, like."

"Ostrich," said Madame Barbeau.

"Yeah, well, that took a really long time. It's four whole floors, this house. A skyscraper, pretty much."

Madame Barbeau was struck by a fit of coughing but still managed to give her daughter a wilting look. "How can you be eighteen years old and know so little?"

Josette ate another cookie.

"And please, stop making a pig of yourself with those packaged sweets. I don't know why Julien insists on bringing them home. Those cookies are made in factories, you understand, not a kitchen. They are no better than food from a restaurant. And as I hope I have made clear…"

She was off, having found an entry point to one of her Subjects, and Josette arranged her expression to look as though she were paying attention, but was instead dreaming of the house on rue Malbec, touching the silk-covered pillows and the heavy curtains, running her hands over a sculpture of a swan that stood in the mayor's bedroom, and leaving the sooty farm kitchen and her scolding mother far, far behind.

2

The *mairie*, where the mayor worked, was only a short walk from his house. His habit was to have coffee and toast with butter and jam at eight o'clock, and then stroll to his office right around nine. It was a pleasure to work at the *mairie*, since the various people who worked under him knew what they were doing and made his life rather easy. They knew which forms to fill out for what occasion—and there seemed to be an infinity of occasions, the French government being extremely fond of forms —but Monsieur Coulon didn't have to worry about any of that, thanks to their abundant expertise.

At the moment, the end of a too-hot July, there was practically nothing for him to do. Sometimes he was asked by the examining magistrate to look into a matter, making inquiries and acting as a sort of policeman. When nothing else was going on he decided his main job should be the promotion of good spirits in the village, and he took that part of his job seriously, walking through the streets and greeting whomever he passed, even going so far as to keep notes in a small notebook he carried about how many people he had spoken to from day to day. At the office, he did not insist on formality, which the others liked him for.

The week after Josette had begun to work for him, Coulon took a call from Charles Mangey, the mayor of Bergerac.

"Maxime, I just heard from a friend, an official in Périgueux who knows about such things, that there's going to be clamping down on black market activity, just wanted to give you a head's up."

"Black market?" said Coulon. "Not sure that's much of a problem in Castillac. I can't imagine anyone trafficking in stolen kidneys or exotic drugs at the Café de la Place," he said with a chuckle.

Charles took a deep breath. "You watch too many American movies," he said. "The black market isn't only for things like that. It covers an enormous amount of ground, from pirated software to cigarettes. Essentially, any transaction where the government is cheated out of taxes, that's black market. How is it possible you do not know this, Maxime?"

"I didn't realize that's what you were talking about," said Coulon defensively. "Perhaps a bit of the work in the village is under the table...ah, you can't blame people, can you? The VAT has gotten ridiculous."

"Maxime," said the other mayor, "I needn't remind you that we cannot hold ourselves up as protectors of the common good while turning a blind eye to illegal behavior, no matter what you might think of the policies coming out of Paris."

"Yes, yes, of course, I wasn't saying that. Though I don't see how much I can do about the kind of thing you're talking about. If a homeowner pays the plumber with cash, or partly cash, what am I supposed to do about it? I'm not present during the transaction and there is no evidence of its having taken place."

"Bank records, Maxime," André said patiently. "Look out for cash deposits. After all, cash doesn't just appear out of thin air, does it?"

"Ah, if only it did!" laughed Coulon. "Thank you for letting me know. As I said, I doubt there is much illegal activity here in

Castillac, at least on any scale worth worrying about, but I will have a word with the bank manager in any case. Now tell me about the music festival next week—are you making any special plans about parking?"

The two mayors spoke for another ten minutes about upcoming events in their respective towns, and then cordially said goodbye.

After hanging up, Coulon sat for a moment looking out of his window. Rue Balzac was empty except for Madame Vargas's dog Yves, who was trotting confidently down the sidewalk before turning onto rue Malbec. "Black market" sounded so exotic, like something in a stylish film, Coulon thought. Perhaps there is money to be made here in Castillac in more ways than I have figured.

A slow smile spread across his face as he contemplated a number of targets that instantly sprang to mind. Candy from a baby, he thought, suddenly hungry for lunch.

ò.

OVER THE COURSE of several months, Josette settled into the job at the mayor's house happily enough, though certain aspects turned a little strange. At first it had been smooth sailing, with Coulon seeming to be the most genial of employers. Each weekday morning, Julien dropped off Josette, and she set about the day's chores with enough enthusiasm and competence to please her boss. She was meticulous with silver-polishing, making sure to get every speck of tarnish even in the crevices of the ornate flower pattern on the flatware. She made the mayor's bed fresh every day, plumping the duvet to cloud-like softness and making sure the pillowcases were washed and dried in the sunshine, as he preferred. Coulon set the schedule of what she was to do when, though he liked to fiddle with it, sometimes changing the day's chores for reasons she did not understand. But what did she care? The job paid well and allowed her to spend the bulk of her day in a stately house, surrounded by beautiful things. It was ten times better than the chicken house, she told Julien, though the truth was that she missed farm life and preferred the company of the birds to that of Coulon by a wide margin.

In the third week, Coulon had led her into one of the guest bedrooms and told her to change into an outfit he had gotten for her to wear during her working hours. "It's the least I can do, providing appropriate clothes for the job," he said by way of explanation. Josette did not entirely understand the concept of 'appropriate for the job,' and with a shrug put on the black dress with a tiny apron hemmed with a frill. The bodice of the dress was tight but not so tight that she wanted to complain, and the skirt was full, short but not too short, and even had an underskirt of tulle, which Josette considered wonderfully fancy, having never had the chance to wear anything remotely like it before.

The outfit was not to last, however. After two weeks, Coulon led her into the guest bedroom once more, and told her that given the heat of August and the lack of air conditioning in his house, he thought it only kind to provide her with a summer outfit that would make her strenuous work more comfortable to perform. She looked doubtfully at the bed, where he had laid out a camisole and pantalettes made by La Perla, a name not familiar to her.

"They are the finest money can buy," he said, trying and failing to sound casually authoritative. "It was cruel of me to expect you to run up and down stairs all day in this heat without any concession whatsoever to your comfort. This should go a long way to ameliorating the situation. And," he added, going to the Empire chest of drawers and sliding open the narrow top drawer. "I have provided more selection, so that you may decide for yourself what you feel like wearing on any particular day."

Josette was taken aback, as any young woman might have been, though other young women would likely have understood

Coulon's motivation more clearly. "You want me to...clean house wearing underwear?"

Coulon chuckled. "Oh, I don't think of it as *under*wear," he said, as though the suggestion was silly. "I think of it simply as something luxurious, something of great quality and high-class, that will make your day much more pleasant. Tell you what: try it for a week, and then decide. If you find there is anything about wearing La Perla that you do not like—if it impedes your work in some way, or you feel self-conscious, anything at all—then I will whisk it all away without another word. After all, the point is to make your day better, Josette. How does that sound?"

Josette did not feel she could go against him, and did not feel especially strongly about it in any case. She was used to the freedom of living deep in the country, where she could skinny-dip in the pond or strip off her clothes to feel the spring sun on her skin. And raising various farm animals over the years gave her that sort of matter-of-fact physicality typical of people whose early years are spent close to nature. Given all that, the young woman did not have an abundance of modesty, and while she regretted the loss of the fancy underskirt, these new items did look very beautiful, and were heavenly to touch.

She agreed to try it. And when Coulon left the room and closed the door behind him, she hurried out of her jeans and T-shirt and into the sumptuous underwear, marveling at its softness. It was like wearing nothing at all, she thought, taking a look at herself in the mirror in the armoire door, and liking what she saw.

Thus the new normal began. Julien continued to drive his sister back and forth to work, even on the days there was no market at which to sell the farm's bounty. On market days, he continued to skim a bit of the profit for himself and usually took himself out to lunch, and Josette spent the five days of the work-week cleaning the mayor's house with industry, while wearing very expensive lingerie.

Neither of them said a word to their mother about what went

on in Castillac. Madame Barbeau asked a thousand questions of them both, but without having to say a word to each other, they answered with a stream of blandness along with a nearly complete lack of detail, and the poor woman was frustrated to the point of apoplexy. She insisted Josette hand over her earnings when she was paid, bi-weekly, but Coulon paid in cash and Josette had learned from her brother to hold back a little each week, gently adding to her nest-egg, which was wrapped in plastic bags and hidden in the rafters of the chicken house.

&

TOWARD THE END of September it was still hot, and Josette was grateful to be wearing something light, especially on the days when her work was strenuous. She kept the black dress hung up in the guest room armoire in case someone rang the doorbell, or she needed to put something on so she could go outside to hang the wash.

On one wash-day, she had the dress on over the La Perla underwear and was on the point of opening the door to go out, holding a heavy basket of wet laundry, when she noticed a woman in the alley, lurking by the back gate. Josette set down the basket and moved out of sight, then peeked from behind the curtain. The wall to the back garden was high, but the woman must have found something to stand on because her head popped up; she was staring at the clothesline, at the silk pantalettes and camisole that Josette had hung out earlier that morning. Josette saw her reach a hand out—was she going to steal them right off the clothesline? The nerve of this strange person!

But one of the neighbors shouted about something and the woman pulled her hand back. She looked up at the house and Josette stayed very still, willing her to move on.

What business is it of hers, she thought crossly, waiting a few minutes after the woman had walked on down the alley and out of sight. She yanked the basket up and went outside, pegging the wash to the line aggressively, then carefully taking the dry La Perla things inside, folding them, and putting them in the narrow drawer where they belonged.

"I'm still not used to village life," she said to Julien on the drive home that day. "Can you imagine, a stranger about to reach out and touch the wash on the line? I didn't know whether to run out and yell at her or say nothing. I don't...I don't know the rules."

"Eh, it's not that complicated," he answered. "It's just the same as you learned in school. How to greet people, when to keep your mouth shut. Just pretend—who was that teacher in primaire, Monsieur Séverin? Just imagine what he would tell you, and do that."

"I don't like people being nosy," she said, raking her fingers through her hair.

"You get that from Maman," her brother said, rolling his eyes. "People are naturally interested in other people. Doesn't have to be a bad thing. Of course, Maman thinks it is bad, but you do know she is crazy as a loon?"

Josette looked out the window and did not answer.

3

2007

A stunning June morning, and Molly Sutton, proprietress of the *gîte* business at La Baraque, was pruning roses when her pal Frances rode a bicycle across the lawn, shouting and zigzagging all the way. Bobo ran back and forth barking her head off.

"I don't think I have ever seen you ride a bike," said Molly, laughing, and kissing Frances on both cheeks.

"I don't remember ever learning. I never had one single day of being sporty my whole life. But Nico dared me. Or not dared exactly, but he said he didn't think I could do it. Can you imagine!"

"Wait, you're insulted because he didn't think you could do something that you can't actually do?"

"But I *can*, Molly, that's point number one. And number two, I never wanted to. So...well, a lot of good you are!" She crossed her arms and pretended to be mad.

"You must be about to die of thirst, picking the hottest day of the year to start exercising. Come get a cold drink."

"I won't say no," said Frances, letting the bike clatter to the ground and sending the orange cat streaking for safety under the bushes. "So let's see, it's...what the hell day is it? Village life has me so relaxed I can't keep track anymore."

"It's Thursday. I *have* to keep track because unlike some people, I work for a living."

"I don't know which people you're trying and failing to throw shade on. I happen to have sent off a new jingle this very morning, for your information. And I expect the renumeration to be quite handsome, thank you very much."

"A lot handsomer than the *gîte* business is turning out to be, though I shouldn't complain. There's a lot to be said about doing work you actually like."

"Cheers," said Frances, clinking her glass of Perrier with her friend's. Molly had left Boston and her fundraising job when her marriage broke up, and come all the way to Castillac in search of a new life. A wild plan, some would say reckless, but so far it had turned out better than she had thought possible.

"So what's your line-up this week? Anybody interesting coming?"

"I have my first repeat customer, which is nice."

"I hope it's that Eugenia Perry, I really wanted to get to know her better."

"Afraid not. It's Wesley Addison."

"The weird dude? The one who killed his wife?"

"He didn't kill his wife. At least, I don't think so. Sometimes the dead bodies pile up so fast around here that we think natural deaths aren't even a thing."

"Good point. I just want you to be a little more careful, after what happened last winter when La Baraque was fully booked and—"

"I know, I know. I *am* more careful now. Much as I hated to do it, I had a lock put on my bedroom door, and a new one on the French doors to the terrace. And while I'll admit that at first

Wesley Addison made me want to poke my eyes out with forks, once I got to know him, I was won over."

"Because you are a marshmallow."

Molly shrugged. "You and Nico want to come over for dinner next Friday night?"

"Who else is coming?"

"You have no manners."

Frances laughed. "I mean, yes, we'd be delighted. Will it be you and Ben?"

"I can invite Wesley if you beg."

Frances laughed. "Make that vegetable thing I adore so much? Listen, I'm glad you invited us, because there's something we'd like to talk to you about."

Molly raised her eyebrows.

"Well, you know..."

"Good heavens, Franny, out with it! This isn't one of your visionary business ideas is it?"

"No, no, nothing like that. It's...it's about the wedding. I'm just...one minute I'm all gung-ho, and the next, I just want to run for the hills," she said, her voice so low Molly could barely hear her.

"For someone who's been married as many times as you, you sure are skittish."

"That's exactly why. Duh."

"Okay, what about it? Have you and Nico set a date? Are you going to have it in Castillac? You know I'd be happy to do it here at La Baraque, if you want to have it outside. Or I can help you find something fancier in Bergerac if that's what you've got in mind."

"I know I brought it up, but listening to you jump in with all those questions...well, you're right, I *am* skittish about the whole thing. It's not Nico, you know I love him to pieces. It's just...my sketchy marital history, you know? Anyway, the idea of having a traditional sort of wedding, with me walking down the aisle and all that—I'm just…not sure I can go through that. *Again*. Seems like for a third marriage, you ought to do something different besides get a new dress."

"The *guy* is different, Franny, that's all that matters."

"Maybe," said Frances doubtfully. "But you can't say symbolism means nothing or why would anyone bother? Anyway, Nico and I were wondering what you and Ben think about an out-of-town wedding. What do you think about going somewhere and celebrating, just the four of us?"

Molly scrunched up her face. "I don't know. Give me some time to think about it?"

"You're not without your own marriage scars, I know."

Molly nodded. Her only marriage had ended in divorce, though her new life in France had done a pretty thorough job of healing most of those old wounds. It was not another marriage she was desperate for, but a child. And as her fortieth birthday loomed on the horizon, her prospects were feeling dimmer and dimmer.

"Want an almond croissant?" she said abruptly, because almond croissants could make anyone feel better, even if they were a little on the stale side.

FRANCES HAD ONLY JUST CAREENED off, looking as though she were going to topple over any minute, when Molly heard a brisk rap on the door.

"Lapin!" she cried, surprised to see her friend on the front step. She almost always saw him at Chez Papa, the local bistro where she had meals or cocktails several times a week.

"I'm sorry to bother you at home," he said nervously.

"Gracious, Lapin, you look distraught! Come in and tell me what has happened. Can I get you something to drink?"

"A glass of something would not be amiss."

Molly checked the half-drunk bottle on the kitchen counter. "Côtes du Rhone okay?"

"Yes, yes," he said, waving his hand in the air. "Oh, Molly, I hope you don't mind my coming to you, but you're the only woman I—I mean, you know I am fond of women, very fond, it's just that—I can *talk* to you. Of course you are extremely lovely, I don't mean—"

"*Mon Dieu*, Lapin. Relax. Just tell me what's wrong." She gave him the glass of wine and they sat down together on the lumpy sofa.

"It's Anne-Marie." Lapin gulped his wine. "She wants...she wants to get *married*."

Was it something in the water? Was the rest of the village going to come trooping through her living room expressing angst about marriage, or was Lapin the last in line?

Seeing his tortured expression, Molly suppressed a laugh. When she first came to the village and met Lapin, he had been the sort of guy who drooled over women but never got very far with any of them, partly because of his boorish behavior and also, Molly and others suspected, because he was actually too afraid for anything to happen. But then he had met Anne-Marie, and she had seen something in him that other women had missed, and they had been happy together for longer than anyone would have guessed.

"Okay, so she wants to get married. Is this actually a problem? From what I've seen, you and Anne-Marie get on like gangbusters."

"Well, yes. Yes, we do. But that's exactly my point. Why change something when it's working so well?"

"Do you want to have a family?" Molly asked, valiantly trying to put her own feelings aside.

"Family? You mean *children?*" Lapin's eyes were like saucers.

Molly laughed lightly. "Yes, children. Has Anne-Marie said anything about wanting them?"

"We haven't talked about it." Lapin took another large sip of wine. "Thing is—you remember, Molly, my mother died when I was just a boy. And my father, he was...difficult. Very tough."

"Abusive."

"One could say that."

Molly raised her eyebrows.

"All right, yes, abusive. I don't want to complain, I'm quite aware that others have had it much worse than I—"

"Lapin, that's neither here nor there."

"Huh?"

"I'm just saying that the fact that others have it worse has nothing to do with how it was for you. It's not a competition."

Lapin's eyes got wide again. "I have to think about that...but on its face, it seems quite wise. I knew it was a good idea to come see you." He polished off his glass and placed it carefully on the coffee table. "But please, tell me how to get Anne-Marie to forget this crazy idea! I was so happy before this."

Molly shrugged. "I'm afraid that's beyond my powers. And yours, to be honest. My advice is to ask her for some time to think it over, tell her how you feel about her, and let the whole thing sink in a little bit. You're freaking out now, but maybe once you get used to the idea..."

"I have never seen myself as a married man," said Lapin. "A roué, perhaps, a man about town..."

Molly somehow managed not to roll her eyes. "Couples need to do what's right for them. Maybe marriage is the thing, maybe it's not. You'll have to figure that out for yourself. Now, I don't mean to rush you out, Lapin, but I've got a long list of chores to get through today."

"Understood, understood. Gîte business treating you right?"

"Not bad. I've got four guests leaving, and three coming this Saturday, including a repeater."

"Quite a compliment! It's not as though Castillac offers a bounty of sightseeing."

"There's plenty within an easy drive," Molly said, feeling defensive even though she realized Lapin was only making conversation and meant no insult. "And some guests come for the peace and quiet."

"Ha! That's what the village used to have, before you showed up. Now that the Master Sleuth is a resident of Castillac, seems like we have a murder every other week."

Irritably, Molly said, "Not fair. There's been nothing since February, and here it is June."

Lapin just laughed. "I think that proves my point more than yours!"

"Like I said, work to do," Molly said, standing up and pointedly walking to the front door. All the talk of marriage had put her in a foul mood, and there was nothing to do about it but spend some quality hours in the garden, preferably hacking at things with a sharp object and working up a good sweat.

❧ 4 ❧

Mayor Coulon tapped his fingertips on the table at Café de la Place, stuck in the uncomfortable ambivalence of wishing his ex-wife would hurry up and get there while at the same time dreading her arrival. He signaled to the Pascal, the server with movie-star good looks, who strolled right over.

"What can I do for you, Mayor?" said Pascal.

"I'm waiting for Odile," Coulon said, not hiding his irritation.

"Would you like a drink in the meantime?"

"Just bring me...do you have a plate of something, crudités?" Coulon made intermittent efforts to control his waistline, and silently congratulated himself on choosing vegetables in such a stressful circumstance.

Just then Coulon caught a glimpse of Odile making her way down the sidewalk. It was Monday and the streets weren't packed, but there were enough pedestrians that she ran into people she knew, stopping to exchange kisses and small talk before continuing toward the café. Coulon saw very well that she was not trying to be on time, was in fact purposely going to be late just to annoy him, and he tapped his fingertips faster and faster until an old woman at the next table shot him a look that made him stop.

"Bonjour, Maxime," Odile said when she finally dropped into the seat across from him.

"Bonjour, Odile," he said, forcing himself to sound more pleasant than he felt.

"Did you order?"

"Of course not. I waited for you. Something that feels quite familiar, I might add."

Odile laughed. She was a put-together woman dressed in a smart suit, her auburn hair in a neat chignon. As the owner of a number of successful beauty product shops, Odile was confident and independent. Her working habits—and failure to defer to Maxime—had been a great source of marital discord.

Pascal appeared with a plate of crudités, a basket of bread, and a pot of pâté. "Maman made her special recipe, don't miss it!" he said with a wink as he passed them each a menu. He took their drink orders and then went on to the next table, where a harried mother and three young children were waving their hands for his attention as though on the point of mass starvation.

"I'm going to cut to the chase," said Odile. "I know you enjoy the fruits of your position, Maxime, including hiring only the prettiest assistants you can possibly find—"

Maxime opened his mouth to argue but Odile held up one finger. "I'm not here to argue about that. I am merely pointing out—"

"Odile, how I run the mairie is none of your business beyond the interest of any citizen of Castillac. And I'll have you know that every single person working in that office is highly qualified. Overly so, actually. And for you to—"

"—what I want is for you to allow the building permits to go through on my store on rue Picasso. All the paperwork has been filed, the staff should have finished its review last month. You know perfectly well you are blocking the project out of spite."

"I haven't the slightest idea what you are talking about," Maxime said airily, though he knew quite well. She wanted to open a third store right here in the village, and Maxime took it as a personal affront. The whole reason for the Castillac shop, from his point of view, was for Odile to flaunt her financial success, as though to proclaim to the village how much better she was than he, even though he was mayor and had been elected, which certainly should count as more—

He was snapped out of his internal rant by his ex-wife, who tapped him on the arm. "Maxime. Look, you're a perfectly good mayor when you stick to your strengths. Go around the village and chat with people. Keep the mairie working efficiently so that we don't all drown in red tape. But these manipulations and underhanded machinations, for revenge or profit or some other motive? Leave that alone, Maxime. I'm telling you. Leave it *alone*.

"Now tell me," she continued, with a stiff smile, "where I can find a few more girls like your house-maid? I hear she's quite the stunner. I could use help like that in my shops."

"Josette? She's quite diligent. I couldn't be more pleased." He was especially pleased that Josette obviously irritated his wife, a side benefit that only occurred to him now that he saw Odile's dour expression as she continued to talk about her.

"She's probably stealing you blind while you stand there drooling," said Odile, with an angry smile.

"I'm afraid your jealousy is showing," said Maxime. "Indeed, it *is* sad when the bloom is off the rose, and there is nothing anyone can do to bring it back, no matter what creams or lotions you use. At least you have your work," he said.

Odile had never despised him more than she did at that moment, which was saying something.

ODILE DID NOT STAY but took off looking as though she had eaten something that disagreed with her. Coulon lingered at the table, savoring his victory as well as Pascal's mother's exquisite pâté, and then deciding to take a stroll around the village before going to his afternoon appointment at the bank.

"Bonjour, Mayor Coulon," said villager after villager, as he made his way along. He was relieved that people seemed happy, as they often do on a beautiful June day, and did not approach him with an endless stream of complaints and problems the way they sometimes did on drizzly gray days with a chill in the air. He stopped to talk to Dr. Vernay, just as he was going back in to see his afternoon patients. He waved at Ada Bellard, who worked at the *cantine* at the *primaire* around the corner. He petted various dogs if their owners were around to appreciate it. All in all, he felt he had bolstered his chances at the next election by ingratiating himself with at least twenty people in a short hour, and went into the bank feeling pleasantly complacent.

The receptionist showed Coulon into a back office, where he sat with Monsieur Lachance, the bank vice-president, for about an hour. The conversation might have seemed rather dry to many, since some of it concerned the hated VAT and matters of taxation —but the local gendarmes would have been very interested to hear what the two men spoke about in low voices with the door closed.

Very interested indeed.

S aturday morning, changeover day. Molly had found, over
several years of running La Baraque, that she got to know
some guests pretty well during their stay, while others remained
complete strangers. Which was fine by Molly, as she understood
that people are different in how much socializing they want to do;
some of the guests were dedicated sightseers and so barely spent
any time at La Baraque except for sleeping.

The group leaving was entirely of the second type, and so the
goodbyes were quick and without any promises to keep in touch.
Molly hoped they were satisfied customers, and reminded herself
to make up a short questionnaire and send it out to her mailing
list of guests, to see if there was anything they might suggest if
they had the chance to do so anonymously. That reminder joined
a rather long list in Molly's head of things she needed to attend to
in the upcoming week: the faucet in the *pigeonnier* was leaking
again; she needed to find a mason to talk about rebuilding the
ruin in the back pasture; a window pane in the hallway was
cracked, and she was sure there were about five other things she'd
forgotten for the moment.

A loud bang on the door, and Constance, Molly's friend and

occasional housecleaner, let herself in. Bobo ran over for a joyous greeting as Constance called out "Bonjour!" in that singsong way the French had. "Molly, I—"

"Don't tell me you're about to get married, too," snapped Molly from the kitchen.

"Whoa whoa *whoa!*"

"Sorry. I've had a stream of people in here telling me how sad they are that their partners want to marry them so desperately. I mean, I'm perfectly happy not being married. Marriage isn't exactly easy, after all. It's just—"

"Oh, believe me, I know. Simone Guyanet? My arch-nemesis since *primaire? She's* getting married. I guess she finally got it through her head that Thomas had made his choice and it wasn't her, so she ran out and got engaged to the first guy to come along."

"Someone from the village?"

"Nope, Bergerac, I think. You'd think he was the Prince of Wales to hear her go on."

"I didn't know you and Simone hung out."

"We don't! But Thomas and I had dinner at Chez Papa last night, and she was there with her fiancé. Talking in a loud voice as usual so that everyone in the whole place could hear all their business."

"Want some coffee before we get started?"

"Sure. And okay, because it's you I'm talking to and I know you know the truth anyway—I *would* like to get married. Wear a fancy dress, throw a party, the whole thing. Or maybe it's really just about having a moment when Thomas says, right in front of everybody, 'I love Constance, and we will be together until the end of time.' Something along those lines."

Molly nodded. It was hard to sort through what she actually felt versus what she wanted to feel. Things with Ben, the former chief of gendarmes, had been going very well lately; they were comfortable with each other, and there was a spark there too. The single thing keeping Molly from being ecstatic about her life was not having any children; even though her fortieth birthday was right around the corner, she mostly kept that worry to herself, at least as far as Ben was concerned. It wasn't fair to unload all that pressure on him—it's not like it was his fault baby alarms rang in her head whenever she spied a little one.

"Okay, shall we have at it?" she asked, after she and Constance had polished off their coffee, both lost in thought.

"I'm ready. So where's the creepo dude staying this time?"

"You mean Wesley Addison?"

"Yeah. I'd have thought you'd have had enough of having murderous guests."

"Jeez! What is it about this village! He did not murder anyone. His poor wife fell off a cliff."

"Right," said Constance, winking.

෴

CONSTANCE AND MOLLY cleaned quickly and efficiently, having accomplished so many changeover days at this point they could do it in their sleep. The cottage, *pigeonnier*, and annex to the house all needed vacuuming and mopping. Refrigerators emptied and cleaned, trash taken out, beds freshly made, smudgy windows washed. Just before the guests were due to arrive, Molly went around to each lodging and left a bottle of red from the Sallière vineyard down the road and a small vase with some June roses, along with a notebook that had listings of emergency phone numbers, places to eat, and sites to see.

She could perform this work without having to think about it, free to wonder why she got so annoyed with Frances and Lapin and their marriage woes, but getting no answers. When she and Constance were done, she asked her if she wanted some lunch, but Constance took off on her bicycle for a rendezvous with Thomas. Which was just as well, because Molly had only eaten a piece of brie with a torn-off bit of baguette when Christophe's taxi pulled into the driveway of La Baraque and Molly saw the imposing body of Wesley Addison inside.

"Bonjour, Wesley, it's good to see you. You're early!" she said, trying to sound jolly.

"If you're not ready for me, I'm happy to wait on the terrace or wherever is convenient. As I am sure you are well aware, traveling is quite tiring and I will require some rest. Please bring me a bottle of Vittel."

Molly stood with her mouth open, unable to form a polite response. She had gotten to like Wesley by the end of his stay the year before, but at the moment she was having trouble remembering why. You wouldn't think the lack of a simple "bonjour" would matter so much, and yet boy, it did.

But like any seasoned innkeeper, she found her good spirits quickly. "Actually, everything's ready and you can have your room right away if you'd like. Or if you'd rather drink your mineral water on the terrace, that would be fine too."

"Excellent, Molly," he said with a rare smile. "I imagine other guests will be arriving soon? In that case, I will go to my room. I would be happy to meet them at some other juncture but as I said, at the moment the stress of traveling must be addressed."

Molly smiled to herself as she got him settled in the same room upstairs he had stayed the year before. It was easily the worst room at La Baraque but Wesley had requested it, not being a fan of change when he could avoid it.

Molly managed to make a salad with greens from her garden, some olives, and a bit of tuna, but before she could eat much of it, Christophe's taxi was chugging into the driveway again with a pair of guests, also early.

"Bonjour!" Molly said, as they got out and looked around. "You are the Vasilievs? Welcome to La Baraque!"

"*Dobryj dyen'!*" boomed the man, who was broad in the chest with short legs. His wife, who had shoulder-length hair bleached platinum, stared at Molly without smiling, then shifted her gaze to Bobo, who was not going up to give them a sniff as she usually did with new guests.

"Ah, I'm afraid my Russian is nonexistent. I'm so glad you are here. I'll show you to the pigeonnier right away, and you can let me know if you'd like a tour of the whole place a little later."

Vasily Vasiliev said something else in Russian. For a moment they all stood awkwardly with frozen smiles on their faces. "I'm sorry," Molly said. "We were emailing in English when you made your reservation, am I right? Or have I lost my mind entirely?"

"I am Fedosia Vasiliev," his wife said finally. "My husband speak only Russian. I fill out form and send money."

"I'm afraid I don't speak a word except for '*do svidaniya*,' and I'm probably saying that wrong," laughed Molly.

"Is no worry," said Fedosia, suddenly warming up and patting Molly on the arm.

"That's good to hear," said Molly. She was thinking, with some embarrassment, that she knew virtually nothing about Russia. Had never been to or even known anyone who had traveled there. She vaguely remembered Brezhnev and communism, and of course knew that Russia became its own country when the USSR split up in the early nineties. But the culture, the people, the language? Molly was utterly ignorant of all of it.

"I just want to say," she said, speaking to Fedosia and smiling at Vasily as they walked to the pigeonnier, "that one of the things I like best about running La Baraque is getting to meet people from so many different countries. I hope we can spend a little time together while you're here, and you can share some things about your home."

Fedosia drew back and Molly said quickly, "I don't mean to sound nosy! I'm just curious about what life is like in Smolensk. That's where you're from, if I remember right?"

The Russian gave a curt nod and dragged her duffel bag

through the door of the pigeonnier. Molly showed them around briefly and made her escape.

I just never know who's going to show up here, she mused as she finished her salad, now wilted. Or why.

§&

MOLLY WAS TIRED and cranky that evening but figured she would take a chance on Chez Papa cheering her up, though she was tempted to burrow in at La Baraque and wallow in her grumbling all evening. It had been that kind of week, nothing terrible, nothing dire, but still, the little annoyances kept piling up, and the Vasilievs' frostiness and Wesley Addison's weirdness felt like the next to last straw. At least she was fully recovered from Lyme disease and had her energy back, she thought as she climbed on her beloved scooter and zipped down rue des Chênes and into the village.

June was a delight in Castillac. Many buildings had flowerpots out front along with window-boxes filled with geraniums; roses popped up everywhere and the streets were perfumed with their sweet scent. It was a time of fêtes, concerts, and ice cream, and it was impossible for Molly's mood not to improve simply by puttering down the cobbled narrow street to her favorite bistro, where she ate so often she joked she should have some sort of meal plan, like a college student.

"*Bonsoir* Nico!" she called out, coming through the door.

Heads at the bar turned around, and everyone spent a few minutes greeting each other with *bonsoirs* and cheek kisses. Molly's best pal Frances sat on the stool at the end of the bar, where she was often found, gazing at Nico with wry appreciation. Lawrence was sitting next to Lapin, who was wearing a striped tank top.

"What is this new fashion you're sporting?" asked Molly, suppressing a grin.

"I don't know why everyone has to make such a fuss," said Lapin.

Everyone laughed.

"Well, it *is* eye-catching," said Molly. "I like it when people take fashion risks."

"You're just teasing me, I know," said Lapin. He stood up as tall as he could and flexed his arms, taking a bodybuilder stance. "Anne-Marie likes it. And that's all that counts."

"Indeed," said Molly. "Nico, you're just standing there. Kir, on the double please!"

"*Oui*, Madame," said Nico, jumping into action.

"So when is Ben getting back, anyway?" asked Lawrence. "Seems like he's been out of town for ages."

Molly shrugged. "Who knows. He says it's the most boring job in the world, but at this point in our private investigator business, we can't be choosy."

"Well, I was sorry you called off dinner the other night. I've got the raincheck right here," she said, patting her pocket.

"I know, sorry about that. I just thought it would be more fun with Ben, and he couldn't get away."

"Where is he again?" asked Frances, sipping her glass of Pecharmant.

"Got a job up near Thiviers. It's forensic accounting, really, so he's at a desk all day looking through files."

"Forensic what?"

"Accounting. Trying to figure out where the money's gone, basically," said Molly. "I don't know why it's taking so long, it's just a little business...a sewing shop, I think? Only a couple of employees and I can't imagine they did that much business. I offered to go with him and help, but in this case my help would be limited to my excellent jokes because math and I are not on speaking terms."

"At least you and Ben can talk on the phone."

"Sure. And text. Just between you and me," said Molly, quietly enough that only her friends could hear, "he may look like a stodgy boy scout but he can write some smokin' hot texts!"

Frances cracked up. "Ben? Sexting? Too funny."

"They don't go that far. They're not smutty, just...deliciously suggestive."

Nico had drifted down to the other end of the bar to serve drinks to two men that looked familiar to Molly. Having lived in Castillac for several years now, she recognized most of its inhabitants but still hadn't been introduced to all of them.

"So? How are things?" Molly asked Frances. "Feeling any better about the you-know-what?"

"Huh? Oh, you mean the wedding. Well, yes, maybe. Hey Nico!" She stood up and waved him over. "Let's ask Molly what she thinks about our idea."

Nico grinned and reached over and took Frances's hand. They beamed at each other for a moment until Molly said, "Okay, speak up or get a room, for crying out loud."

"You're very grouchy," said Lapin.

"I am," agreed Molly. "That's how it is sometimes. Frances knows not to take it personally."

"So listen," said Frances, "you know I was talking about an out-of-town wedding? What would you think about coming to the Maldives with us, and our having the ceremony there? It's seriously paradise on earth, no joke."

Molly's mouth opened but nothing came out.

"I'd love to!" said Lapin, who had been leaning over so he wouldn't miss what Frances said.

"I was talking to Molly. But you're welcome to come too, Lapin."

Nico's eyebrows went up but he said nothing.

"Molls?"

"Right, I—"

"You don't want to."

"It's not that, it's just...it's hard for me to get away. I have guests pretty much every week now, and the Maldives isn't just around the corner, you know?"

"I suppose it's a lot to ask," said Frances.

"And, well...I'm not quite as flush as I was a few months ago. The new pool turned out to be way more expensive than the estimate—my fault, because I kept making changes—anyway, if I'm going to hold on to any of my nest egg, I just can't spare the extra dough for a resort vacation right now."

Frances nodded. She knew Molly was something of a spendthrift; even as children, she would be the one to blow all her allowance on candy the minute her mother gave it to her. So when her friend had come into an unexpected windfall, Frances had figured it wouldn't last all that long.

"Let me offer again to have the wedding at La Baraque," said Molly. "It could be so beautiful this time of year! We can decorate any way you want, have a theme—or not—have a big seated meal, or heavy hors d'oeuvres and cocktails, whatever. How do the French handle weddings, Nico?"

"Most of my friends aren't married. A few have been to the mairie, and I know some with religious parents who have gotten married in the church. Usually there's a big raucous party the night before, with costumes and drinking strange drinks, you know—silliness! But generally, it's not like in America where people spend huge amounts of time and money on them."

"I hope to go to the Maldives with you someday," Molly said to Frances. "But what do you say—will you consider letting me do the wedding here?"

"How do you know you won't suddenly get a big case and not have time?"

"Franny! Once we have a plan I'm not going to bail on you if something else comes along! And plus, things are quiet now. That bad run of murders must have come to an end," she added, not entirely happily.

Frances looked at Nico, who grinned at her. "Whatever you want," he said. "I just want you to be my wife."

The whole bar groaned and then burst out laughing. Frances went around the bar and put her arms around him, and then kissed him like she meant it.

"Okay then!" she said brightly. "Um, can you pull it together in a few weeks? Not that I'm in a rush or anything."

Molly agreed and they all clinked glasses. The two men at the other end of the bar bought Frances a Negroni, Lawrence ordered his third of the evening, and the friends settled in for a long conversation that swerved occasionally into serious topics but mostly was about making each other laugh as much as possible. When Molly finally climbed back on her scooter to go home, she was smiling and full of love for her adopted village and its inhabitants, and a tiny bit tipsy, so the things that had been making her irritable had shifted into the background, enough out of sight that she slept a deep and restful sleep. Bobo crept up on the bed and the orange cat curled up on Molly's pillow, but she did not wake.

❧ 6 ❧

Unbeknownst to almost everyone in Castillac, Maxime Coulon had more than one ex-wife. When he had been at the university in Rennes over twenty years earlier, he had met another young student, fallen passionately in love, and married her without telling his family or any of his friends from Castillac. Noelle, his new wife, had immediately become pregnant, but unfortunately the couple fell just as quickly and passionately out of love before the child was born. Noelle left for Laval before she was even showing, and they had had no further contact beyond the logistics necessary for completing the divorce.

Though Noelle was so indifferent to Coulon that she never had the slightest desire to see him again, their child, now a young man, was understandably curious about his father. His mother either refused to give him any information or had none, and so Daniel spent some time online devoted to finding out about his father, and easily identified him as the mayor of Castillac, a small village in the southwest that no one had ever heard of.

It's hardly surprising that a son might want to track down his biological father—no reason to raise an eyebrow. And the fact that the son had also seen where Coulon lived and correctly surmised that he was comfortably well off, plus the additional fact that Daniel was in need of funds sooner rather than later—all in all, it was no mystery why Daniel Coulon was having breakfast that Friday morning at the Café de la Place in Castillac. He was dressed in worn jeans and a T-shirt that had seen better days, but at least he had managed to shave and shower at the hostel in Périgueux before making his way to his father's village. His hair was cut with a nod toward a mohawk; no matter how little money he had, he always kept his hair neat, even if it meant offering to clean up the barbershop in trade for a cut.

Daniel had ordered the Spécial, and was trying to formulate something to say when his father answered the door. Should he come right out with it, and identify himself as his son? Or would the door slam in his face? How best to play on the man's guilt for never even bothering to ask after him, much less meet him?

Difficult questions, thought Daniel, sipping his orange juice and watching a pretty young woman walk by. He felt himself go a little off-kilter, just thinking about the way his father had behaved towards him. How could he never have had a moment's curiosity to meet his own son? That thought, which for years had repeated on an endless loop in Daniel's mind, felt like a burning hole in the center of his chest, a wound that never healed.

The prospect of getting rejected again was a frightening one. Maybe I should invent some other reason to run into him, and get to know him a little before introducing myself, he wondered, biting into his croissant.

The problem with that plan was that it would take time, and time was another thing, in addition to money, that Daniel did not have nearly enough of.

❧ 7 ❧

When Josette returned home from work that Thursday, she changed into a pair of shorts and went outside. The thing she disliked the most about working for the mayor was that she was inside almost the whole time. She walked to the chicken coop and talked to the birds, telling them what her day had been like, and then went into the back field hoping to find that some mushrooms had spouted up after the night's rain.

Madame Barbeau watched her daughter through a grimy window. She did not know what went on at the mayor's house, though she had her suspicions. Josette might be an ignorant fool but Madame Barbeau was more sophisticated, at least in the ways of men. Adolph Barbeau had been a brute and she had not shed any tears when he dropped dead while cutting down a tree next to the house, and not on the children's account either, since they had suffered from his brutality as well.

"Josette," she said when her daughter came back inside. "Sit and tell me about your day. I want you to be forthcoming, *chérie*. Do not feel that I'll judge you, no matter what you have to say."

Josette was confused. "Maman? It's not like I got this job yesterday. It's been almost three years, can you believe it?"

"It's time you asked for a raise."

"Oh, Maman, you are always so dissatisfied!"

"What is not satisfying is that I have the idea there is some mystery afoot. I have felt that way almost since the beginning of the arrangement. There's something you're not telling me." Madame Barbeau turned away from her daughter as though the thought of this was terribly painful.

Josette sighed. "I've told you about the schedule and described my duties. Honestly, Maman, I clean the house, there's really not much more to say about it. Today I polished silver. I like polishing silver. Monsieur Coulon gave me some special tools so I can get every last bit of tarnish."

"How much silver is there, exactly?"

"It takes me almost all day. The candlesticks go pretty quickly because they're smooth without a lot of details. But the flatware!" Josette shook her head. "The forks and spoons have this really complicated decoration on the handles. Flowers and swirls and all kinds of curlicues. Tarnish gets in those tiny cracks and it takes a lot of work to get it off."

"You do a good job? Because if you don't—"

"Maman! If he were going to fire me, he'd have done it by now."

"You have a point," said Maman, and Josette smiled. A rare victory.

"If there is so much silver," said Madame Barbeau, taking an offhand tone, "perhaps he would not notice if a piece or two went missing?"

Josette's eyes got wide, but in fact, she had thought the same thing more than once. The mayor's house was filled to the brim with so much stuff—why should he not share a bit of it with her family that had so little? And certainly nothing as beautiful as silver. Josette did love her job, and silver-polishing day was her favorite. She liked the sense of accomplishment she got from making the flatware and special pieces gleam. She liked handling it, feeling its expensive weight in her hands, and pretending that she was at a glamorous dinner seated at a beautifully-set table with an embroidered lace tablecloth and an enormous bouquet from Madame Langevin's shop, not some raggedy collection of wildflowers yanked from the fields as her mother sometimes put on the table at home.

It would make dinners at the farm so wonderful if they could eat their stew with silver forks, Josette had thought, but pushed the thought away.

Madame Barbeau could see from the expression on her daughter's face that the seed had been properly planted. Now the thing to do was leave it alone, with only the sparest watering, and see whether it would sprout without any further prodding.

It had been tricky, after Josette got to be around thirteen, to get her to do what Madame Barbeau wanted. She often found that pretending not to notice or care about something was helpful in leading her daughter where she wanted her to go. Now that Josette had finally opened up just a little, Madame Barbeau desperately wanted to continue asking questions—a full accounting of the valuables in the house, for starters—but she used all of her considerable will to change the subject, and talk instead about the hen whose favorite nesting place was on top of a pile of junk in the barn, very inconvenient for gathering eggs.

But Josette had had enough of Maman for the moment, and went back outside, letting the door bang behind her. When she was sure her mother wasn't following, she went to the chicken house and climbed up in the rafters to count her money. Her imagination was somewhat limited on the subject of what she would do with it, but she added to the pile every week without fail, trusting that the right path would occur to her eventually.

THE VERY NEXT DAY, Josette was anxious for the mayor to leave in the morning so she could begin the day's work with a somewhat different perspective, that of thief instead of loyal housemaid. But Monsieur Coulon dilly-dallied, as he often did, chatting to her about the people he had seen the day before on his rounds through the village—Castillaçois being famous for loving gossip in all its variety—and as she washed the mayor's dishes from the night before, he stayed seated at the kitchen table drinking another cup of coffee, his eyes lingering on her backside since she was turned the other way and could not see him, so he thought.

But she *could* see him, since the sink was in front of a window and the light at that moment caused his reflection to be nearly as clear as if it were in a mirror. Over the years Josette had gotten used to the mayor's glances, especially since he never said anything improper or made any sort of advances. She very much enjoyed the new finery that he bought every so often for her to wear. Every single piece was high-class, in her opinion, and not the least bit slutty. Even the balcony bra that lifted up her breasts and had a thin edging of delicate lace was, to Josette's mind, an article of underwear fit for a countess, and nothing to be ashamed to wear as she went through the day's chores.

Of course, the mayor was no aristocrat—only the beneficiary of a grandfather in trade who had worked very hard and been lucky enough to make the money to buy the house and the silver, and the further luck (more unusual) to have had a father who had not squandered the inheritance, even though, to Maxime's regret, he had not added to the fortune either.

"Maybe you would like to sit and have a coffee with me this morning, for a change?" the mayor said, cringing a little because he could hear in his tone how desperate he was for her to say yes.

Josette smiled before turning around. She wriggled a little in a way that she had found the mayor liked, and said, "Oh no, Monsieur, I couldn't. Here it is Friday, and so much left to do! I want your house to be perfect for the weekend." She saw his eyes fall on her on her chest and she leaned towards him, bending forward and picking up the jam from the table and then moving away to put in back in the refrigerator.

Maxime gasped slightly at the sight of her. It was torture, having her prancing about in La Perla day in and day out, but it had been his own idea, so how could he change his mind? And the truth was, of course, he didn't *want* to change his mind. Yet this pretty young woman, so delectable and just out of reach, was a daily torment of his own making.

"All right then, the duties of the village call," he said, standing up and then moving close to her as he put his coffeecup in the sink. He heaved an enormous sigh, said goodbye, and was out the door.

Josette washed his cup and dried it. She always felt, when Monsieur Coulon left in the morning, that he might turn around and come back at any minute. Even though that had not happened even once, she never felt assured of her privacy until at least an hour had passed after his departure.

On Fridays she vacuumed the second floor where his bedroom was, and cleaned the bathrooms, one on each floor. The bathrooms on the third and fourth floors were never used since no one ever went up there, but Josette cleaned them all the same. That day she moved about the mayor's house with less daydreaming than usual. Instead of imagining herself dressed in beautiful clothes (which in her mind almost always had voluminous underskirts of tulle as though she were living in 1870), she studied the mayor's things, trying to decide what he might not miss.

If I take something special to him, she thought, he'll notice, and of course I'd be the obvious suspect. Well, the only suspect, since I'm the only person with access to the house. Monsieur Coulon did not entertain at home and there had been no workers or repairmen at the house, except for an electrician who came over a year ago when the washing machine was shorting out the lights upstairs.

But how can I know which things he cares about? He never

talks about any of it. He doesn't even seem to notice that any of it is there. One more reason why just a few of these beautiful things would be better off at the farm, where we'll pay attention to them.

In Coulon's bedroom, Josette stood in front of the mirror and looked at herself. She was not a vain woman, or concerned very much with her appearance, but she would have had to be unconscious not to have noticed the effect she had on her boss.

Maybe I could just ask him for something, she thought. Maybe he would give me some silver, if I just asked him for it.

All during the rest of the day she thought this idea over, imagining Coulon smiling broadly and opening the drawer of the sideboard and telling her to take whatever she wanted, and how happy he was that she had asked. She finished the vacuuming and was just fluffing up the comforter on his bed when she saw it was almost time for Julien to show up for her ride home. She took off the La Perla balcony bra and lacy bikini she was wearing that day and put on her jeans and T-shirt.

On the way to the front door, she passed through the dining room. And as quickly and easily as though she did it every day, she opened the drawer of the sideboard, took out a soup spoon, and slipped it into her bag.

❦ 8 ❧

Molly was on her knees in the front flower border when a battered Renault swung into the driveway.

"Ben!" she cried, jumping up and running over.

He got out quickly, opened his arms with a grin, and Molly nearly bowled him over as she went to hug him. Laughing, they went inside, Bobo jauntily following behind.

"I didn't expect you!" she said. "There's nothing in the house to eat. I was trying..." she looked away, uncharacteristically embarrassed.

"Trying what?" asked Ben. He looked healthy and tan for someone who had been working at a desk for two weeks. His brown eyes were full of affection for Molly as she mumbled something about trying to lose a few pounds.

"Oh, *chérie*," he said, wrapping his arms around her. "Don't do anything drastic, please, especially not on my account." He leaned down to kiss her on the mouth and she hugged him more tightly.

When they came up for air, Ben said, "Speaking of food, I'm starving. Didn't want to stop for anything on the road. Have you eaten? Can we have lunch together?"

"Well, sure, but like I said, there's not much in the larder. Will a salad be enough? I have some eggs I could hard-boil to give it a little more substance. And I can throw in some sardines too, if you like. So tell me how it went in Thiviers? Did you get any damning evidence? Is the client happy?"

"It was a curious case," said Ben, sliding onto a stool at the counter and watching Molly assemble their salad. Then he hopped up to pour them glasses of rosé. "The owner of the shop, who hired us, was suspicious that the man doing the accounting for the business had been embezzling. So I went through the accounts all the way back to 2003. Laborious work, especially considering I had to study up on accounting beforehand. Not exactly an expert as you know, but the owner had heard good things about us so she was willing to give me a shot.

"Well, that decision made more sense once I was there for a few days and could get the lay of the land. Turns out there was probably no embezzling, and the owner was perfectly well aware of this. But she and the accountant had had a brief affair, the accountant had ended it when he took up with a younger woman, and the owner was hurt and wanted revenge."

Molly chopped some fresh herbs to sprinkle over the salad and shook her head. "But how was she going to get any revenge if he didn't actually do anything wrong?"

"I suppose just the word getting out that he was being investigated might be damaging? It's a business that depends largely on reputation, after all."

Molly blew out some air, still shaking her head. "People are strange, aren't they? What happened to dealing with heartbreak by just eating a quart of ice cream or drinking-and-dialing?"

"The what?"

"Oh, you know. You get cheated on or broken up with, you're at home feeling sorry for yourself and drinking too much, and you decide calling up the person who broke your heart is a good idea."

"Which it never is."

"Right. Here you are," she said, pushing a plate in front of him. "Well, I'm glad you're home. I missed you!"

Ben smiled and dug into his salad. "I hope you're going to tell me we have some more work lined up? Anything?"

"Nope. Nothing. I was hoping you had some leads."

Ben shook his head. They sat in silence for a few minutes, eating but in an un-French manner not paying any attention to what they were putting in their mouths, as they considered the dreary prospect of their private investigation business going belly-up before it had a chance to get started.

"Something will come along," Ben said finally.

"I just...I'm worried you won't..."

"Be able to make a living here in Castillac?" He shrugged. "I'm not worried about that. Not yet. I've lived here all my life, remember. If our business doesn't make it, someone will give me work. I can always go back to Rémy's."

Molly said nothing. After Ben had quit the *gendarmerie*, he had worked on his friend Rémy's organic farm for some months. No one involved had thought it was a success.

"It's a little weird to be hoping someone does something bad, so we can try to catch them," she said finally.

"I would like to do something bad right now. With you," answered Ben, with a twinkle in his eye.

"Right in the middle of lunch?"

Ben stood up and took Molly's hand, pulling her toward the bedroom. "Lunch can wait. I want to show you how much I missed you."

They broke into a run, laughing all the way.

❦ 9 ❦

The next day Coulon waited longer to go to the mairie. He wasn't sure whether his suspicions were the result of actual wrong-doing. Josette might be upset about something at home, or simply not have been feeling well, but over the last week he had noticed a change, and he wanted to stick around and keep an eye on her, if only for an hour or so.

Josette arrived at the usual time, dressed in her usual jeans and T-shirt. She greeted him cheerfully and went straight upstairs to the guest room to change into her La Perla. The mayor was always tempted to try to find a way to peek in on that process, but he had restrained himself, leading to no small amount of self-congratulation. He helped himself to another croissant, having walked over to fetch them at *Pâtisserie* Bujold that morning, and spread it with a generous spoonful of strawberry jam. After gobbling that up and finishing his coffee, he waited for Josette in the foyer, wondering what in the world could be taking her so long. The elections for city council were right around the corner and he didn't have time for nonsense.

"Josette!" he called up the stairs. "I'd like you to come down, please!"

He could hear the drawer of the bureau close and he smiled to himself, thinking she had spent the last half hour contemplating her finery and feeling extremely grateful to him.

"There you are!" he exclaimed, as she came trotting down the curving staircase. "It just occurred to me—is your farm outside the commune limits? I'm afraid you won't be able to vote in the elections."

"I...I haven't ever voted for anything," said Josette, slowing to a walk, her hand lingering on the bannister.

"What? Don't ever say such words to a politician, chérie! What blasphemy!" he chuckled, pleased with the idea of himself as gracious and quick with a suitable pleasantry. His eyes flicked over to Josette, who had chosen a pair of ice-blue pantalettes with a slit up almost to her hip, and a matching bra that was unfortunately rather modest.

"I wanted to have a word with you before leaving. I've noticed lately...well, you seem...you seem rather pre-occupied, I suppose that's it. I'm wondering if there is anything wrong, anything you'd like to talk to me about? I have been quite pleased with your work, and if there is anything..."

Josette blushed and looked at the floor.

Charming, thought Coulon.

"It's my mother," said Josette. "She's always after me to ask for a raise. And I...it makes me uncomfortable, like you say."

"What kind of raise do you—or your *mother*," he added with a snicker, "have in mind?"

"Oh, I couldn't say," said Josette. She looked up at him with wide eyes. He didn't know, she thought. For a minute there, I thought he did know, somehow. But now I think he doesn't. *Whew.*

"Would an extra ten euros a week please you?" he said, as though offering her a chest of jewels.

"Oh yes, monsieur," said Josette, dipping that curtsy her

mother had so carefully taught her. Ten measly euros, she thought, nearly rolling her eyes.

"Maxime, please. Call me Maxime."

"Thank you, Maxime," Josette said softly. Well, she would take the whole ten euros and add it every week to her stash in the henhouse. She had decided to save for a trip to America, and any little bit helped.

"All right, then," said Coulon awkwardly. He desperately wanted to take the girl in his arms and carry her up the stairs to his bedroom, and the force of his desire made polite conversation difficult. Finally he mumbled an awkward goodbye and went out, leaving Josette to her Tuesday duties.

It was nearly ten in the morning, and rue Malbec was empty save for a young mother pushing a baby carriage and a stray dog Coulon kept seeing around. He hurried to the mairie, anxious to find out anything he could about the state of the upcoming election.

The system for municipal elections was straightforward enough. The council had twenty-seven seats, evenly divided between men and women, based on the size of the commune Castillac belonged to. The citizens voted for council members in two rounds with proportional representation, and then the council members elected a mayor from their number. So if Coulon was to be mayor a third time, he would have to be reelected to the council, and then that group would have to reelect him to the top job. He thought he had the second part of that sewn up pretty well, having dispensed plenty of favors to the right people over the course of his two terms. The commune vote was a trickier business, since it involved around six thousand people, far more voters than he had favors. He seemed to be well-liked, as far as he could tell. In his daily walks around the village, he usually met with smiles and people did seem genuinely glad to see him.

But Coulon knew as well as anyone how fickle people could

be. Sure, they had supported him for the last twelve years, but that was no guarantee at all. A few good-looking charmers find their way in, and that could spell the end of his mayoral career. He was usually more confident, but he had heard some gossip about a new candidate that disturbed him a great deal. He reached the steps of the mairie and stood for a moment gazing at the stately building, a nineteenth century edifice that conferred a sort of grandeur on all who worked there, Coulon had always believed. Clamping his teeth together, he strode in, trying to push away the image of Odile taunting him if he were no longer mayor. *I must not lose*, he said fiercely to himself. Above all, *I must not lose.*

"Annette!" he said, kissing the receptionist on both cheeks after coming inside.

"Maxime, I've been looking for you," Annette said. "I don't know if you've heard," she said, lowering her voice, "but André Lebeau has officially entered the race. You just missed him; he came in this morning to file the forms."

"*Merde*," said Coulon under his breath. "Did he...how did he seem? I mean, just generally."

Annette shrugged. "I don't want to say it, but he is...he is an impressive man, Maxime. Physically, I mean." Annette looked as though she might need a drink of water.

"All right, yes, he is well-built. That is not a crazy, never before seen occurrence, yes? And I will add that muscles are not part of the job requirement for civil service."

"And he's tall, quite tall. Imposing, you might say."

"I believe we do most of our council work sitting down, so I don't see how that will be of advantage to him. Too bad he is not running for a position on a basketball team."

Annette heard the bitterness in the mayor's joke and did not smile. Coulon took a deep breath and pulled himself together. "Thank you, Annette, I appreciate the heads-up." He stalked into his office and closed the door.

Just when everything was finally starting to come together, he thought. If I lose, it will be years of work down the drain! I bet Odile urged André to run against me, just to humiliate me. Well, she'll see. I'll beat her pretty boy, and anyone else who tries to push me out. I didn't get to be mayor for almost twelve years because I don't know how to fight.

His words were strong but he slumped in his chair, staring at the door instead of getting a start on the pile of papers on his desk. He opened a drawer and reached in for a handful of Haribo gummy worms, and chewed on one thoughtfully as he worked out how to fatally maim André LeBeau—politically speaking—as quickly as possible.

৯৯

ONCE MONSIEUR BARBEAU had died and was no longer around to torment his family, life in the Barbeau household improved rather dramatically. Madame Barbeau and her children suffered no beatings, and did not have to tiptoe around, fearful that any sound would set him off in another unpredictable rage that would end up being taken out on them.

But growing up in such a violent home, the children failed to learn the most basic lessons of trust. Though their mother had been a victim of Monsieur Barbeau as well—even the primary one—after his death she did not prove capable of trying to heal her family with warmth and loving kindness. She was a different sort of mother, more interested in how her children could be used for her own ends now that she was free to indulge her ambitions. Unfortunately for Josette and Julien, these ambitions did not include happiness for them, though it could generously be thought that Madame Barbeau assumed they were happy enough and she needn't worry about them. For herself, she wanted *more,* and *better*—ideally, some way to escape the farm and the backbreaking work necessary to run it. Julien was helpful enough, and more or less dutiful; he tried to relieve his mother of the chores she could no longer accomplish because of her arthritis.

But still, even if the children somehow managed to do all of the work—the ambitious woman was stuck in a dreary, cramped house way out in the country, far from the village where she had grown up and still considered, in the way that a childish perspective is slow to erode, to be the center of all that was sophisticated and glamorous. Josette and Julien's stubborn refusal to open up and relate the details about what was going on beyond the farm was making her crazy.

"Josette!" she said, letting a cast iron pot of beef stew drop to the dining table with a loud thump. "I've been doing some thinking. You have been working for the mayor for years now. Obviously he is happy with you or he would have gotten rid of you long before now. I do congratulate myself for having raised you with a good work ethic so I am confident you are not slacking off. So where is the raise? You did ask him?"

"Well, I—"

"You wouldn't be holding out on me, would you? Taking the money for yourself, after all I have done for you? I've made peace with your ignorance, out of necessity, but I never thought you were devious on top of it. And think for a moment, daughter, where you would be without me?"

"A lot happier?" muttered Julien softly enough that only Josette could hear. Josette giggled and put her hand over her mouth.

"I'm not joking," said Madame Barbeau, ladling out the stew into three shallow bowls. "I have a mind to call the mayor and have a few words with him myself."

"Please don't do that, Maman!" said Josette. "You'll make me look like a child. I promise to talk to him, I've just...um...I've just been too shy to ask for more money. It's embarrassing, you can understand that, right?"

"No," said Madame Barbeau. "I don't see what could possibly

be embarrassing about asking for what you are worth. That man depends on you, and there's an election right around the corner. He might bring people home for meetings, or want to entertain. He may want you to stay late helping him with these kinds of things. If he had any sense, he would be using that grand house to his advantage, instead of treating it as though it were nothing more than a cheap apartment not worth showing to anyone.

"I hope you have had the sense to make yourself indispensable, and if so, I congratulate you for that," their mother continued. "It's too bad the experience of practically living right in the center of the village is wasted on you. You'd probably be happier in a pig pen."

"There's nothing wrong with liking the country," said Josette.

"Oh, sure. Nothing at all," sneered her mother.

"I've been wondering about getting a different breed of chick next time," said Julien, bringing up something to divert Madame Barbeau's attention from his sister.

"Fool," said Madame Barbeau. "Why would you even suggest such a thing? Do you not sell out of the meat nearly every single market day? Josette, how are the layers doing?"

"Fine, Maman," said Josette, helping herself to more stew, having cleaned her bowl.

"And hold it right there. I plan to have this stew for my lunch the rest of the week, and you don't need any extra padding. If you get too fat, the mayor will replace you in the blink of an eye, I can tell you that right now."

"He...he said he likes..."

"Mon Dieu, speak up!"

"He said he likes girls with some meat on their bones."

"Excellent. A man who talks of women as though they are cattle at the auction. Delightful." She pushed herself back from the table, her appetite diminished.

Julien winked at Josette, who choked down a snicker. Her habit of privacy was so strong that she never shared with her brother what had happened between her and the mayor, or how well her campaign to lure him into marriage was going. They both finished second helpings and then began clearing the table, while Madame Barbeau smoked a cigarette and stared at the floor, the corners of her mouth turned down.

After the kitchen was cleaned up, the siblings separated without a word, each going to the place where they kept their private stash. Josette clucked to the hens and talked to them while she reached up to the rafters and took down the small bag stuffed with money that she thought of as her whole future. This moment, every evening, when she was alone in the henhouse, was the only time she felt almost happy. It was time to find a better place to keep it, now that it was such a big pile, she thought with pleasure, imagining herself climbing the long stairway up to an enormous jet that would take her to the bright and brilliant shores of America, far away from the intrusive clutches of Maman.

10

By three-thirty, Coulon had had enough of the office. The workers kept talking about André, and when Coulon went into his office and shut the door, just knowing they were out there still talking was making him crazy. So with a falsely cheerful wave he said his goodbyes, inventing a story about something pressing he needed to do at home, even though if he had left without a word no one would have given it a thought.

On the short walk home, he daydreamed about Josette's staying to have dinner with him. Her brother was sometimes late; maybe today he wouldn't show up at all and they could have a nice, intimate dinner together, and then he could gallantly drive her home. Or even invite her to spend the night.

Coulon paused at his front steps, considering what to do for the rest of the afternoon. Since he had told his co-workers he needed to get home, it would hardly do to wander about the streets, and in any case, he wouldn't mind another sighting of Josette in her ice-blue La Perla. Instead of going in the front way, he walked down the block to stretch his legs, then around and down the alley, wanting to get a screwdriver from the workshop in the backyard so he could tighten a wobbly hinge on a kitchen cabinet.

His father had been a great one for spending hours and hours in the workshop, fiddling around with one thing or another. He had never invited Maxime to join him, or taught his son any of the prodigious mechanical skills he had developed over the years. The workshop, with its tiny windows and concrete floor, was a place Maxime had been excluded from during his formative years, and all these decades later, he entered the building tentatively, as though his father were going to rise from the dead and bark at him to leave at once.

Somehow it still smelled like his father inside. Or more precisely, it smelled of oil and sawdust, which his father always smelled of. Maxime had a quick clear picture of his father sitting at the breakfast table, his face obscured behind the newspaper, grumbling about politics. I'm not in the mood for any maudlin memories today, Maxime said to himself, grabbing the screwdriver and making his way up the back steps to the house. Through the window in the door he saw Josette's back, and he smiled even though it was late enough in the day that she had changed back into her jeans and T-shirt. He paused for a moment with his hand on the latch, admiring her backside for the millionth time.

He must have walked up the porch stairs without making noise, or perhaps Josette was not expecting anyone to be at the back door. Perhaps she was so intent on stealing the silver sugar bowl that she had blocked out everything else. In any case, she did not hear Coulon, and he saw her take the sugar bowl off the kitchen counter where it had sat for decades, and put it right into her straw bag.

He gasped. She was about to add a silver salt shaker when he yanked the latch and barreled inside.

"What did I just see?" he cried, his face reddening.

"Nothing," said Josette, backing away.

"Don't tell me nothing! I saw you! I saw you take it!"

"I'm sorry! I didn't mean to!"

"Oh, my sugar bowl just jumped into your bag of its own accord?" He lunged forward and grabbed her by the wrist and twisted it just enough to hurt.

"Let go of me!"

"I don't think so," said Coulon. "You do know what will happen to you now? You've been caught stealing from the mayor. Obviously you are prettier than you are clever, because the penalties for such a thing are dire, Josette. Quite dire."

She looked afraid, and he found, somewhat to his surprise, that he liked it.

"The silver left to me by my family is extremely valuable, though perhaps I needn't point this out to you. But their value only makes the penalty worse, you see? If you had only stolen something cheap, well then, maybe the penalty wouldn't be terrible. But as it is, family heirlooms and worth so much money...."

"Monsieur! Please, it was a mistake!"

Coulon laughed. "I am the *mayor*," he said, having to push a pang of anxiety over André Lebeau out of his head. "And I can make things very, very bad for you. I work with the courts and know all the judges, or did you not think of that before you started pilfering?"

Josette moved to ease the pressure on her wrist but Coulon twisted it again so that she cried out. "Please, monsieur! I will return all of it. There's more, at home. My mother—my mother forced me to do it. I never wanted to. I'm so sorry after everything you've done for me."

Nice try, thought Coulon, but *no*.

"Prison is so uncomfortable," he said, emphasizing the word. "And it does make me sad thinking of you that way. You did say only last week that you didn't like asking me for a raise, which I gladly gave you, am I right? And this is how you repay me?"

Josette turned her face away and whimpered. She thought fast.

"Maxime," she said quietly, her voice quavering just a little.

"I...I am more sorry than I can find words to say. For me to take advantage of you, who have been nothing but kind—I am a terrible person. To hurt you...who mean," she lowered her voice even more, "who mean so much to me..."

Coulon's grip on her wrist loosened. He narrowed his eyes at her.

"I deserve whatever punishment I get," she said, quickly glancing up at Coulon to see how he was reacting. "I only wanted to have a little bit of you at the farm, a reminder during the long weekends away from here. I know it was silly of me. It was wrong. But you must understand, Maxime...you must have realized how I feel about you?" she lifted her eyes to his, her dark lashes charmingly shining with tears.

"Well," he said, "well." He let go of her wrist and instead stroked it with his fingers. "I had no idea you were such a sentimental sort," he said gruffly.

Josette nodded meekly. She stepped so close to Coulon that there was only a centimeter between them. "Kiss me," she whispered.

And he did. Tentatively at first, and then ardently, years of pent-up desire finally allowed some release.

"You are a very bad girl," the mayor said, taking her hand and pulling her toward the stairs and on to his bedroom. "A very beautiful, very bad girl."

❦ II ❦

11

At the sound of raucous laughter, Frances looked at Molly with wide eyes. "What in God's name is that?"

Molly grinned. "Probably the guests in the cottage. Two women, old friends in their mid-sixties. They are seriously enjoying themselves. Kind of thinking we'll be like that when we get to be their age."

"I don't plan to," said Frances, taking a sip of her wine. "Got any cheese?"

"As a matter of fact, I saw our favorite cheesemonger, Lela Vidal, at the market on Saturday. Got a *brébis*, a fantastic sheep's cheese—help me eat it, it's perfectly ripe. And what do you mean, you don't plan to? You'd rather the alternative?"

"Oh, I don't know, it was just something I said without thinking. I prefer to exist in total and complete denial that I will ever get the least bit old."

"You are forty. I'd say that counts as 'least bit.' We'd certainly have said so when we were twenty."

"Twenty-year olds know absolutely nothing."

"That's exactly what old people say," said Molly. "At least your skin isn't wrinkled. My face is starting to look like my grandmother's knees."

Frances cackled. "Okay, I'm feeling momentarily strong thanks to this amazing cheese—let's talk wedding, if you're up for it. I would like to have it here, but only if you're not just willing but actually enthusiastic about doing it. And I won't for one second be put out if you've changed your mind."

"No, no, I'd love to do it!" Molly said, mostly telling the truth. "Do you have any thoughts about how you want it?"

"No. Absolutely not. Except…I don't want the usual thing, you know? I don't want what everyone else does, little sweet bouquets and lace and all that. It's just not me."

Molly had to agree. Frances was entirely more exotic, and after all, she had done the white dress and lace thing twice already. "We'll put the decorations to the side for now. How about food? Hors d'oeuvres or sit-down?"

Frances pondered. She looked up at the ceiling, had another sip of wine, sliced a bit of cheese and ate it on a cracker. "Oh, I don't know," she said finally. "Every time I try to picture it, I think of my parade of ex-husbands, and the whole idea of marriage just seems hopeless and misguided and I want to forget the whole thing."

"Have you tried quickly sweeping the exes out of your head and replacing them with thoughts of Nico?"

"Well, of course. I'm not a total moron, you know. But it doesn't seem to do any good. And I can't help wondering whether my brain is trying to tell me something…sort of like a mental 'Go No Farther' sign with a skull and crossbones, does that make any sense?"

Molly sighed. She loved Frances, and Nico too, but the tedious work of having to bolster Frances's optimism about getting married in the face of her two divorces was rather wearing. At the moment she felt like snapping, *Okay fine, don't get married then!* but of course she restrained herself. "It is tricky, knowing one's own mind," she said, helping herself to some of the *brebis* and moaning softly at how good it was.

"What, are you like the Dalai Lama now? Sprinkling your bits of wisdom all over the floor for the rest of us to gather up like rose petals?"

Molly looked at Frances. Frances looked at Molly. They cracked up laughing.

"Why don't I talk to Nico? Maybe he has some ideas, and whatever he wants is fine with me. Thanks for stepping into this nightmare," Frances said, standing up.

Loud shrieking from outside, and the two friends went out through the doors to the terrace to see what was going on.

The guests staying in the cottage were outside, sitting at a small metal table Molly had set up just outside their front door, so that guests could sit outside without having to use her terrace. The women had a bottle of wine, more than half gone, and were bent over in hysterics.

"If that was a joke, you're going to have to tell it to us," said Molly, having walked over to say hello.

The women sat up, wiped their eyes, and dissolved again into helpless laughter.

"Frances Mayes, let me introduce Emily Scribner and Nancy Hackenberry. They're from Portland."

"I always said the worst thing about living in Oregon is how far it is from France," said Emily. "Now that we're finally here, we're enjoying ourselves so much we may never leave."

"Hey, that's what happened to me," said Frances. "She'll start plying you with croissants from that place in town—"

"Pâtisserie Bujold? Yeah, we found that right off. Emily can smell a good bakery from miles away."

Emily patted her belly. "Yep, though if we keep up this pace, I'm going to have to buy more clothes. My pants are already feeling a little tight and we only just got here."

"Thing is," said Emily, "we're sort of celebrating. Well, celebrating and mourning both at the same time. Nancy's husband died a few months ago after a long illness."

"Oh, I'm so sorry," said Molly, reaching to touch Nancy on the shoulder.

"Don't be," said Nancy. "He was a mean son-of-a-you-know-what, and there is not a person in this world who was sad to see him go."

"Oh!" said Frances, taking to Nancy right away.

"I would have loved to take this trip years ago, but he wouldn't let me. Well, it wasn't like he forbade it or anything like that. But he would put me off, saying we just didn't have the money that year, just to be patient. I'll be sixty-five next month so I'd say I've been patient long enough!"

"That's for sure," said Emily. "And she was a fantastic nurse to that stingy man all through his illness. Leave it to Abner to linger on forever. Anyway, we're here now. Nancy and I went to grade school together. This nut has been making me laugh for over fifty years. How about that?"

"We're old friends too," said Molly, gesturing at Frances. "There's nothing better. If there's anything I can do to make your vacation wonderful, please ask—you can knock on my door anytime." She was about to head back to the main house with Frances when Emily said, "We've looked through the brochures for local sites, and some of them look fabulous and we'll be sure to go see them: Beynac, Domme, and I think there's a monastery somewhere that looked worth investigating. But..."

Molly smiled and waited, but neither woman said anything.

"Well, we're interested in sort of...*dark* things, if you under-stand me, the uglier, stranger parts of history," Emily continued. "Could you steer us to anyplace with, I don't know, some kind of spooky tale that goes along with it, or a site where something terrible happened?"

"Now you're going to think you've got a pair of weirdos on

your hands," said Nancy, pouring the rest of the wine between their two glasses.

"I'll think about it," said Molly. "One thing that springs to mind is the Museum of Torture, but it's all the way down in Carcassonne, which is about three hour's drive from here."

"Torture?" said Nancy, her eyes lighting up.

"From the Inquisition," said Molly. "It's quite something. First, the ingenuity people have for causing pain is remarkable. And also, of course, the way they used religion as an excuse for their sadism..."

Emily and Nancy were looking at each other. "We said when we planned this trip that we would stay flexible," said Nancy.

"Yup. I don't have to be home for at least another month. Slow time at work, they don't really need me until August. If you're thinking what I'm thinking."

Nancy nodded. "So, what's your booking schedule looking like, Molly? Could we have the cottage for another week, maybe two?"

"You're in luck, actually—just had a cancellation. I'd be happy to have you! As long as your interest in torture is purely theoretical?" she added, smiling.

They all laughed. Molly was grateful for the extra money and liked the women very much, and while she could understand an interest in the museum—she had been to it herself, after all—who was she to say that their interest was perhaps a little over the line? And what was that line, exactly? She closed her eyes, remembering some of the more chilling artifacts in the museum, and shivered at the memory.

"Molly!" shouted Frances. "You're drifting off like a dotty old lady!"

"Excuse me?" said Emily, eyebrows raised.

"Joking," said Frances.

Molly went off to find them a map, Frances left to find Nico and stress about the wedding, and the two guests went inside, tipsy from the lunchtime wine they weren't used to, and planned their trip to Carcassonne.

❦ 12 ❦

André Lebeau, candidate for a seat on the council, had decided to do a bit of campaigning on rue Malbec in the late afternoon, hoping to catch people on their way home from work. He had a stack of printed flyers with his photograph on them along with a few bullet points of what he intended to focus on once elected, such as environmental concerns and improved tourism.

At first there were few people on the street, and André passed the time having a long conversation with Madame Vargas, who told him about how her husband kept wandering away from home and had to be found and brought back by the gendarmes or helpful neighbors. She wanted to know what, if he were elected to the council, he proposed to do about this problem. Old Madame Gervais came by, carrying a few provisions she'd bought at the *épicerie* in a string bag; she wished him well and asked him to say hello to his mother, whom Madame Gervais had known many years earlier when she taught school.

But eventually word got out that André was there, and a small crowd congregated on the sidewalk in front of the mayor's house.

"I guess my question to you is, why are you running for

office?" said a young man around André's age. "You look like you're mainly interested in working out. And *les femmes*," he added with a wink.

"I haven't lost interest in those things," André answered, smiling. "But I'm glad for the chance to explain why I want to get on the council. It's because of this: a friend of mine wanted to open a business over in Salliac. Nothing fancy, just a little shop where you could buy or rent sports equipment. He was buying second-hand skateboards, tennis rackets, all sorts of stuff, building up an inventory. But when he was all set to go, he couldn't get the permit. He was at the mairie like a hundred times, trying to find out why his application kept getting rejected, and he couldn't ever get a straight answer.

"Now we all know the country's got an enormous bureaucracy, and you can like that or not, but when that bureaucracy is infiltrated by corruption, well then, somebody's got to do something about it. And so that's when I decided to throw my hat in the ring. Things like building permits, licenses, commercial permits—it may not be exciting or sexy, but that stuff has got to be dealt with fairly, don't you all agree? Tell me if you think otherwise, I would like to hear what you have to say."

Several people smiled at hearing the handsome candidate sincerely ask for their opinions, and the conversation went on for some time, with villager after villager talking at length, giving their thoughts on building permits, and sometimes losing track of the subject at hand and ending up talking about a movie they had just seen or what kind of cheese was best in fondue. André listened carefully to everyone. The younger women managed to get in the front of the crowd and gazed at him with unabashed interest. He had lived in Castillac only for the last year or so, having moved there from Poitiers or perhaps as far as Tours; no one was quite sure. His return to his mother's village was a definite positive, to judge from the warm expressions of the crowd surrounding the young candidate.

"So besides corruption, I want to take good care of our land and water, and develop more opportunity for tourism right here in the village."

"What on earth would anyone want to see here?" said a young woman, and some of the others giggled.

"Oh, there's so much beauty here in Castillac," said André, looking at her and smiling, and the woman blushed furiously. "I can imagine tourists from all over the world wanting to flock here, if they only knew. Look how charming it is!" he said, gesturing at the street, which was certainly not objectionable, though rather ordinary for the most part. The mayor's stately house was by far the most attention-getting thing in view, but the houses on either side of it were not in especially good repair or very lovely in any case. But the villagers were proud of Castillac, understandably, and they were pleased to hear such a good-looking fellow pay it compliments.

"You've got my vote," said one of the young women, and the crowd murmured agreement.

"But for you to actually get anything done," said an older man, "being on the council isn't enough. You're just one of seventy-odd. To have any real power, you'd have to topple the mayor himself."

All eyes went to the mayor's house, looking up to the fourth floor and back down again. The shutters were open, but standing on the sidewalk the villagers were too low down to be able to see inside, except for some sumptuous-looking curtains at the front windows.

"Eh, Coulon's had his turn," said André dismissively, as though he expected no competition at all from that direction despite the mayor's three terms and being a native of Castillac.

"I don't know," said the older man dubiously. "He's had time to grease a lot of palms, if you know what I mean."

"Life is unpredictable. Maybe he'll drop dead and make it easy for me," laughed André, and some in the crowd laughed with him, perhaps at the ridiculousness of such a notion, the mayor not being an old man by any stretch.

&

"Is ANYTHING WRONG, MONSIEUR LACHANCE?" the assistant asked the banker, who was standing in the doorway to his office with an especially sour look on his face.

"No, no," Lachance said, going into his office and closing the door. The meeting with Coulon had not gone the way he might have wished. Oh, the mayor was game, all right. He wasn't going to cause any trouble with the case in front of the examining magistrate, at least he claimed he would not.

But the mayor's services did not come cheap. Lachance sank into his chair and put his head in his hands. He was deep in a hole, yet all he could think to do was keep digging.

❧ 13 ☙

The next morning, to Bobo's great disappointment, Molly got out of bed and zipped into the village on her scooter without having coffee. She wanted to pick up fresh pastries for her guests at Pâtisserie Bujold and have a leisurely breakfast at the Café de la Place before starting in on the day's chores.

The sight of the red-enameled shop made her mouth water, and as she parked the scooter she was already struggling to decide which pastries to get.

"Bonjour, Edmond!"

Edmond Nugent, proprietor of the bakery, gave Molly a wink and a wave as he finished helping a customer who was buying a dozen beignets.

"*Au revoir*, Malcolm," Molly said to the young man, and he mumbled a goodbye to her on his way out.

When the man had left, Nugent leaned across the counter and said, "Look out for that one. He's something of a sneak. When he comes into the shop I don't dare turn around or he'd manage somehow to have all the éclairs stuffed in his pockets in the blink of an eye. Though he might be good to know for whatever you and Ben are working on—you know, part of the criminal element—who could have some information for you from time to time." He let his eyes drift to Molly's chest but remembered himself and looked out the window.

"I'm rather fond of Malcolm actually, he helped out with a case awhile back."

"Well, I never would have guessed you'd be friendly with the likes of Malcolm Barstow. He's well known to all the shopkeepers because he'll steal anything that isn't nailed down. I heard the Barstows were in hot water back in England, but they haven't improved their conduct here. Father's in and out of jail."

"Sort of a sad case."

"There is nothing sad about Malcolm, believe me. He's the type of thief who enjoys the whole thing immensely."

"Well, thanks for the tip, Edmond. Though the way things are going, I'm going to be out of the private investigator business before long."

"How come?"

"Pure and simple: no clients."

"At least you have your gîte business to fall back on. Can't you simply be patient until something comes up? Not that I'm hoping for anything to come up, to be honest. I mean, um, I wish you every success but at the same time, I am not in favor of crime, you understand? Oh dear, this is awkward."

Molly laughed. "Not at all, I've had the same thought myself. The trouble is, yes, I have the gîtes—and I love doing it, so that's all good—but Ben is another story. He needs work, and he can't just wait for it indefinitely."

Edmond shrugged, not feeling especially warm towards Ben Dufort since he, Edmond, could quite easily imagine himself in his place as Molly's boyfriend. He allowed himself the fleeting hope that Ben would be forced to leave town to find work, leaving the field open...

"Edmond? Hello?"

"Oh yes, so sorry," he said, reddening. The doorbell tinkled and Lucie Séverin came in, at least Molly thought that's who she was, the wife of the principal of the primaire who had been part of a case Molly worked on the year before. Everyone in the village understood that Lucie had struggled with depression, so Molly was glad to see her out and about.

"Bonjour, Lucie!" said Edmond, with a big smile. "Have you made your decision?" he asked Molly, gesturing at the pastry case. She was unused to being hurried along and quickly chose a variety of deliciousness—napoleons, éclairs, and lemon tartlettes—hoping to hit on something that would tempt Wesley, the Russians, and the pair from San Francisco. She was halfway out the door when she remembered that Wesley did not eat sweets, and asked Edmond if he had any small spinach quiches.

While he went in the back to check, Molly gave Lucie a quick smile and looked away. Though she had moved to Castillac almost two years earlier, it was still tricky navigating the social customs of the village; as an extroverted American always up for talking to anyone, Molly had learned some restraint, and though she wanted to start chatting away with Lucie and asking how she was doing, she understood that Lucie would most likely find that to be intrusive. So they stood next to each other, both of them staring at the pastries for something to do, until Edmond returned with a quiche and slipped it into a bag.

"No charge," he said gaily, causing Molly to wonder what in the world had gotten into him. Though his joyful expression as he turned to Lucie, all twinkly-eyed and intense, gave her a pretty good idea.

With some effort she managed not to eat any of the pastries as she walked to the Café de la Place, taking a seat in the sunshine, and once again thinking that despite whatever problems arose—as they would anywhere, simply being life—she had managed to find paradise. The plane trees made a dappled shade over most of the café's terrace, and some sort of spiky-leaved palm grew next to the Presse across the street. A few tourists drifted through on their way to the church, which was an interesting example of its type but not so interesting as to draw very many people out of their way to see it. Window boxes and hanging baskets were everywhere, brightening up the stone buildings with splotches of red and yellow. She saw her friend Manette going into the hardware store, and several other familiar faces that she couldn't quite match to names.

Molly loved Castillac with all her heart. If only the investigation business would take off, and allow Ben to stay, life would be about as perfect as it ever gets.

Pascal appeared, bestowing a warm smile and a view of his dazzling white teeth, and took her order, the usual Spécial. Circling back to the problem at hand—she couldn't help wondering—was *she* the problem with the P.I. business? Did people not want to hire them because she was a foreigner, and worse, devoid of any real credentials beyond a few lucky breaks in some local cases? Maybe she should suggest that Ben drop her name from the business and try to make a go of it by himself. He was the one with all the local connections, along with a stellar reputation as former chief of the gendarmerie.

It was the last thing she wanted to do, since solving the various cases that had cropped up in Castillac had been one of the main reasons she was so happy there. It felt so good to set things right as well as give back to the community she adored. And yes, admittedly, the successes weren't half bad for her ego, either.

Pascal arrived with her freshly squeezed orange juice, croissant, and long overdue coffee. As Molly sat still, rather like a child unable to decide which thing to have first because they all looked absolutely divine, two women sat a few tables away, deep in conversation. An inveterate eavesdropper, Molly tuned in right away.

"—and the thing is," the woman with dark auburn hair said,

"he's only doing it to annoy me. As though he hadn't gotten quite enough of that while we were married!"

Molly nodded to herself. One of the best things about moving to France after her divorce was that she and Donny, her ex, led completely separate lives now, and any ideas either might have for tormenting the other in the ways exes sometimes do were nullified by the distance between them. Molly actually thought mostly fondly about Donny now, much to Frances's horror, but she was pretty sure that would not be the case if she had stayed in Boston where he still lived.

Enough ruminating, and back to eavesdropping!

"Do you think he will win? He always seems to. Honestly, I don't think it's because anyone likes him that much, Odile. It's more that no one ever runs against him who isn't some kind of nut. The truth is, no one wants to be mayor. It's a lot of work, after all. For me it would be a nightmare of a job."

"Well, Maxime adores it. It gives him delusions of grandeur, you know. Don't you see him swanning about the village, greeting people as though he were wearing an ermine stole and a giant crown on his head? Though I suppose if he wore a crown, maybe he wouldn't need to have that comb-over."

"Odile, you are *terrible!*" tittered her friend.

It didn't take a crack detective to figure out that they were talking about Maxime Coulon, thought Molly. She had shaken his hand and exchanged a few pleasantries with him at some point, but never met his wife. Her impression of the mayor had not been negative...or positive either, come to think of it. He seemed to be a mild sort of man, very much wanting people to like him—at least that was her impression from the brief contact she had had.

"Just between you and me, I wouldn't be sorry if someone pushed him in front of an oncoming train. Do you know he has blocked my business permit for over six months? We all accept a certain amount of bureaucratic lethargy but this is just ridiculous.

It's obviously on purpose. He's costing me gobs of money and absolutely reveling in it."

The two women then engaged in a long discussion about facials and various skin creams, and Molly got bored and stopped listening. Breakfast eaten, she hurried back to the scooter clutching her bag of pastries, hoping that the guests all slept late and her timing would then be perfect.

❧ 14 ❧

Madame Barbeau had called the mayor Thursday morning to let him know that Josette was not feeling well and would not be coming to work that day. She tried to pressure Josette into making the call herself, but her daughter rolled over, pretended to be asleep, and did not respond to Madame Barbeau's entreaties.

Which were half-hearted, in any case, since the older woman was glad of an excuse to talk to the mayor himself. If she were not so arthritic she would have paid him a visit long before—how she would love to get inside that house and see it for herself! Josette was utterly deficient when it came to relating any sort of detail. Well, utterly deficient in most things, her mother thought, except looks. And those will go soon enough.

Madame Barbeau stroked her chin, thinking carefully about what to say before she made the call. Perhaps if she took a hot bath and rubbed her knees with ointment, she might be able to make the trip? She was still young, only in her fifties...if her joints would just behave. It's not as though she had lived her life avoiding pain; she wasn't afraid to suffer if the reward was worth it. For a moment she thought greedily of the mayor showing her around the house on rue Malbec, while she made note of the paintings, sculptures, fine plate, and who knows what other valuables might be there that Josette was blind to?

But with a sigh, Madame Barbeau returned to reality. Though she was no stranger to fantasies of fortune, she was a practical woman always, and knew that if she tried to go to Castillac and climb the mayor's three flights of stairs, she might be stuck in bed for days after, barely able to move, with her joints on fire. There was too much work to do on the farm to allow it.

The phone call was brief and disappointing. She told him Josette wasn't well and he thanked her for calling and hung up before Madame Barbeau could get out another word.

She did not believe for a moment that her daughter was sick. Either something had happened to upset her or she was just looking to have a day off so she could lounge around doing nothing.

As she swept the kitchen floor, she pondered the situation. Truthfully, Josette had never been lazy. Sure, sometimes she put off doing her chores until the last minute, but overall her mother couldn't really complain about her daughter on that score. With a groan Madame Barbeau put a dustpan on the floor and swept dirt and tracked-in bits of straw into it.

I wonder, she thought slowly, if what I feared has finally come to pass. It's no good putting a young woman like Josette alone in a house with a man—men are beasts, plain and simple. They will do the worst if even given half a chance, as I very well know.

She stood up straight, for once not noticing the pain in her knees, imagining Maxime Coulon taking advantage of her innocent daughter. It felt as though an electrical storm unleashed in her head, a raging fury interspersed by fleeting memories of her husband Adolph's savagery, which she had been forced to endure until his death.

Madame Barbeau clamped her teeth together and went off to find Julien, who might be able to shed some light on the truth. It had been several years since Josette began to work as a housemaid, and Madame Barbeau had felt, right from the beginning, that there was more going on than she was being told by either of her children. And now she was almost certain something had shifted, exactly in the sordid way she had anticipated, and she did not intend to submit to it, not this time.

§

BY THE NEXT morning Josette had made a miraculous recovery. She fed the chickens and made the coffee as she usually did, then waited for Julien to load the truck.

"Glad to see you are still among the living," said her mother unpleasantly, watching for a reaction.

"Guess I needed to rest," was all Josette would say. Cheerfully, she kissed her mother on both cheeks and said goodbye before getting into the truck with Julien.

"I hate her," Josette said simply.

"Yeah," said Julien. They said nothing further, and did not need to.

Once on rue Malbec, Josette began to feel nervous. She had not wasted her day of rest but done a lot of thinking, trying her best to come up with a plan, some way of salvaging the disaster that had ensued when the mayor had caught her stealing the silver sugar bowl. His threats had scared her so completely (and she had not even considered whether he might not be telling the truth) that she was sure she faced years of living as his virtual slave, with the constant sword of prison hanging over her head if she did not keep him satisfied enough to keep quiet.

Josette liked life on the farm, and while she enjoyed working in a grand house and being surrounded by beautiful objects, she did not crave that world the way her mother did. She had always expected to marry a local guy and have a family somewhere nearby, to go on raising chickens and keeping a large garden. Once out of her mother's house, she expected to be happy.

But obviously life had taken a different turn. There had been no local guy that her mother would agree to her seeing, and so instead of her own farm and family, she was stuck living with her detestable mother and now found herself desperately under the thumb of Monsieur Coulon.

But maybe, she thought, knocking on the door with renewed confidence, maybe there was a way to turn everything around. If he likes me so much, she reasoned, why not marry me? Then I would be able to leave Maman for good, and he will not want to see his own wife go to prison. He has so much money, he might even buy a little place in the country so I could have some animals, maybe another goat like the one I had when I was little. He's ugly, but so what? And as for what had happened in his bedroom...it certainly hadn't been romantic, but at least it had been over quickly. All in all, being married to him might be better than living with Maman. Almost anything would be.

Josette was pleased with her plan, if only because it is always better to have one than not. She did not have any specific ideas for how to put it in motion, but felt reassured nonetheless.

Anxiously, she knocked on the door. The mayor had mentioned giving her a key years ago, but never seemed to get around to it, instead leaving for the mairie only after she had arrived, even the times she was late.

Would he kiss her? Take her upstairs again? Or would things settle back down to normal?

The door opened and Coulon waved her inside. "Come, come," he said briskly. "I'm glad you're on time, I have a series of crucial meetings this morning and I must get to the mairie right away."

Josette glanced at his face but he did not look at her. When they had last seen each other, the events had been so momentous that neither one knew how to act.

"Well, good luck!" she said, trying to sound like a supportive wife. "Let's see, it's Thursday...I'll be doing the laundry and all the usual things, unless you have something else in mind?"

"No. No, that would be fine," said Coulon.

They stood awkwardly in the foyer for a few seconds, then he leaned over, inhaling the air next to her neck, and kissed her wetly on the cheek, while reaching around and giving her backside a squeeze.

When he had closed the door behind him, Josette wiped her cheek with the back of her hand. Getting straight to work, she gathered up the laundry and washed it in the washing machine in the kitchen, dusted the ground floor, and after lunch, lugged the basket of wet things out to the yard to hang them to dry.

Hanging the laundry was one of her favorite jobs, probably because it was an excuse to go out and feel the sun on her back. She liked the feel of the wooden pegs in her fingers, and the smell of the clean sheets and clothes. She had just gotten back in the kitchen, about to close the door, when she heard someone coming down the alley behind the house. Quickly she closed the door and stood behind the curtain, waiting a few seconds before peeking through.

It was that red-haired woman again. Just as before, she stopped, poking her head up over the back wall and looking intently at the clothesline. Who *was* this nosy person, anyway? She did not look like anyone from around there, thought Josette. It wasn't her clothes, or her hair, but something... something about her was not French at all. Josette did not trust her and wished she would turn her attention somewhere else.

After a few moments, the woman kept walking. Josette wanted to chase her down the alley, shouting at her to mind her own business, but she was in enough trouble with the mayor and did not need to go looking for more.

The pastries had been such a big hit the day before that Molly scootered into the village on Friday morning to get more. She always liked her guests to leave on a high note, and though the other guests were all staying for two weeks, the Vasilievs were due to leave the next morning. She would not be sad to see them go. After her long struggle for fluency in French, Molly found it very entertaining to try to talk to people when they did not share a common language. It turned into a game of deduction and charades that almost always led to hilarity and a feeling of warmth between the participants.

But apparently the Vasilievs did not feel the same way. Fedosia had knocked on the door of the house several times, asking for instructions on how to run the washing machine and what place had the best exchange rate for changing currency. But she did not linger, gave the barest thanks, and was gone. Molly could not remember seeing Vasily even once since they moved in on changeover day the Saturday before.

Meanwhile, she had shared several cocktails with Wesley Addison, after remembering from his visit the summer before that cocktail hour was a sad time of day for him, when he missed the ritual of making his wife a drink every day at five. Molly invited him to join her on the terrace and asked him if he would be so kind as to make her a kir, and one for himself too, of course, though he usually stuck with mineral water.

He regaled her, after a fashion, with stories from his work in linguistics, which could actually be quite funny after a kir or two. He told her that in Mississippi, people called a fat person a "squab." In Missouri, a coat rack was a "hall tree," and in Oklahoma, if something was delicious you could call it "larruping."

"Well, have some of this larruping cheese, then, Wesley. You know, the French never serve cheese before a meal and they probably have very good reasons for that. But some of my American habits die hard."

Often Molly organized a get-together at some point during the guests' stay—an *apéro* the first night, or possibly a dinner later in the week if the group seemed to be hitting it off. This week, though never intending to skip it, she kept coming up with reasons to put it off, and here it was their last night. Honestly, the prospect of socializing with the Vasilievs seemed like such an uphill slog, and she was in no mood, having been plagued all week with worries about Ben and their failing business.

Eh, maybe if I invite them, they won't even come, she said, on her way to the cottage to ask Nancy and Emily first.

§▲

BUT THEY DID COME, all of them. And not only that, Fedosia asked Molly if it would be possible to stay another two weeks, and the question came as such a surprise that she couldn't think of a graceful lie fast enough.

Two more weeks of the Vasilievs. *Ugh.*

Molly hustled in the kitchen to come up with a suitable meal for seven, giving Ben a quick call to press him into service. She went with simplicity, making an enormous salad, steak Diane, and garlic mashed potatoes, and sent Ben to Pâtisserie Bujold to pick up dessert.

"Thank you for inviting us," said Fedosia graciously enough, as Molly poured kirs for her and Vasily. Wesley was drinking mineral water on the terrace, where Emily and Nancy were giggling about something—probably their latest discovery of a cache of bones somewhere—and Molly suggested the Vasilievs join them while she and Ben finished preparations for dinner. Vasily said nothing and remained expressionless as usual.

"He gives me the creeps," Molly whispered to Ben as he dressed the salad and she whipped the potatoes, splashing in some extra cream.

"Is he always so stone-faced?"

"Always. Well, to be fair, I haven't seen him much. And he doesn't speak English, so I guess it makes sense that he doesn't react to what's being said. But still...usually when I'm around people and we don't share a language, people's faces are *more* expressive, not less."

"What are they doing in Castillac, anyway?"

Molly shrugged. She picked up the bowl of potatoes and turned to see Fedosia standing in the doorway, looking at them. Molly had no idea for how long, or what she had heard. Her face got instantly red, not being in the habit of insulting her guests and being overheard doing it. "Dinner's ready!" she sang out, sounding like a complete idiot. "Ben, you'll bring the steak? I think we've got everything we need at the table."

The weather was that perfect temperature of warm but not at all too warm, and the lightest breeze skipped along the treetops surrounding the meadow. Everyone was bare-armed and comfortable, and the sounds of an oriole and woodpecker were easy to pick out since no one was saying anything. Even the usually jolly Emily and Nancy were quiet.

"So, what brings you to Castillac?" Ben said to Fedosia, giving Vasily a smile.

"We are tourist," she answered, and applied herself to cutting her meat.

An awkward silence. Molly remembered with longing the many glorious dinner parties she had thrown back in Boston, full of laughter and serious conversation. Her success rate in France had not been not great, though she had to work with whoever showed up at La Baraque and didn't have the luxury of picking guests who would complement each other.

"How was Carcassonne?" Molly asked Emily.

"Oh, it was amazing. It's just like you said—such ingenious ways of hurting people! Though I suppose we like to think all that's long past. Don't think it is, really."

"We don't have to get into that right now," said Nancy softly. She looked around the table. "Sorry, it's just that Emily and I can get going on world affairs in a way that's not really meant for polite company."

"Are you on different sides?"

"Heavens, no! But we direct a lot of cursing at people we don't approve of."

Molly nodded and grinned. "I understand!"

"Cursing is interesting, from a linguistic perspective," said Wesley, but then applied himself to his steak and did not elaborate.

"We saw a reliquary in Cadouin," said Emily. "You're familiar with them?"

"Mummified body parts, right?"

"Yes. Of famous people—holy people. The one in Cadouin was less grisly, only a wisp of fabric claimed to be a headwrap of Jesus. At any rate, reliquaries were quite the hot commodity in the Middle Ages. Churches fought over them because they had the power to draw a lot of visitors."

"Money, in other words," said Ben.

"Exactly!" said Emily brightly. "Nothing like having a bit of the Pope's toe to really bring in the crowds."

"Or the Pope's...." Nancy could not finish the sentence before dissolving in laughter.

The other stopped eating, waiting to hear.

"*Private parts,*" Emily managed to gasp between cackles, and Molly and Ben laughed too.

Wesley looked uncomfortable. Vasily had eaten his steak and potatoes and sat looking at the older women with a scowl. Molly tried to come up with some way to make him laugh, to reach him somehow, but could think of nothing. She could sense Ben keeping an eye on him even when he was talking to someone else and not looking in Vasily's direction.

Molly knew it was considered impolite in France to ask someone what they did for work, but she was desperate for something to say and figured Ben would forgive her. "So what do you do back in Smolensk?" she asked, using every bit of willpower not to look at her watch.

Fedosia just stared at her and said nothing.

Oops, thought Molly. Guess it's rude in Russia too.

Never had a dinner dragged on like this one.

She and Ben managed to limp through the rest of the evening, with the help of some pineau after the meal and some slightly off-color jokes told by Emily. And there was no scowly guest on earth that could dim her pleasure in the perfect June evening, with that magical feeling left over from childhood—the soft air and bird-song meant that wonderful things were right around the corner, any problems would somehow solve themselves, summer would last an eternity, and all they really had to worry about was what delicious thing to eat next.

❧ 16 ❧

For Molly, it was strange to have a Saturday morning in June with no changeovers. The Russians, Nancy and Emily, and Wesley Addison were all staying over, so Constance came over for only about an hour to empty trashcans, change sheets, give the bathrooms a quick cleaning, and that was it.

"How's the wedding planning going?" she asked Molly on her way out the door.

"I don't know! Frances has been working under a deadline for the last week and I haven't seen hide nor hair of her. I guess it's still on? But I haven't lifted a finger with the planning yet."

"I know you love a mad scramble more than anything on earth," said Constance over her shoulder as she wobbled down the driveway on her bike with Bobo running alongside.

Do I? Molly thought, turning to go back outside. Maybe just a little.

She told Bobo to stay and took the scooter down rue des Chênes right after Constance, wanting to go to the market before it got too late to get anything good. On June Saturdays the market was crowded. Most of the tourists in the area were sure to be there, and almost everyone in the village and the surrounding area came, if not to buy, then to gossip and have lunch. The cafés around the Place were full to bursting and the mood was palpably joyful. And why not? The weather was absolute perfection—sunny but not ghastly hot, and there had been enough rain to keep the farmers and gardeners happy. Castillac had apparently returned to its peaceful self, with no apparent work for the gendarmes for months beyond the odd traffic ticket.

Molly parked the scooter and went straight to her friend Manette, who ran the largest fruit and vegetable stand. She was leaning against the truck with one hand on her lower back, while her older brother waited on customers.

"Bonjour, Manette!" said Molly loud enough to be heard over the bustling noise of the market-goers. "Are you all right?"

Manette looked up and smiled. "Bonjour, Molly." She shook her head, still smiling. "Just...just a bit of a surprise."

Molly waited, wondering.

"Turns out the family's going to get a bit larger in about six months," said Manette. "Turns out...forty-two is not too old to get pregnant."

"Oh my! Congratulations!" said Molly, kissing her friend on both cheeks and gripping her arms maybe a bit too strongly. A flood of mixed feelings swept through her so quickly that she was unsteady on her feet. "Are you...you're glad?"

"Not so much at first. Our youngest is eleven, so we really had moved beyond...the idea of diapers...but you know, we've come around. I do adore babies."

"Me too," said Molly softly. She rubbed Manette's arm and gave a quick glance to her belly which was just a little bigger than before. "So happy to see you and hear your good news. Now I'll hurry with my order because of the crowd." She filled her basket with eggplant and strawberries, an impulsive combination that betrayed her discombobulation, and moved off to look for the next items on her list, soap and chicken.

She always bought soap from a lovely deaf woman who made

it herself using plenty of lavender and goat's milk. Then on to Julien Barbeau, who had very good chickens if you were lucky enough to get there in time to snag one.

"Bonjour, Julien!" said Molly when it was her turn in line. "How is everything at the farm?"

"Good, thanks," he said. "Tell me, would you be willing to pay a little extra for an unusual breed? I've been thinking about adding some Bresse to the flock, do you know it? It's a breed that's actually been given the AOC designation, just like wine."

"Um," said Molly. "Can I ask you a slightly embarrassing question? I should know this by now, but what exactly is this magical AOC I see all over the place?"

Julien laughed. "It stands for *Appellation d'origine contrôlée*. It just means some agricultural product that is special to a certain *terroir*, or place. Like—Roquefort cheese, right? It only gets the AOC label if it is made in the caves at Roquefort. Any old blue cheese won't qualify. Now, strictly speaking? Bresse chickens come from eastern France, not the Dordogne. But a breed of chicken will travel pretty well outside its *terroir*, though purists might insist the feed won't be the same. Maybe more than you wanted to know!" Julien added with a laugh.

"Well, the main question is, are they tasty?"

"Depends what kind of cook you are. But I hear you're not half bad, for an American."

Molly took this as the good-natured teasing it was meant to be. "You don't have to graduate from Cordon Bleu to roast a chicken. All right, give me that one," she added, pointing to a nicely plump roaster, one of only five remaining. "How early do you run out, anyway? I don't want to miss you."

"Usually by eleven at the latest," he said. "You're back already?" he said to a pretty young woman approaching, whom Molly had never seen before.

"Molly Sutton, this is my sister, Josette. Molly has roast

chicken every week without fail. She's almost singlehandedly keeping the farm above water."

Molly laughed. Josette stared, instantly realizing she was the redhead who peered into the mayor's backyard in that annoying way.

"Kidding, Josette, kidding. Five—no, four—more birds and we can get on our way. The lettuce and eggs were gone by nine thirty."

"Oh, your eggs! If only I didn't have to hustle down here at the crack of dawn before you run out."

Julien grinned. "It's not a huge flock because our henhouse isn't that big. If we could only shake loose some money from our mother, we'd expand, right Josie?"

Josette mustered a hint of a smile, and nodded.

Molly paid and stuffed the chicken into her straw bag. "All right, I'm off! Put me on your list for the Bresse, Julien. And good luck with the henhouse," she added to Josette.

A bottle of rosé, some late asparagus, and dinner was practically made. She might have some difficult guests, her friends were getting married and having babies at a ridiculous rate, the P.I. business might be languishing...but Molly would have a wonderful meal, perfect in its simplicity, with Ben that night. Not half bad indeed.

❦ 17 ❦

Molly was long gone, already back at La Baraque thinking about whether to put a lemon in the chicken cavity or possibly take a swim in the new pool, when André Lebeau started making his way through the crowded market. He had waited for the moment of peak crowd size and judged it perfectly. He moved along, kissing cheeks and exchanging greetings, smiling at everyone, and throwing out a few winks at young women who watched him with big smiles.

Since he had no government position—and no job either, to be precise—he could not do much more than make promises about what he would do if he were elected, but he made sure that every small business owner he met got an earful about how much better his business would be with Lebeau on the council.

Less red tape! Lower taxes! More flexibility to expand! Lebeau was not entirely sure the council had that much control over some of the things he promised, but he figured that even if the specifics were a bit shaky, the overall idea was that he was in favor of supporting the little guy, as opposed to the giant stores that were beginning to crop up at the edge of towns all over France.

"Why should a giant supermarket be allowed to build right

here in Castillac, when we already have the best food available to us right here at the market?" he boomed out, stopping by Julien's stall as he was beginning to pack up. "I bet your chickens are far better than anything you could buy in a supermarket, right?" he said, clapping Julien on the back.

"Of course!" Julien answered.

"And how about you, *ma beauté*," Lebeau purred, turning to Josette. She lifted her eyes and saw how his chest muscles showed through his tight shirt. His arms were so big she thought he could pick her up with one hand. She giggled. André slipped an arm around her small waist. "And no one can say that the French do not have the most beautiful women in all the world!"

"Don't know what that has to do with running for council," muttered an old woman trying to get close enough to see whether there were any chickens left.

Josette put an arm around Lebeau and he squeezed her closer so that she could smell his cologne. Suddenly she was struck with a pang of anxiety—what if the mayor were to come by, and see her with Lebeau? He might fire her on the spot. Or at least be very, very angry. And what would that do to her campaign for marriage?

But she pushed those worries away and snuggled close to Lebeau, delighting in the firmness of his body and wondering if he had a girlfriend.

Lebeau kept talking politics to the crowd but he did not take his arm away from Josette's waist. He gripped her tightly when making an especially strident point, his fingers digging almost painfully into her flesh.

"Lebeau for mayor!" someone yelled, and without giving her any warning, Lebeau picked Josette up and put her on his shoulders as though she were no heavier than a doll.

"Lebeau for mayor!" Josette cried out, in all the excitement forgetting entirely her matrimonial plans for the current mayor.

THE NEXT MORNING Josette arrived at Coulon's feeling very conflicted. On the one hand, she was guilty for her flirtations with Lebeau the day before. On the other, however, she had enjoyed her moments with Lebeau and was resentful of having to spend any time with Coulon, much less trying to butter him up all the way to marriage.

Perhaps it was Josette's somehow expressing these contrary feelings that put Coulon in such a bad mood, but whatever it was, his face was unusually grouchy and he snapped at Josette and told her the coffee wasn't hot or strong enough.

"I'm sorry," she said, but it came out sulky instead of meek. Coulon reached for the newspaper and knocked into his cup, spilling some coffee on the table. Josette looked at the coffee spreading across the table and at him, but did not move.

"What has gotten into you?" he said. "Do you think you don't have to work anymore? You're too good to wipe up a spill, is that it?"

"No, I—" Josette could not find the right words but she moved close to him, and dared to slip her hand around his shoulders, wanting him to forget about talking. "I love...I *love* you, Maxime—"

Coulon scrinched up his face as though the sun had flashed into his eyes. "You love me?" he said. "What am I supposed to do with that?"

"Well," said Josette, lowering her eyes, a flush coming up her neck. "When people love each other..." but she faltered, unable to finish.

"When people love each other...?" Coulon said. "Are you—are you suggesting that I should *marry* you? Really? Is that what you're saying?" He got up from the table, taking a rag from under the sink and mopping up the spilled coffee himself. "Why in the world would *I* ever marry *you?*" he said condescendingly, wanting to hurt her. "So that's what you're up to? Ha! I will never do it," he hissed. "Never!"

❧ 18 ❧

Later that afternoon, André had a meeting with his friend Alain in the basement of Alain's house on the edge of the village. "It's so dead around here," said Alain. "Why Castillac, for God's sake? Why not someplace with a little size to it, make the operation easier to hide, you know?"

"The small size is part of the plan," André said impatiently. "We try to set up in Bordeaux or Toulouse, the gendarmes will be on us in two seconds flat. Here in charming Castillac, we've got nothing more than a few bumbling fools to deal with. If I can just get on the council and unseat that insufferable Coulon, we'll be on easy street, I promise you that."

"You're never short on promises," mumbled Alain, getting settled on a rowing machine and doing a few perfunctory rows. He was short and lean, in good shape, but without the bulging muscles of his friend. His hair was cropped in a military style, but his face had a softness to it, with full lips and a weak chin.

"Look, once that permit got blocked, we had to change strategy just a bit. That's what winners do, Alain—hit a roadblock, figure out a way around it. Never give up."

"Who said anything about giving up? I just don't think it has to be so complicated. We've got suppliers, all we need is customers. If the sporting goods shop is a no-go, we'll find 'em some other way, right? How about some local ads for body-building training, something like that?"

"Right. Sure. If you want to get one or two at a time, go right ahead. We need bigger numbers than that and you know it. If we don't move a certain amount of product, we're gonna get squeezed."

Alain shook his head. "I don't know why you wanted to get involved with those thugs in the first place," he said, too softly for André to hear. "And if we need such big numbers, what the hell are we doing in Castillac?"

"Ever thought about online sales, my friend?" asked André. "The stuff is small—a months's supply will fit into a cheap mailer. There's just no need to take the risk of being in a city when we can reach customers that way."

"So you're talking about online ads? And who's going to pay for those?"

But André was paying no attention to him. He had opened a small bag and taken out a syringe, a small glass bottle, a bottle of rubbing alcohol, and a box of cotton balls. Then he looked at himself in the mirror that covered one entire wall of the room, flexing his arms, and then lifting his shirt and twisting to the side, watching his abs pop.

"You gotta admit, the stuff really does the job," he said, grinning.

Alain shrugged. He had readily agreed to go into business with André, but the idea had been to make some quick and easy money, that's all. Taking illegal drugs to turn himself into some over-muscled freak—not his thing, not at all. Nor was getting entangled with a bunch of Russians whom he did not trust not to stab him in the back and toss him into the Dordogne on some moonless night.

André drew air into the syringe and then plunged it into the oil in the glass bottle, drawing it up to a black line on the syringe. Then he put the needle on the table and disinfected a place on his thigh with a cotton ball dipped in alcohol.

"I don't even want to watch," said Alain, doing a quick sprint on the rowing machine to distract himself from any thought of needles.

André laughed. Then he picked the syringe back up and plunged the needle into his thigh, grunting as he pushed the plunger in.

"Once they get their operation up and running, we'll be getting this stuff so much cheaper. Keeping up this physique is costing me a fortune."

"How long do you think we'll be able to keep this thing going?" asked Alain, panting.

André shrugged. "That depends. If I get elected mayor? Then we'll be sitting pretty no matter what. If I don't—and how I could lose to that pathetic slug?—then maybe a year...and we reassess. The Russians won't be sticking around that long, either way. They're just here to get the ball rolling, get the shop up and running. Once they do that, we can take over."

"But they'll still take a cut."

André shrugged again. "Well, yeah. Cost of doing business. They're the ones who know how to run a business like this. We need them right now. Later...anything can happen."

Alain laughed nervously. "You talking about skipping out on payments to those guys? You kidding me? I don't even want to guess what they do to deadbeats."

"I can take care of the Russians, and Coulon too," said André, gazing at himself in the mirror, more confident than any man in all of Castillac.

❧ 19 ❦

It had started out a Monday like any other Monday, Annette thought to herself later. She was the first to arrive at the mairie as she usually was; she unlocked the front door and made herself an espresso with the machine the mayor had kindly bought for them with his own money. Claudine and the others had come in and settled at their desks, everyone reasonably productive, everything as normal and regular as could be.

Except that the mayor did not arrive. He was known to miss the occasional workday, as everyone did, but he always called or emailed, usually the day before unless it was a matter of illness keeping him away.

Annette was worried. But she said nothing until the following day, when she could no longer convince herself that nothing was the matter. She had called, texted, and emailed, and gotten no response. So finally, when the time for an important meeting had come and gone with still no word from Coulon, Annette decided to take action. Without discussing it with her co-workers, she stepped outside to the street and called Maron at the station to tell him that the mayor was missing.

20

Molly was making a salade Niçoise for her and Frances to eat on the terrace while they talked wedding plans. She cut some romaine and added a few handfuls of baby greens, and was bent over looking for olives in the refrigerator when Frances breezed in, looking glamorous as ever in skinny jeans and a white silk top that set off her jet-black hair beautifully.

"Bonjour, Franny," said Molly, standing up with a crick in her back. "Jeez, you're looking fab. I would hereby like to give myself some major credit for being your best friend all these years. It's not exactly easy standing next to you, you know."

"What has gotten into you?" said Frances, genuinely wondering.

"I don't know." Molly scrunched up her face. "Ignore that. What I meant to say was, that outfit looks amazing, and what are you going to wear for the big day?"

"Let's call it a medium day, please," said Frances, a note of panic in her voice.

"Okay!" laughed Molly. "Bring the glasses and I've got the rest. I already put a pad and paper on the table so I can take notes."

"Notes? You're taking the whole thing way too seriously,

Molls."

"My best friend doesn't get married every day." She paused. "Oh, wait..."

Frances did not crack a smile. "Not funny. Okay, well, it *was* funny, but also not helping. I'm barely able to make myself go through with this. Maybe lighten up on the teasing until after the deed is done?"

"I'm sorry. Truly. Let's have some rosé and talk about something else and then we can start fresh. Have I told you I've been on a massive rosé obsession lately? I like drinking it with pretty much everything, especially things you're not supposed to drink it with. I don't know what it is about the wine-drinking rules, but all I ever want to do is break them."

"You do have a streak of willfulness."

"Doesn't everybody?"

"I always thought it was particular to redheads, but maybe," said Frances, flashing the first smile since she'd arrived. She took a deep breath. "At the risk of being exceedingly tiresome, tell me again why I am getting married for the third time?"

"Because you and Nico are made for each other, and it will make him happy."

"Isn't it weird that it's the *guy* who has his heart set on getting hitched?"

"Sexist pig."

"And why mess with something that's working so well? That's what I keep coming back to. We're so ridiculously happy at the moment. Why not sit back and *wallow* in it, instead of..."

"Oh, Franny, it's just a quick ceremony and then a party right here at La Baraque with all your French friends. Celebrating your incredible luck in coming for a visit and finding someone you love with all your heart. Anyone would be thrilled to be in your shoes!"

"Not literally," she said, pulling off a new loafer that was giving her blisters. "And if you're so big on getting married, why aren't you doing it?"

"It's not the same thing at all."

"Oh no? You and Ben are obviously totally smitten. There's no complication standing in your way that I can see. Or are you holding back about something?"

"No, not holding back. Just...we've never even talked about it. I..."

Frances put down her fork and waited.

"...I guess in the back of my mind, I've been thinking at some point he would dump me and look for someone younger. Not because he's a jerk," Molly added, seeing Frances's expression, "but because he probably wants to start a family. He's younger than I am, you know, and I'm staring forty in the face in a couple of months."

Frances let out a cackle. "Honestly, Molls, the crazy stuff we come up with! From over here, that whole story you just spun is nothing but a pile of b.s. And um, how about just talking to him about the children stuff for crying out loud?" They munched their salads for a few moments in silence. "What about Lapin? Isn't he about to jump the broom too?"

"Haven't been to Chez Papa all week and didn't see him at the market either. Maybe he's in hiding," Molly said, laughing.

"Just between you and me? It's Lapin's getting married that was the last straw for me to go through with my own wedding. I could stand plenty of indignities, but Lapin having more courage than me...oh the shame, the shame."

Molly snorted and picked up her pen. "All right, then. Decisions must be made, Madame Courage. Pick a date, first of all, and then I'm going to need to know how many people you want to invite, and whether you want a full dinner...and how about music?"

Frances turned even paler than usual as she poured herself another glass of wine. "Please tell me you have some dessert," she said weakly. "I'll get to all that in a minute. After a pastry and maybe three more glasses of wine?"

❧ 21 ❧

Paul-Henri Monsour, junior officer of the Castillac gendarmerie, was feeling queasy. "If it's all right," he said, officious as usual, "I'll just trot downstairs and let Nagrand know where we are?"

"Yes, fine," said Gilles Maron, smiling to himself because he understood very well why Monsour wanted to leave the room. The sight of Maxime Coulon lying on the rug in a gigantic pool of blood was enough to put anyone off, no matter how experienced in the grisly matters of murder one might be.

Chief Maron crouched next to the body, looking at it from different angles. A clear slit on the side of the neck, but Maron could see nothing lying around that could have made it. He stood and went into the bedroom across the hall, apparently Coulon's own, noting a sculpture of a swan and a few framed photographs on a bureau, a pair of pants draped over a chair. On the bedside table was a dirty coffee cup and a bookmarked novel. An undistinguished painting of a sunset at the beach hung over the bed.

The chief gendarme, as he often did, thought for a minute about what the former chief, Ben Dufort, would have done next.

Dufort had given him the best training of his career, which could mostly be summed up as listening to what people are saying that they do not mean to tell you, and following protocols to the letter. Maron stood in the Mayor's bedroom and tried to see if there was any statement, any meaning to the small items already catalogued, but he could see nothing. He made a note to find out who was in the photographs, and went downstairs to wait for the coroner and the forensics team.

"Well, we got a call from the mairie," Paul-Henri was saying to Florian Nagrand as he bustled through the front door carrying his big black bag. "I guess there was an important meeting this morning and Coulon never showed up. Never came in all day yesterday, which Annette—you know Annette? Receptionist at the mairie. Always most helpful. I once had a problem with the—"

"Monsour," interrupted Maron. "Let Florian get upstairs and do his job."

"Of course. I was just saying that Annette sounded the alarm and so we came over to check. The front door was wide open, that's one thing right there, and we called and so forth, and, well, you'll see..."

"Well, for once in your life you called when I wasn't just sitting down to the table," growled Nagrand, huffing as he went up the long set of stairs to the second floor. "It's been, what, four whole months since the last murder? Was beginning to think the village had gone back to its sleepy old ways."

"Carotid artery was cut," said Maron just as they got to the second floor.

Nagrand pressed his lips together, irritated as always that the gendarmes refused to keep their untrained opinions to themselves and let him do his job in peace. He stood quietly for a moment, looking at Coulon. "Impressive pool of blood, eh? Reminds me of the baron. Remember—"

"Not a château this time, but a pretty nice house neverthe-less," said Maron.

"In Paris, as I'm sure you know, houses like this are a dime a dozen. My mother always says—"

"Monsour, go downstairs and wait for forensics." Maron waited until Paul-Henri was gone before saying to Nagrand, "Sorry about him. He's not as dull-witted as he seems, actually, just doesn't know how to keep his mouth shut."

Nagrand made a wheezy chuckle. "All right then," he said, with some difficulty squatting down next to the body. "Yes, a cut to the anterior left side of the neck. Quite deep. At first glance I don't see any other wounds, though the autopsy might find otherwise. If the intent was to kill him, that slice to the neck did the job quite nicely. Preliminary finding is death by loss of blood caused by trauma to the neck." With a groan he stood up and wiped his hands on a rag taken from the black bag. "Maron, this isn't turning out to be an interesting case for me at all. Next time try to do better, huh?"

Maron smiled grimly. He had learned to stay out of the way and let Nagrand and the forensics team do their job, and was already starting a list of potential suspects in his mind. First stop, he supposed, was the mairie, so he said goodbye to Nagrand, left Paul-Henri nominally in charge, and strolled over to see who might be able to tell him something useful.

"Annette," he said softly to the woman at the front desk, her eyes glued to her computer screen.

She looked up and blanched, able to tell in an instant that the news was not good for the mayor. "Is everything all right?"

"I'm afraid not. Coulon is dead. Murdered, unless you have any reason to think he would have any desire to cut his own throat?"

Annette looked horrified.

"Sorry," Maron said hurriedly. "That was unprofessional of me. We at the gendarmerie tend to develop dark senses of humor, perhaps you can understand? At any rate, I *am* sorry. Would you be able to answer a few questions? I know it's a difficult moment for you, but we need to move quickly. Can you tell me Coulon's habits, regarding when he came to work, when he left, that kind of thing?"

"Yes," she said, and then put her hands on either side of her face. "Wait. Can I...the others should know..."

"This won't take long. As you might know, speed is critical in a murder investigation. As I said, I am sorry for your loss, Annette. The best thing you could do for Coulon now is help us catch his killer."

She looked down at the floor for a moment, trying to get control of herself. It's not that she had been close to Coulon, or even liked him very much. But he was her boss, he had been there every workday for nearly twelve years, and she was used to him. The thought that someone had killed him—it was hard for that to sink in. "He—we weren't exactly friends. But he was okay to work for. Fair, even generous sometimes. The office is going to be terribly upset."

"I understand," answered Maron, trying to keep impatience out of his voice. "Just quickly—did the mayor stick to a schedule? What time did he come in to the mairie usually?"

Annette sighed deeply. She fluttered her fingers on her forehead, trying to focus. "He is mostly quite regular, getting here by 9:30 most mornings. Lately...he's been a little more erratic. So when he didn't come in at all this morning, I didn't think at first... could...would it have made a difference if I had called sooner? Could he have been saved?"

Maron shook his head. "I believe he was dead in a matter of minutes, perhaps even seconds. The coroner will be the one to determine that with any precision. But whether you called yesterday or today—wouldn't have made a bit of difference. Now, what about the afternoons? Did he go out for lunch? Did he leave at the same time?"

Slowly and methodically Maron went through a list of questions with the distraught Annette, writing the answers down on the same brand of notepad Dufort had used. At first glance, nothing the receptionist said seemed to shed any light on what had happened the day before on rue Malbec. Maron worried that the investigation might take a long time, since it was not lost on him that a mayor might have all sorts of enemies that a regular citizen would not. He and Monsour might have to comb through council business and endless files at the mairie to find out who wanted the mayor dead; and who knew, there might well be more than one.

As had happened before since becoming chief, Maron felt an unpleasant buzz in the back of head, an anxiety that this time, he would not be up to the task and the murderer might go free. He would never admit it to anyone, barely to himself, but he hoped that somehow the team of Dufort and Sutton got on the case, because you couldn't ask for better backup than that.

❧

NEWS OF COULON'S murder whipped around Castillac like an out-of-control forest fire. His unacknowledged son, Daniel, stood down the block from his father's house for hours, watching official-looking people go in and out. He saw Maron and Monsour arrive first and sail in through the open front door. Next came Florian Nagrand with his black bag. Daniel waited a long time, long enough to see a stretcher at last leave the house, carrying a covered body.

Eventually, worried that someone might get suspicious about a stranger hanging around, the newly-half-orphaned Daniel made his way back to the Café de la Place and ordered a coffee even though he could not afford it.

His body was on edge, despite having stood for so long in the same spot, and his mind kept racing around to the same thought:

that his father was considerably more valuable to him dead than alive. A living father could reject him, as he already had. A living father could turn him away without a *centime*. But dead? Surely a biological son had some claim on the estate, whether he had met his father or not? Daniel did not know the specifics, but had an idea that French inheritance law was quite favorable to the children in almost every case. You couldn't just disown your flesh-and-blood son on a whim, no matter how negligent a father you were.

Daniel grinned and ordered a crème brûlée to eat with his coffee. He felt expansive, almost rich, as though the money were already filling his pockets. As far as Daniel knew, he was the sole heir. As it hurtled toward an abyss of stark poverty, his life had just come to a screeching halt, wheeled in the opposite direction, and was careening straight for that lovely mansion and all that was in it. And surely, anyone who lived in a house like that would have multiple bank accounts and investments, he told himself.

As he dug into his crème brûlée with gusto, he began to pay attention to what the other diners were talking about. Behind him sat two older women, who were of course discussing what had just happened to the mayor.

"I heard he was shot with some sort of automatic rifle," said the first woman.

"I don't know who you've been talking to. Someone making up a pack of lies just for sport! I have it straight from my neighbor's cousin, who works in the office next door to the coroner: the poor man had his throat cut! She didn't say what the weapon was though. I'm not sure they know. But get out of here with your automatic rifles!"

Daniel leaned in their direction so he wouldn't miss anything, sucking the last bit of sweet sticky goodness from his spoon.

"I bet anything it was Odile," said the first woman, lowering her voice but not enough to prevent Daniel from hearing.

"Hm. Maybe. They did have that big row on the street a few

months ago. You'd really think the mayor of all people would have a little more self-control! But why do you think Odile did it? She doesn't need his money, that's for sure. Her shops are popping up all over the place. And have you tried that new eye cream? I don't know what's in it but it takes ten years off," she said, tilting her face as though being photographed.

The first woman rolled her eyes. "She was *married* to him," she said, like it was obvious. "*You've* been married. Do I need to give you the illustrated version? Who doesn't want to kill her husband from time to time?" The other woman giggled. "And he was an *ex*-husband on top of it. Who knows what might have broken up their marriage and left her seething with revenge?"

The other woman threw her head back and laughed. "What an imagination you have! Odile may be a hard-charging business-woman, but she's always been perfectly nice whenever I've had dealings with her."

"You mean been one of her customers? Of course she's nice then. How many euros did you throw away on her eye cream? That stuff is *murderously* expensive."

The other woman hooted. They continued to discuss the mayor's case, the lack of any solid information not deterring them from making wild guesses and suppositions about any of the details. Finally, when Daniel was just about to leave, one of them mentioned Molly Sutton.

"Well, you may disapprove of her for whatever reason, but you have to admit she's the best when it comes to finding killers."

"Which we have seen far too many of lately...since she's moved here, I might add."

"No argument there. Do you think Chief Maron can just outright hire her? I admit I don't really understand the protocols involved."

"Don't be ridiculous. The Chief's job is to handle crime and arrest perpetrators, right? He can't go around hiring outside people to do it, and an American female detective on top of it. That would be like admitting he was a total failure at his job."

Daniel was listening intently. Quickly he paid his bill and rushed out into the mild June sunshine, intent on finding someone who could help him understand a bit about tax law—and how quickly a murder victim's estate might be expected to settle.

᛫ 2 2 ᛫

"Okay, so tell me *everything* you know about him," Molly said to Ben, who had come over to La Baraque after a day walking around the village talking to people, just like he had in the old days when he was chief at the gendarmerie. "I can't believe someone killed the mayor. This is so crass to say, but I know you'll understand: this could be a seriously juicy case, don't you think?" Molly's eyes were bright and she couldn't help grinning.

"Could be. Can't say this early. And I don't have to remind you that we have zero business sticking our noses into it."

"But we will anyway, right?" said Molly, crestfallen.

Ben shrugged. "Maybe Maron will ask for our help, but honestly, he's not going to want to. It doesn't look good, the chief running to the American gîte owner and former chief for help solving cases."

"I'd be more than happy to meet with him on the sly, if that's the problem. I don't do it for the glory."

Ben gave her a wry look.

"Well, maybe a teensy bit," she admitted.

"That doesn't matter. If our business is ever going to get off the ground we need all the glory we can get, and word of mouth to go with it."

"Well, we're getting a little ahead of ourselves. Let's *solve* the thing first," laughed Molly. "So come on, tell me about the mayor. Coulon, right? I met him a few times but don't know him at all. I've seen him working the crowds at village fêtes, that kind of thing. Was he a good guy? Did you like him?"

Ben popped the top on a beer and joined Molly on the sofa. "I can't say that I did, no. Not that I have any particular reason for not liking him, I mean, nothing solid. I just always had the feeling that he…was an operator, you know what I mean? Out for himself, above all. Oh, he pretended to be interested in the needs of the village, of course. Politicians always talk a good talk."

"Married?"

"Not anymore. His ex-wife is Odile Dupont, who has a store in Bergerac and I think some other places. Beauty stuff. He didn't have any girlfriends, that I ever noticed. I always had the idea that Coulon was more interested in money than anything else."

"What makes you say that?"

Ben thought for a moment. He reached over and stroked Molly's arm and then held her hand. "Just an impression, I suppose. I often saw him going in and out of the bank. Whether that was managing his own money or something to do with village business, I have no idea. It just struck me as odd."

"When Lawrence called to tell me—because of course he knew about the murder before almost anyone, practically before Coulon himself—he said the body was found in his house on rue Malbec. Which house is it—the nice one with the blue shutters?"

"Yes," said Ben. "I asked a few questions today in the village— just idle curiosity, of course," he added with a quick smile. "Apparently his family had some money—his grandfather bought that house, then his father had it and left it to Maxime when he died about five years ago. You don't get rich on a mayor's salary, that's for sure."

"Did his father make a lot of money?"

"I can't say. But that's one thing we might be able to check out without bothering Maron. Maybe Coulon got involved in a business deal with some shady characters to supplement his income, or something along those lines."

"Lawrence said the front door was wide open. That struck me as odd, how about you? Say Coulon interrupted a burglar who killed him in a panic—the last thing you'd want after killing someone would be to leave the door open, attracting attention."

"Yes, a murderer with any sense would want that door closed. Presumably the longer it took anyone to find him, the better."

"You make me nervous, saying 'presumably.' That's what gets us into trouble."

"Right you are, chérie," said Ben affectionately, scooting closer on the sofa and putting his hands in her hair. "Have I told you today how beautiful you are, carrot top?"

"No."

"I could look at your freckled face all day."

"Benjamin! We've got work to do!" Molly was unused to such romantic remarks from Ben and she felt a bit off balance. She grabbed the pad with the few wedding notes on it. "Can't we make a list? That'll at least give us the feeling that we're getting something done."

"I'm afraid that until we get some kind of standing in the case —and by that I mean someone actually hires us, or Maron swallows his pride and comes knocking—we're no better than the gang at the bar of Chez Papa making wild guesses."

"Well, I'm not as resigned as you. I'm going to head into the village and poke around a little, swing by the house, talk to whoever I can find, see if I can turn up any good nuggets."

"You are the best nugget-finder in the département, no doubt about that," he said, smoothing her tangled hair out of her eyes and kissing her on the forehead.

"Glad you think so. Now tally-ho, there's not a moment to be lost!"

❧

AFTER MOLLY TOOK off on the scooter, Ben walked back to the village by himself. He was in no hurry. Coulon was dead and nothing was going to change that; neither had he any particular worries that the murder posed any danger to the rest of the village, though to be sure, that was more of a wish than a fact.

He walked straight to the gendarmerie and went in, feeling the slight sense of dislocation one sometimes experiences when returning to a familiar place under different circumstances. "Bonjour, Paul-Henri," he said to the junior officer, who was sitting at his desk. "I hear Castillac just woke up from a nap."

"You could say that," Paul-Henri said, standing and making a slight bow, which embarrassed Ben. "Maxime Coulon, our mayor, as I'm sure you realize. Did you know him, Monsieur Dufort?"

"In passing. Is Maron in, by any chance?"

"I'm afraid not."

Ben waited to see if Paul-Henri would elaborate but he did not.

"All right, please tell him I dropped by. If there's anything I can do, please let me know."

Ben looked at Paul-Henri and wondered how a person could seem so smug without even saying a word. They said goodbye and Ben went back on the street, pausing to think about his next move.

It was murder that eventually had chased him away from his career at the gendarmerie, or more specifically, a bad case of anxiety that routinely cropped up during investigations. It was't so much that the anxiety itself was so terrible (though it was uncomfortable and deeply unpleasant); it was more that he began, as a consequence, to doubt his powers, and to mull over rather obsessively the few unsolved cases in the files, and conclude that he was simply not competent enough to do the job. But he had gotten past all that, thanks to a trip around the world and a lot of thinking, and enthusiastically started the private investigation business with Molly—in part, hoping to make up for those unsolved cases (only one remaining now) by bringing other wrong-doers to justice.

The mainstay of detective work, as anyone involved in it will tell you, is the tendency of people to blab. Castillac was something of a jewel in this regard; its inhabitants adored gossiping about each other, and more than once a case had been rescued from oblivion by the willingness of someone to share what he or she had seen or overheard.

One villager in particular, Madame Tessier over on rue Simenon, was known for having the best information. For three seasons a year, she sat outside her small stone house on a folding chair, talking at length to anyone who would stop by. And nearly everyone stopped, because she could be counted on to give them a delicious morsel or two about someone they knew—not maliciously, at least most of the time.

June was one of her favorite months, the weather being so encouraging for everyone to be out and about, and as Ben rounded the corner he could see her down the block, sitting in her chair talking to an old woman leaning on a cane. When he got closer she called out, "Chief! Come pass a bit of time with me. Madame Gervais has to rush off to do her shopping and I'm hoping you can answer a few questions for me."

Bonjour, Madame Tessier, Madame Gervais," said Ben, kissing cheeks all around. "I was hoping the same from you," he said. "Of course you've heard…"

"Oh, everyone has heard. I have to tell you, Monsieur Dufort, that I wish you were still chief. I don't think we'd be in the middle of such a crime wave if you were. Maron is all fine and well, I can't say I have anything concrete against him and I don't like slandering the man without cause—but you must admit, since you've gone, the situation in Castillac has become quite alarming!" Madame Gervais finished by raising her cane up and shaking it for emphasis. Ben suspected she did not actually need the cane to walk but liked having a handy prop. "Anyway, *au revoir* to you both, I've got to run off."

Madame Gervais was a hundred and four, and "run" might have been overstating the case just a little, but she took off down the street and disappeared around the corner faster than a lot of villagers much younger than she might have managed.

"So..." said Ben hopefully.

"Yes. I'll tell you right off, I'm not terribly surprised."

Ben's eyebrows flew up. "Really?"

"Maxime was always...a bit on the shady side."

"How so?"

"My memory is long, as you know. A boy gets detention for cheating in primaire—I file that away. It may seem like a small thing to most people, but to me, something like that is a mark of character."

"You don't think sometimes people make mistakes?"

"Of course they do. We all do. I'm merely saying that the flavor of those mistakes tends to be of a piece. It would not surprise me one whit if it turns out that Maxime was involved in something illegal, and got himself killed."

"Interesting. Any ideas on what that illegal thing might be?"

"You don't want me to do your entire job for you, now do you?" said Madame Tessier with a smile. "And tell me, how is Molly doing? Did the money go to her head?"

Ben laughed. "Yes and no. She's the same Molly, for sure. But it turns out she's something of a spendthrift, and the whole lot is practically gone."

"Tsk tsk," said Madame Tessier. "I pride myself on my frugality. I was born just before the war, you see, and my gracious, money was tight. My parents saved every bit of string, paper—we reused practically everything instead of throwing it away the way they do now. Different world."

"It is, it is."

"All right then, if you've got nothing to share..." said Madame Tessier, pretending to be irritated.

"I just told you Molly has nearly spent her fortune, isn't that enough of a tasty bit for one morning?"

Madame Tessier laughed. "I suppose. Have you talked to Maron? Any idea how the case is going?"

"No idea yet. One thing I was wondering—how long ago did Coulon's marriage break up?"

"First or second?"

"What?"

"Really, you must keep up, chief! Of course you know Odile Dupont, I believe that ended not long ago, last year perhaps? But he was married long before, when he was at university in Rennes, I believe. A quickie marriage and quickie divorce, is what I heard. She never even moved back to Castillac with him."

"Hm."

"Odile despises him, but I suppose that's not exactly unusual."

"Any particular reason?"

"All of the usuals," said Madame Tessier with a cackle. "Oh look, Monsieur Vargas, lovely to see you! Come sit with me a moment on this fine day."

Monsieur Vargas, suffering from dementia, looked confused but came and sat in the folding chair next to Madame Tessier. "I'll make you a cup of tea," she said to him, giving Ben a wink.

Ben said his goodbyes and walked away, lost in thought. Was Coulon's murderer an angry ex-wife? Or had he cheated someone out of something, and crossed the wrong person? Tessier had opened up vistas of possibility but offered nothing substantial as evidence. The questions tumbling around in Ben's brain were, number one, what was Coulon up to that got him killed (because since he disliked him, Ben would bet anything that the mayor had somehow brought the murder upon himself), and number two, how were he and Molly going to get in on the case, and, crucially important—get paid for it?

❧ 23 ❧

"Look, it didn't take an investigative mastermind to figure it out," Maron was saying to Monsour. "The second person I talked to told me that the girl had been working for Coulon for years. She's the sister of—you know Julien, who sells chickens at the market? No? Paul-Henri, you *do* go to the market on Saturdays? What, are you eating pizza every night?" he said, shaking his head. "Oh never mind, I sound like somebody's grandmother. Anyway, the point is, Josette Barbeau has been working five days a week for Coulon since 2005. The Barbeau family lives on a farm, way out toward Riberac. Julien gives her a ride into the village every morning and picks her back up in the afternoon.

"And you assume...?"

"I assume nothing. But if Josette was in the house the day of the murder, which would fit with her normal schedule, she could have seen or heard something. Or done it herself, for that matter. Come on, it's a long drive out to the farm."

"Does it make sense for us both to go?" asked Monsour, whose idea of a good time did not include out-of-the-way farms with their funky smells and pretty much guaranteed manure on your shoes.

Maron stood still, trying to decide whether to chastise Monsour for his insubordination. It was tempting to go without him; the prospect of a long drive listening to him talk about his mother and her Paris connections was not appealing, to say the least. "Someday," he said finally, "it would be good if you would simply do as I tell you, and not attempt to make every single thing a subject for discussion. Do you think you can do that?"

"Yes, chief," said Monsour.

"All right, stay here in the village. Keep your ears and eyes open."

"I could go over to the mairie and talk to more people there?"

Maron sighed. He couldn't be everywhere at once, after all. "Do that," he said finally. "I won't be back for some time, depending on how things go at the Barbeaus. Just the drive there and back will be nearly two hours."

Monsour brightened up and Maron went out and got on the police motorcycle, happy to have an excuse to ride it on the lonely country roads where he could go fast, clearing his mind and enjoying the thrill of leaning into sharp turns, the wind whipping into his face.

❧ 24 ❧

Malcolm Barstow, Castillac's most promising young thief, realized early on that he had gotten in over his head with these Russians. But in the optimistic way of young people, he believed he would be able to figure out an escape at some point down the road. So rather than admit his mistake and extricate himself right then, he pretended to be enthusiastic about helping the Vasilievs.

He had met Vasily and Fedosia on Sunday, when they had spied him stealing a magazine from the Presse. Fedosia walked up to him and grabbed him by the arm, suggesting that they take a few steps into an alleyway where they could talk in private.

Malcolm whipped his straight brown hair out of his face by jerking his head to the side, giving the woman the side-eye. He was good at sizing up strangers, and this one looked dangerous. He knew from the start that she was not going to turn him in, but rather use witnessing his theft as leverage. But for what? Castillac's foreign visitors were usually on the trail of obscure historical sites or rare cheese, not illegal activity.

His interest was piqued, perhaps more than it should have been.

He kept an eye on Vasily, who made him a little nervous, rightfully so since he had a dead-behind-the-eyes look about him and was strong enough to tie Malcolm into a pretzel if he felt like it. Malcolm's father was in jail again (fraud this time, having gotten carried away with impersonating an itinerant roofer and taking checks while doing no actual roofing) and the family would be in even worse shape if Malcolm followed him, but on the other hand, his mother, as usual, was in somewhat dire need of money. Fedosia promised him a sizeable wad of cash, so in the end, given the circumstances, she did not have to do much convincing for Malcolm to agree to help them with their project.

At first, it seemed an easy enough job. All they asked was for Malcolm to help them secure a rental on an empty building—first scouting for the kind of building they had in mind, and then coming up with a believable false name to use on the rental agreement, so as not to attract attention.

"But the thing is," Malcolm had warned them, "I understand why you want the building on rue des Chênes. It's out of the way, like you want, and convenient to where you're staying and everything. But what I'm trying to tell you is, if you're up to anything a little bit outside the law? And I'm not saying you are? But that building is bloody well right next door to Molly Sutton. And I want to let you know, mates, that you'll want to keep as far away from her as possible. I would advise not renting that particular building and changing where you're staying, if at all possible. Seriously."

Fedosia waved a hand dismissively. "You forget, boy, we're staying at La Baraque. We've been there for over week now. We know Molly Sutton. She thinks Vasily and I are a pair of stupid foreigners who can't speak anything but Russian. And she is easily distracted, a scatterbrain."

"Ha," said Malcolm under his breath. "She's caught a pile of murderers since she moved here, I can tell you that."

"Who said anything about murder? That is not why we came

here. We know her reputation. And anyway, don't you think it's the policeman boyfriend who solved those cases?"

Malcolm shook his head. There was no reasoning with some people.

"We want to make it clear," continued Fedosia, shaking her head quickly like she had something in her ear. Malcolm noticed that her platinum hair was so stiff it barely moved. "Privacy is very important to us. You get chatty...you'll be very sorry."

Even right then, when he had only just met the Vasilievs, Malcolm chastised himself for getting mixed up with them. But the lure of quick, easy cash proved too tempting, and he figured all he could do was hope they did whatever they were going to do and left town as quickly as possible.

But still, he was curious about what they wanted that building for. His criminal senses tingled anytime he thought about it. Perhaps there was more money to be gotten from them, and it could be quick and easy like the fat wad padding his pocket as he jauntily headed for home, anticipating the relieved smile on his mother's face as he held out enough cash to cover the rent on their dilapidated house for the next two months.

❧

A WINDOW in the downstairs corridor was cracked, and rather than luxuriate in the new swimming pool, Molly forced herself to go to the glazier's for a new pane of glass and some putty so she could replace the damaged one. That errand was delightfully accomplished without any trouble whatsoever, and she decided to swing by Pâtisserie Bujold on the way home, just to say hello to Edmond Nugent and check out the contents of the display case.

Well, she hardly fooled herself with that little lie, and soon enough Edmond was packing a small white box with an array of pastries that Molly claimed were for her guests. And she would share, really she would, as long as the guests happened to be available at La Baraque and not napping or out sight-seeing.

"They're just impossible to resist," said Molly, gazing at the display case. "The strawberries in that tart look unreal."

"They do have a glaze, you know, that gives them that shine," Edmond said proudly. "Now tell me, chérie, are you hard at work on the mayor's murder? You know we depend on you to root out all the bad elements here in Castillac. Which frankly, there seem to be an alarming number of."

"Well, *comme ci comme ça*," she answered, a bit glumly. "Of course, Ben and I have our eyes and ears open, but we haven't been hired by anyone. And really, who's going to, anyway? He's not leaving behind a bereaved family. I doubt his ex-wife is going to call."

"I gather she's delighted by the news."

"Is that so?" Molly felt a quick shiver. It verged on nearly imperceptible, but a shiver nevertheless.

"I exaggerate, don't take me literally. I adore Odile, she's one of the most fashionable women in the village—nothing on you, of course, Molly—and I don't mean to imply she's bloodthirsty. But it's no secret that whatever love existed between her and Maxime died a long time ago, and then turned into pure poison. Very acrimonious divorce."

"That's what I thought. You know of anyone else that Coulon had bad blood with?"

"Hmm," said Edmond, pleased that Molly was asking him. "Actually, Maxime spent much of the day strolling about the village trying to ingratiate himself with everyone. That worked, in some cases. Others of us, not so much."

"Not a fan?"

"Molly, he shopped at *Fillon*," he said, as though the taste of the word in his mouth made him want to throw up. Fillon was the other pastry shop in the village, which the highly competitive Edmond Nugent considered beneath contempt. Molly had never sampled their wares, rightly fearing Edmond's wrath if he ever heard of her disloyalty.

"Ah," said Molly. "All right, well, I should head home and get this window taken care of. Nice to see you."

"You too, dearest Molly."

She leaned across the counter to kiss cheeks, quickly turned and nearly bumped into Daniel Coulon, who had somehow managed to come in the shop without the bell tinkling.

"Excuse me!" said Molly, taking a step back.

Daniel cocked his head. "You wouldn't be Molly Sutton, would you?"

Molly summoned a fake smile. Very occasionally she found that her reputation had preceded her and it always made her quite uncomfortable, as though it meant that any moment she was going to be exposed as a fraud. "I am," she said. "Who are you?"

"Daniel Coulon." He moved to the side and looked into the display case as though the conversation was finished, tucking his worn T-shirt into his even more worn jeans.

"Pardon me for intruding, but are you related to the mayor?" asked Edmond.

"I am his son," said Daniel, and broke into laughter.

Molly and Edmond exchanged a look.

"I'm so sorry for your loss," said Molly. Daniel said nothing, but continued to look over the pastries in the display case. He licked his lips, still smiling.

Molly did not remember anyone saying anything about the mayor's having a son, but could not think of a way to broach that politely. For a long moment, the three of them stood in silence, until Molly decided to hell with manners, she needed some answers.

"I didn't know Monsieur Coulon had a son," she said, trying to soften the rudeness with a mild tone. "Perhaps you're from out of town?"

Daniel turned quickly to face her, glowering. "Some people

don't go around talking about every detail of their personal lives," he said. "That doesn't mean anything. Some people like to keep the things they care about the most a secret."

"Are you saying no one knew you were his son?"

"I'm suggesting that perhaps you shouldn't poke your nose in someplace that doesn't concern you." He turned back around, and pointed at the éclairs but did not say anything to Edmond.

"One more question, Daniel. If you don't mind my asking, how did you know who I was?" she said, picking up her box of pastry.

"Well," said Daniel, with a smug chuckle. "I didn't know. But I have heard of your exploits. I'm sure anyone around the département has, right?" he said, looking at Edmond for corroboration. "So when I heard him call you Molly, with the village being fairly small, I just made a guess."

Molly nodded. "Well, it was nice to meet you. I'm sorry for intruding, and also about what happened to your father."

"It's not sad to me," said Daniel. "I would like a caramel éclair, if you please," he said to Edmond.

Molly stood with her mouth open.

"I never even met my father," he explained. "My mother married Monsieur Clary when I was so little I don't even remember it, and I've always thought of him as my father. And we live in Laval, a long way from Castillac."

"Ah," said Molly, relieved he had opened up a little. "Did you come to meet him for the first time, then?" Molly asked. Information was coming in faster than she could process it. Did the rest of the village know that Coulon had an estranged son?

Daniel bit into his éclair, his eyes closed. When he opened them again, he stared at Molly as though trying to memorize the details of her face. She stepped backwards, wondering if he had heard her question.

"Everyone should be able to eat éclairs," Daniel said, smiling oddly as though he had just made an incredibly important announcement.

"Excuse me?" said Molly.

A group of schoolchildren came in the shop, doorbell tinkling like mad and the sound of chatter filling the small room. Molly bit the side of her cheek, wishing Daniel would talk more, but in the moment she could think of no way to make that happen, and watched helplessly as he paid Edmond and left Pâtisserie Bujold with a short nod of farewell.

III

❧ 25 ❧

The next day, Maron and Monsour went to the Barbeau farm together, no one having been home when Maron had gone out there the day before. Maron climbed into the car with a sigh, not at all looking forward to the long drive with his junior officer.

"I'd been looking through the old files, trying to find something to work on. But I guess poor Elizabeth Martin will just have to wait," said Monsour, fussily adjusting his seatbelt.

"I guess so." Maron jerked the car into reverse and screeched the tires just a bit as he accelerated forward. He would have found an excuse not to bring Monsour but he wanted to talk to Josette alone, and would need Monsour to keep the mother busy.

"So, is the housemaid a suspect? Josette, is that right?"

"Josette, yeah. We're only a day into the investigation, Paul-Henri. We don't exactly have a suspect list yet. At the very least the girl had opportunity, which I've been telling you is more important than anything else. We'll see what she has to say. I want you to interview the mother. She's suspicious of strangers, or gendarmes anyway—barely opened the door to me yesterday."

"Maybe she's covering up for her daughter."

Maron shrugged. "Well, keep her out of my way so I can talk

to the daughter without her interference. And don't be complacent. She looks like the type who'd stick a knife in your back without giving it a thought."

"You're saying the Barbeaus are a family of criminals?"

Maron sighed again. "I just meant...don't grab onto some small remark and run with it like that."

"What about a remark like someone made about the mayor the day before he died, let's see, I have it in my notes but I believe it was, and I quote: 'maybe he'll drop dead.' Followed by chuckling."

"Who said this?"

"Someone...let's see...a political competitor of Coulon's."

"You mean someone running for council?"

"Right."

"Where did you hear this?"

"Well, I performed some informal canvassing yesterday, hoping to turn up something helpful. Just some off-hours extra duty," he said, unable to resist the opportunity of making himself look good to his boss.

"Who told you this story?"

"Um, I believe it was...not Madame Tessier...oh right, I remember now. I was over by the primaire, and Ada Bellard was on the sidewalk talking with Georgina Locatelli, you remember, who used to be the housekeeper out at the chateau. I struck up a conversation. And they told me that a few days before the mayor was killed, André—*that's* his name, André Lebeau—had said maybe Coulon would drop dead. Seemed pleased by the idea, actually. Chuckling, as I said."

Maron chewed on his lower lip, thinking this over.

"Probably just talk, trying to make a joke."

"Maybe," said Monsour, not wanting his tip to lose value. "But still, pretty remarkable view into the future if that's the case."

"I'll grant you that."

They drove in silence for some kilometers. "Do you know Lebeau?" asked Monsour finally.

"I do not." He did not add that Castillac was full of people he did not know. "I only know his name because I've seen the slate for the election."

"Well, apparently he is aptly named. Ada and Georgina were positively drooling over him. 'So tall, so fit,' they said. More than once."

"Hard to imagine anyone getting killed over a council election. Stakes just aren't high enough."

"Maybe that's not all there is to it."

"Also, if you were planning to kill someone, why announce it to everyone on the street?"

"You've told me over and over that very often people who break the law are not the most intelligent."

Maron nodded reluctantly. "Okay, look, when we get back, you're on Lebeau. Find out whether that was just an offhand remark or something more meaningful."

"Are we going to search the farm at all?"

"Not officially. Keep your eyes open, though. Murder weapon would be nice," answered Maron, ironically.

"You think Josette killed him?"

"I don't think anything until we have some evidence. But we have to look for it and find it first, right?"

Monsour straightened his jacket and looked out the window, silently hating Maron for his condescension.

Maron speeded up, anxious to get to the farm and put some distance between himself and Monsour.

"One time, when I was no more than nine or ten, a man living in the apartment building next to our—"

"Paul-Henri? If this has nothing to do with the case, just save it, okay?"

Monsour pressed his lips together. He did not understand why

Maron disliked him so much, but at the moment, the feeling was entirely mutual.

❦

FINALLY, Maron turned into the short driveway of the Barbeau farm. The farmhouse sat by the side of the road, squatty and old, not charming. There was a dilapidated barn and a henhouse out back. The place did not have the air of neglect so much as want of funds; the grass was cut, and a neat stack of wood stood near the door, though paint was peeling and the roof had sections of orange tile that were cracked, with pieces missing.

"Remember, keep the mother busy," said Maron. "If Josette is home, I'd like to ask her some questions without Madame Barbeau hanging around and butting her nose in. Obviously I don't expect a murder weapon to be lying around in plain sight, but keep an eye out anyway. Look for things that seem out of place, anything that might have been pilfered from the Coulon house, understand?"

"Got it," said Monsour, resigned to getting the worse assignment every time.

The driveway was empty, no truck in sight. Maron worried that he might have missed Josette again, but just as he was climbing the two steps to knock on the front door, it swung open and a pretty young woman smiled at them.

"Bonjour, Messieurs?" she said. "What can I do for you?"

Maron felt his irritation at Paul-Henri melt away at the sound of her voice, which was not particularly melodious but had a scratchy quality he found instantly seductive. Even more than her voice, however, was the rest of her; she was dressed in a grubby pair of jeans and a T-shirt, but the jeans were tight in all the right places, and the shirt might have been custom made for the way it flattered her bountiful, curvy figure. Her chestnut hair fell to her shoulders, charmingly tousled as though she had just rolled out of bed.

Maron opened his mouth but no sound came out.

Monsour was similarly struck by Josette's good looks, but did not lose his footing. "Bonjour Mademoiselle. You are Josette Barbeau? We are Officers Maron and Monsour of the Castillac gendarmerie. We would like to ask you a few questions about the unfortunate death of your employer. Why don't you come outside on this beautiful June day, and we can talk here?" Monsour gestured to the unkempt yard as though inviting her into a serene garden.

"I...oh, it's just terrible," breathed Josette, quickly leaving the house and closing the door before Maman saw them. "Monsieur Coulon was very good to me. I can't believe it! I was so sad to hear the news." Her coloring brightened and the men both noticed tears beginning to gather in the corners of her dark brown eyes.

"It must have come as quite a shock," murmured Maron. He blinked his eyes hard, trying to block out the distraction of her sensual presence. "Is your mother home? Monsour, go ask Madame Barbeau if she objects to our having a look around. Josette, why don't you show me the farm, and I can run through my questions as we walk?"

"Sure, Officer," said the young woman.

"I'm chief, actually," said Maron, the first time he had ever said such a thing. Her eyelashes were thick and dark against her cheek when she looked down, he noticed. And her bottom, generous and round, her waist so narrow...he blinked again, feeling himself almost on the verge of panting, she was having such a dramatic effect on him. It's just an animal reaction, he told himself: now pull yourself together and do the interview.

"Now then," he said gruffly. "Tell me about the morning of June 13th, this last Monday. Was anyone at the Coulon house besides you? Did you let anyone in…any workers, delivery man, anyone at all?"

"Oh, that's the strange thing. I wasn't there. I've barely missed a day of work in all the years I was the mayor's housemaid. Not quite three altogether? Anyway, on Monday I wasn't feeling well so I didn't go in. I guess that's lucky in a way because otherwise maybe the murderer would have killed me too! But on the other hand, maybe, somehow? I might have been able to save him." She looked off into the woods and a tear trickled down her rosy cheek.

"I see," said Maron. "You were home with your mother? How about Julien? Where was he?"

"You know my brother?"

"You do have the best chickens."

"Thank you, chief!" she said, with a warm grin. "So let's see, Julien is usually gone most mornings. He goes to get feed, things for the barn, I don't know all of what he gets up to. You know how men are," she added, giving Maron a shy smile.

"Indeed," said Maron, nearly choking. He had lost virtually all professional distance, and instead of concerning himself with the mayor's case, he was thinking about the completely inappropriate things he wanted to do with this potential witness.

He cleared his throat and tried to get back on track. "Well, all right. Let's see…in the time you have worked there—over two years, you say?—have you had any occasion to think someone had a major beef with the mayor for any reason? Have you overheard arguing, anything like that?

Josette put a finger on her chin and looked up at the sky. She tapped the finger, and Maron stared at it, mesmerized. He stepped closer so that he could inhale the scent of her body, unmasked by any perfume.

"I don't think so," she said finally. "I was wondering if it was a burglar who killed him. He had plenty of valuable things in that house, you know."

"Like what?"

"Oh, silver things. Lots of paintings. There was even a silver knight on a silver horse, up on the third floor. I kept asking him, why don't you bring it downstairs where people can see it? And he'd say he was afraid someone might steal it." She finished with an air of finality, as though that anecdote clinched the case, and all the gendarmes had to do was find the thief who had come into the mayor's house and killed him.

As they talked, they had moved away from the house a little ways, over near the henhouse. Maron pointed to it. "What's in there?"

"The chickens, silly," she answered, unable to believe anyone wouldn't know such a thing.

"Did you work on the farm before getting the job at the mayor's?"

Josette laughed. "I worked on the farm before, during, and after! You're not from Castillac, right? A big city somewhere?"

Maron nodded. "My family is from Lille." He started to say something more about his upbringing, things he had never told anyone, but stopped himself in time. "And what are your jobs on the farm?"

"You're easy to talk to. I could talk to you all day," said Josette. "But what do my chores have to do with the mayor?"

"I'm just curious. I'd like to know how you spend your days."

They had passed the henhouse and gone into a field. The sun was shining and the grass in the field a strikingly bright green thanks to an overnight rain. It felt deeply peaceful on the Barbeau farm, with only the bucolic sounds of clucking hens and a donkey trotting over to them to break the silence. Josette chattered about farm work and her love of animals as they approached a small pond, where she fell silent. She turned to face him, her eyes tearing up again from emotion, and it was all Maron could do not to throw his arms around her and kiss her deeply on the mouth.

The moment tested him like no other since he had joined the

gendarmerie, but he did manage to resist, even if for a long moment he couldn't form any words.

§⟡

WHILE MARON WAS ALLOWING Josette to stomp on the last shreds of his professional objectivity, Monsour was ensconced in the dingy farmhouse, drinking a terrible cup of coffee with Madame Barbeau. He may not have been the most competent junior officer the Castillac force had ever seen—the much-missed Thérèse Perrault probably took those honors—but he believed he had one skill that came in handy more than occasionally: Monsour understood older women, and knew how to handle them.

"So you didn't grow up in the country at all? It must have been so difficult for you to adapt to life on a farm, after growing up in Castillac."

"Oh, it was, it was," said Madame Barbeau, nodding and fixing her large gray eyes on him. "You know how young love is," she said, giving a wink that sent chills through him. "I thought Adolph was the moon and stars! Turned out he was nothing but a mean, penny-pinching... well, that's over and done with, long ago. I suppose you want to know anything I can tell you about Monsieur Coulon. But I'm afraid I don't have much to tell. My Josette was very happy at the mayor's. He treated her well, paid on time, wasn't a difficult employer. She's quite upset by the news, as you can imagine. Do you have any leads, any idea about who could have done this horrible thing?"

"We're completely in the dark," Monsour said, with a confidential tone. "Did Josette ever mention anything like...someone coming over and arguing with the mayor? Did she tell you about overhearing any angry phone calls, anything like that? Or did the mayor talk about anyone in a negative way, someone feuding with him or something along those lines?" He broke away from

Madame Barbeau and walked slowly through the large room as he spoke, looking around for anything that seemed even a little bit suspicious.

"She never did. You think it was some bad blood that got him killed? I don't know how you gendarmes ever get anywhere with a case like this. Seems like the possibilities are literally endless. There are psychopaths that wander the country, killing people at random, you hear about that from time to time. Or someone might have been blackmailing the mayor, and they got into a tussle. And who knows what kind of business dealings he was involved in! Not to say the mayor was crooked—like I say, he was always good to our Josette, so I won't say anything against him. And of course, there's an ex-wife. She probably had a hundred reasons to kill him. Is it allowed—can you tell me how the mayor was killed?"

"Throat cut."

"Ouch," said Madame Barbeau, but Monsour turned back to her and thought he saw a slow smile creep over her face.

"Was Josette very upset when she got home from work that day? I understand that it was someone working at the mairie who found him. Why wasn't Josette there when it happened, if you know? Of course, if she knew the mayor had been attacked, she should have called us immediately. But I do understand," he said, giving Madame Barbeau a sympathetic look, "that sometimes in a moment of crisis, we flee instead of thinking clearly about what must be done."

"Oh, it wasn't anything like that. She was home sick," said Madame Barbeau. "I don't mind telling you, as you seem to be a decent young man, that I'm glad she wasn't there. You never want your daughter mixed up in anything like this."

"Of course. Quite understandable," said Monsour, running his eyes over everything he could see in the kitchen, but seeing nothing at all that didn't fit with the generally rundown feel of the house. "Was anyone outside of the family here that day, who might have seen Josette?"

"Are you saying she's a suspect?" said Madame Barbeau, drawing back in surprise.

"No, madame. I am only asking the usual questions and making an effort to have corroboration for every statement anyone connected to the case makes. Standard procedure, that is all."

"Well, now that you mention it—talk to Rémy, the organic farmer. He was out here that day, and he and Josette spent a little time together in the henhouse. He's looking to expand and asked if we were interested in growing some out-of-the-way vegetables he claims there's a market for."

Monsour was not interested in vegetable farming, but he made the note to talk to Rémy. His gaze lingered on a set of knives hanging from a wire strung below one of the few kitchen windows, especially noting the cleaver. Not being a cook or a butcher, he had never wielded one, and he guessed correctly that Madame Barbeaus was an expert.

But it was not Madame Barbeau who had killed the mayor, unless this case was more tangled than they knew, and Monsour kept looking.

"You sell eggs, as well as chickens?" he said, seeing a large stack of egg cartons on the kitchen counter.

"You don't shop with Julien?" said Madame Barbeau, pretending to be affronted. "Yes, although not as many as we'd like. They sell out quickly, believe me. Maybe now that Josette has lost her position, we can increase the laying flock. She was limited for time, you understand, while she was at the mayor's, and I'm afraid I don't have that many hours of work in me a day. Arthritis," she said holding out her gnarled hands for Monsour to see.

"Oh, my," he said, taking them in his own, and giving them a light rub. "I'm a city boy, as you've no doubt figured out, but anyone knows that running a farm takes many hands and many hours!"

If her mind were not racing in ten different directions, Madame Barbeau might have enjoyed Monsour's visit more than anything in along time. As it was, she was wracked with worry about Josette outside alone with that other officer, whom she could tell in the few minutes she had seen him the day before, was very much more a force to be reckoned with than the mealy-mouthed excuse for a gendarme taking up space in her kitchen. Josette will never know how to handle herself, she thought. And it wouldn't be the first time that an innocent person gets blamed for something she did not do.

"I want to speak with the chief," she said moving for the door, and despite her arthritis, was spry enough to get out before Monsour could think of a way to stop her.

❧ 26 ❧

With some trepidation, Odile Dupont pulled her late-model Peugeot into the driveway of La Baraque. After parking, she checked her makeup in the mirror on the underside of the sun-visor, and got out of the car. A large pile of pulled weeds stood wilting in the sun by the front flower border, and the well-dressed woman scowled at it, never being one to tolerate any sort of messiness at her own house. Nervously she twisted a ring on her right hand, an understated but beautifully cut sapphire flanked by diamonds.

Molly answered the knock quickly. The two redheads looked at each other for a moment in surprise.

"Bonjour?" Molly said at last.

Odile jerked her head. "Oh! I'm sorry, bonjour madame, I am Odile Dupont. Former wife of Maxime Coulon?"

"Nice to meet you. Molly Sutton." She held out her hand and they shook. "Please come in. And excuse my clothes, I've been working in the garden."

Odile looked at the grass-stains on Molly's pants and said nothing.

"Is there something I can do for you?"

"Yes. Well, maybe. I hope so. I'm sorry to bother you like this, showing up unannounced, but somehow the telephone just did not seem..."

"Come in, come in," said Molly, praying that the chance to get in on the Coulon case might actually be standing right on her doorstep. "Can I make you a coffee? Tea?"

"No, no thank you." They walked to the somewhat disheveled living room and sat down, Molly inwardly cringing at the sweater flung over the back of the sofa and the sloppy pile of gardening magazines on the floor. Surreptitiously she snatched an empty glass from the side table and shoved it under the sofa.

"I'm so sorry to hear about Maxime," Molly said. "I'm divorced myself, so I understand it's somewhat complicated...of course, just because you separated doesn't mean you wished for something terrible to happen. Obviously." *Jeez, did I not drink enough coffee this morning? I sound like a fool.*

"Yes, you're exactly right," said Odile, her face visibly relaxing. "I'm grateful to hear you put that into words. Our divorce was not a friendly one, as I'm sure anyone in the village will tell you. And that's...that's why I'm here."

Molly met her eyes and waited. She thought back to the conversation she had overheard, between Odile and a friend at the Café de la Place, when Odile had said something about her husband getting pushed in front of a train. Surely that had just been exaggeration, an attempt to be amusing?

Odile looked away and fidgeted with the sapphire ring. "You see, I have my own business. Perhaps you have seen them, or been a customer? My shops are called *Beauté Simple*, so far in Bergerac and Brive. More to come, I hope."

"Congratulations. I'm sure that's the result of a great deal of hard work! Speaking as someone running my own business here at La Baraque, I know a little of what you're up against."

"Oh yes? What sort?" Asked Odile, glancing around doubtfully.

"A gîte business," said Molly. "Of course it's not nearly as complicated as what you're doing. But you know, still the constant need to take care of problems, worry about the bottom line, plan how to improve, all that. Is the problem you're having related to *Beauté Simple?*"

"Sort of. Well, not exactly. Let me explain. It's only that...in retail, image is everything. *Everything*. The design of the shops, the tubes and bottles, the way I dress—everything gives customers an impression, you understand? And let me tell you, murder is most definitely *not* something I want associated with my brand!"

Molly noticed Odile's hands trembling, and she was fairly certain it was not caused by sorrow over her ex's fate.

"This business with Maxime needs to be wrapped up immediately or I'm worried it may cause permanent damage. This sort of scandal—and I don't pretend to have the slightest idea who killed him or why, but whatever the story is, it's something terribly seedy and low, that's obvious enough—this sort of scandal can ruin a brand. Just ruin it—to the point where it cannot be salvaged."

Molly held her breath. She thought, this woman hated her husband. And is not sorry about his death.

"Thankfully, thus far my business has done very well, so I have the funds to hire you. Name your price, Molly. You come with the highest recommendations from every person I have spoken with. Lapin Broussard especially."

"You know Lapin?"

"Oh, most of us in the village know each other. Lapin and I were in school together, and occasionally I buy something from his antique shop. He calls me when he thinks something's come in that I might like. In any case, what do you say, Molly Sutton? Will you take the case? I need this thing wrapped up as soon as possible. Sales are already down and if rumors start to swirl about some of the public fights Maxime and I had, I'm afraid that will only get worse."

Molly, of course, readily agreed, deciding on the spur of the moment to ask for about thirty per cent more than the fee she and Ben had decided on. Odile assented without hesitation, and rushed off to a meeting in Bergerac she claimed she absolutely could not miss.

All very curious, thought Molly, settling back on the sofa with a cup of fresh coffee after the Peugeot had disappeared down rue des Chênes. Never a word about all the reasons most people want to find a killer: nothing about justice, or making the village safer, or avenging Coulon's murder. Odile's only concerns were business and branding. For an instant Molly wondered whether hiring Dufort/Sutton Investigations was anything more than a public relations move.

Then she grinned. They were on the case! And she dug out her phone to text Ben the news.

✣ 27 ✤

The ride back to the village was quiet. Maron was embarrassed by his conduct with Josette; even though he had said or done nothing untoward, he knew he had been embarrassingly distracted by her feminine charms.

Well, it wasn't her charms exactly, to be honest. It was her animal, physical presence he had responded to, her shape and her smell. Unable to imagine any man not similarly affected, he had a quick flash of pity for Coulon, having her in his house day after day.

Josette claimed she wasn't at the house the day of the murder, and all that remained was to check with Rémy, and double-check to see if any of the neighbors had seen her. Perhaps the delivery boy for the *épicerie* might have been on the streets and noticed something, or the postman.

Typical legwork, that's all that was required. He welcomed the tediousness of it, in a way. Just a long list of boxes to tick off, precisely and thoroughly, and by the end of the process, there was your killer. Though he suspected Molly Sutton operated somewhat differently.

"So what did you think?" asked Monsour, after they had driven for a good half hour without speaking. "Do you believe the girl?"

"Same as any witness at this point in an investigation—I don't believe or disbelieve."

"Hm," said Monsour. Having eyes in his head, he had seen how Maron responded to Josette, but wisely he kept his thoughts to himself for once. "The mother is certainly of a piece of work."

"Suspicious of outsiders, for sure. You get anything from her?"

"I did not. I thought I was successfully softening her up, when suddenly she said she wanted to talk to you and barreled out the door. I'll say this though: if Madame Barbeau had been the housemaid to Coulon, I'd bet a Louis XV armchair that she was the murderer."

Maron was happy to talk about someone other than Josette. "I told you I sensed a violent streak in her."

"I kept glancing at the set of knives dangling from a wire in the kitchen, and thinking that if she had reason to, she would pick one of those up and slit my throat without a moment's hesitation. Just, you know, just a feeling I got."

"And what kind of feeling did you get from the daughter?"

Monsour shrugged. "A pretty girl, a bit dim. I suppose we should talk to the brother as soon as we can—doubtless he will back up her story, but Madame Barbeau said Josette doesn't drive. If she was in the village on Monday, he would have driven her."

"And driven her home after the murder."

"When we get back, let's find André Lebeau," said Maron. "Interview him. He may be a much better suspect than Josette, given that he was Coulon's competitor in the election and as you said, making death threats."

"Though you said that if you were going to murder someone, probably best not to announce it in public beforehand."

"And I believe you answered and we have previously noted on innumerable occasions, criminals are often idiots. What else do you know about Lebeau?"

"Not much. He's a loudmouth." Monsour was pleased to have been given the interview to do on his own, and already feeling protective of any information. He had gathered from Ada Bellard and Georgina Locatelli that André's interest in running for office had something to do with small business interests, but Monsour wanted to understand that angle more completely before bringing it up with Maron. This was his first real chance to impress his boss, and he wanted to give it a wallop.

❧ 28 ❧

"I thought you would be thrilled," said Molly, mixing lettuce with a mustardy salad dressing as she put the final touches on lunch for her and Ben.

"Who said I'm not thrilled?"

"You didn't crack so much as a smile."

"I suppose my mind had already run ahead and gone around the bend in the road."

"Which road is that?"

"The road lined with the ever-growing list of suspects in the case, and the huge amount of legwork we need to put in before we can hope to get anywhere at all. Of course I'm very pleased, just anxious to get at it."

"Now you're talking my language. What's the list look like so far, in your opinion? The chicken's ready, would you scrape the rice into a bowl and set it on the table? And bring the drinks."

Ben came around the side of the kitchen counter, kissing Molly on the ear as he passed by on his way to the rice. "In no particular order: his son, if indeed Daniel is actually his son. Also, I'm interested in the banking angle...I've got little to go on besides noticing Coulon seemed to go into the bank unusually often, but speaking generally, you know how time and again money turns out to be the motive for murder. At any rate, that's where I'm going to continue digging for now. Monsieur Lachance at the bank has not been very forthcoming, claiming privacy restrictions, but I may be getting somewhere with his assistant. There's Josette the housemaid, of course. And I don't think we can leave our client off the list either."

"Right, I had the same thought. I wonder if it would be terrible for business if we ended up getting our own client arrested?"

"It could definitely have a chilling effect, at least as far as more criminals wanting to hire us," Ben said wryly.

"About Josette—I made a few calls this morning, itchy to get started. Turns out Rémy was out at the Barbeau farm the day of the murder, and corroborates Josette's story about being home sick that day."

"Rémy and the Barbeaus? I wouldn't have thought they'd have anything to do with each other."

"Something about AOC chickens and some strange vegetables he doesn't have room to grow? You know Rémy, in two seconds he was off talking about soil composition, drainage, and all the flap about new EU rules for organic certification. Anyway, he says he talked to her at the farm on the day of the murder, so that's one less person to worry about. I'll go ahead and interview her in case she has something to tell us about who the mayor hung out with, his habits, all that jazz."

"All right, good, keep going. Tell me more about running into Daniel Coulon."

"He was a bit strange," said Molly.

"His father was just murdered."

"Right. *If* he's actually Coulon's son. I guess it would be a little unorthodox to ask Maron to ask him to take a DNA test? Should we call Nagrand and ask him to swab some of Coulon's cells, or is it too late for that?"

"Not too late, I don't believe. But maybe to avoid asking a favor of Maron, how about contacting Daniel's mother—Coulon's first ex-wife—and see if she can shed some light on the family situation. Who knows what you might be able to get out of her."

"I hope you like lemon. This sauce will turn your mouth inside out."

"I adore lemon, actually—have you forgotten how Frances has infected me with her addiction to fresh lemonade?"

"Oh yeah. I'm...sometimes not that great with...I get distracted..."

"By murders, instead of your boyfriend's tastes?"

"You could put it that way."

"Excellent. That'll be good for business."

They smiled at each other, a warm, loving smile of appreciation, and dug into the food.

"So Daniel was a little odd, as I said. He looked...poor. He expressed zero sadness about his father, but maybe the fact that they didn't know each other explains that? There was definitely something chilly about him. But more than that—he zigzagged all over the place, one minute chuckling, the next minute super defensive. I don't know if it was instantaneous mood swings or he was hiding something. But he was definitely off somehow."

"Hmm."

"I was thinking, if he's as poor as he looks, there might be a financial angle."

"Right. Though you don't want to go around assuming if someone's not well off, they're automatically a candidate for murderer."

"Not what I meant. He was *weird*, Ben. Not only not grief-stricken, but seemed to be almost happy about the death."

"All right. Let's hear from Daniel's mother before we go too far with this. She may say there is no son and this guy is a con man or something."

Molly nodded, chewing thoughtfully and thinking about

Daniel. She made a mental note to ask Edmond what his impression of the young man had been.

"Okay, let's lay out our first steps, shall we?" said Ben.

Molly nodded. "I was thinking I'd head out to the Barbeau farm tomorrow morning, talk to Josette, and get her view of Coulon as well as anyone who came to the house over the last few months."

"Want company?"

"Of course. But maybe you should follow a different lead. Can you meet with that bank assistant again? Talk to Odile, maybe? Do you know her?"

"I used to. We were in school together, all the way through lycée. She was always a sharp one, winning math contests and things like that. No surprise she's made such a success—she's one of those people you can tell early on will accomplish something."

"But you didn't know Coulon?"

"He's a little older. You know how it is with kids, a few years can make a big difference. I knew who he was, vaguely, but we weren't friends or in the same classes. And he was definitely not one of those people who have success written all over them. He was sort of a...nobody. That's my slim bit of memory about him, anyway. Not someone you wanted to be around."

"You find out anything on your stroll around the village?"

"I did not. Even Tessier had nothing of interest."

"What about the method of killing? I know we always talk about means, motive, and opportunity, so I guess this sort of fits under means...what I'm wondering is, what circumstance, or personality, brings about a throat-cutting? Is it a crime of impulse, or something planned? How much force would it take?"

Dufort grinned at her. "It is a joy to watch you in action, chérie."

"Oh," said Molly, coloring a little. Ben had been so full of compliments lately that it was making her a little uncomfortable.

"To answer, I'm not sure you can say much that's definitive.

Could be an impulsive act or not—obviously it would help to have the murder weapon. In this case I lean toward planned, because in the guest room, what would be at hand to slit a throat with? The knives presumably were in the kitchen. Guest rooms don't tend to have much of anything in the way of weapons, do they?"

"We need to get in that house and find out."

They ate quickly, anxious to get going. They left the dishes in the sink, kissed goodbye, and went their separate ways, Molly on the long ride to the Barbeau farm, and Ben to the gendarmerie to see if he could find Maron and arrange a look inside the mayor's house, before heading back again to the bank.

The owners of Dufort/Sutton Investigations were feeling energized and confident that beautiful Thursday in June, not so complacent as to think the murder was nearly solved, but they had outlined the steps to get there, and soon enough the latest evil to threaten Castillac would be arrested, giving their business a welcome boost.

They had no idea, not yet, that the mayor's case was going to become quite a lot more complicated—and dangerous—in very short order.

❧ 29 ❧

The air was sweet and warm, the sky an intense blue as Molly revved up the scooter for the trip to the Barbeau farm. A long solo drive is a perfect time to do some clear thinking, thought Molly, zipping down rue des Chênes away from the village and whipping around a corner. But the case was so new, there wasn't much to turn over in her mind. The mayor had been killed on the second floor of his house, in the guest room. Did the exact location matter? How often would you go into a guest room if no one was staying there? Had he been preparing the room for someone—Daniel Coulon, for example?

She made a mental note to ask someone at the mairie if Coulon had an appointment book they could look at, and to ask Ben if there was a way to access his phone records.

Having little else to consider, for the rest of the forty-five minute drive Molly made a mental list for Frances's wedding party: she needed containers for flowers, because there *would* be flowers, no matter what Frances said. A long linen tablecloth, snowy white, that would look so lovely with fallen petals scattered across it. The food—oh, what in the world could she make that would be extraordinary but not take too much time away from working the new case?

When she got close, Molly began to slow down at each farm, looking for house numbers sometimes in vain, but she recognized Julien's truck parked next to an ancient stone house with some outbuildings scattered behind it, and pulled into the driveway. She smiled to herself, having discovered that she had an effortless, almost photographic memory when it came to cars and trucks, which was rather a surprise since she wasn't especially interested in them.

The farm was quiet except for a rooster crowing over and over somewhere behind the house. Molly went up to the front door and knocked hard several times, hoping Julien would come to the door, since she knew and liked him.

But instead, the door cracked open just barely, not enough for Molly to see anything except a narrow stripe of face and dark clothing below.

"What do you want?" asked a voice. Molly was at least relieved that the woman's accent wasn't unusual and she could understand her without any difficulty.

"Pardon," Molly said, and then used what she had found to be the magic words when she wanted to enlist someone's help in France: "Excuse me for bothering you, but I need some help."

The door did not budge.

"My name is Molly Sutton, I live in Castillac. Ben Dufort, the former chief of gendarmes, is my partner." She paused, this being the first time she had introduced herself that way, and thinking it sounded like she was talking about a boyfriend. "I mean, he and I have an investigation service. We are looking into the mayor's case and I would like to talk to Josette."

She was about to ask if Josette was home, but held back, not wanting to give the woman an easy out.

The door did not move and the woman did not speak. Molly

shifted her weight, waiting, and just as she was about to try to say something reassuring, the door swung open.

"Bonjour, Molly," said the old woman, smiling. "I am Alicia Barbeau, Josette's mother. Of course your exploits are famous, even as far away from the village as we are here. I grew up in Castillac, as a matter of fact, but it's a simpler life we lead, you understand, in the country. Up with the sun, physical labor all day. Not much extra time for following the goings-on in the village, or anyplace else for that matter."

"I understand. I've never done farm work myself, having grown up in Boston, but I'm very grateful for your hard work. I benefit from it directly—I'm a longtime customer of Julien's. Your chickens are amazing and I try to get one every Saturday. And your eggs! Oh, they are the best anywhere. I can't tell you how many double yolks I've gotten! And they are the deepest, most beautiful orange. One of my favorite colors."

Madame Barbeau was taken aback by this outpouring of verbiage, not used to being around Americans who will sometimes share their personal opinions with you only seconds after being introduced.

"If you will wait here for a moment, I will tell Josette you are here. She is up in her room, where she spends much time these days, I'm afraid. The death of her employer has hit her very hard, especially as sudden and violent as it was."

Molly nodded. She listened as the old woman slowly made her way up the stairs, then heard murmuring between mother and daughter. In a few moments a young woman came downstairs, her gait not sounding lugubrious to Molly, but rather light and energetic. Molly remembered how pretty she was, and held out her hand to shake.

"Nice to see you again," said Molly, "I'm so sorry for what's happened. You must feel rather shaken.

Josette nodded and shook Molly's hand.

"Would you like a cup of tea? Or coffee?" asked Madame Barbeau.

Molly was hoping the old woman would leave to do some of that constant physical labor she had talked about, but she showed no sign of budging.

"Coffee would be lovely," said Molly. "Then maybe we could take a walk around, you can show me the farm?" she said to Josette.

"That's what the chief wanted to do, too," said Josette.

"Ah, Maron's been here?" Molly was not surprised but was looking for Josette's reaction to the gendarme's visit.

Josette only nodded.

Madame Barbeau bustled in the kitchen as though preparing a great feast. "I'm wondering—since I was born and raised in Castillac, you see, and only got this far away—what brings a person to change countries? I don't mean to be rude, but isn't that sort of drastic? Were you running away from something?"

"Maybe," said Molly with a laugh. "A bad marriage was part of it. But mainly, I moved here because I love France so much. The first time I came I was a teenager, and it felt—I know this will sound corny—but it felt like I was coming home. Then for years I sort of buried that feeling, and went on with my American life. When that fell apart, and the marriage breaking up wasn't the only thing, I was unsatisfied in my job too...well, it seemed like the moment to come home had finally arrived."

Madame Barbeau and Josette looked at Molly with wide eyes.

"I know, I know, in France it is considered strange, perhaps impolite, to say so much when we've just met. But you did ask," said Molly with a laugh, as she took the cup of coffee from Madame Barbeau. The cup was fine china, a chip on the rim, with a faded gilt pattern and a delicate hook.

"Please excuse me for asking," said Madame Barbeau, drawing herself up. "I wish Josette had something to tell you about the events concering the mayor. Of course we would be happy to further the cause of justice if we were able. But unfortunately, as you may have heard from your friends at the gendarmerie, Josette woke up that morning with a bad headache, and did not go in to work that day. So she is not in a position to give any evidence whatsoever about who came into the house the morning of the mayor's murder."

"I guess that was lucky for you," said Molly, with a small smile at Josette.

Josette relaxed a little. She pulled her hands out of her jeans pocket and smiled back. "Yeah, I'd rather be far away when murderers are on the prowl!"

"Will you give me a tour? Since you weren't there on Monday, I don't have a ton of questions, but I'd like to see where those delicious chickens are raised, if you don't mind showing a city girl around?"

Madame Barbeau stood still, and Molly thought she looked something like an owl as she blinked her large gray eyes and swiveled her head around to face her daughter. "Go on, Josette," she said. "I'm going to finish up in the kitchen and clean the upstairs. Then we need to sit down with Julien to talk about expanding the henhouse."

"Yes, Maman," said Josette, sighing.

"Is Julien around?" asked Molly as she and Josette left the house. "We've gotten to be friends, from meeting at the market week after week."

"That's what he told me," said Josette. "You're sort of famous, you know. Solving all those cases and all."

"Eh," said Molly, both pleased and embarrassed. They walked around the dilapidated barn and out of sight of the house. Molly felt relieved to be out in the open air, and away from the penetrating gaze of Madame Barbeau.

"Do you mind answering a few questions about Coulon—what sort of man he was, things like that? Maybe it will be easier without your mother listening? I know at your age, I wanted to be as far away from my mother as possible."

Josette giggled. "Oh, I don't know. That's what the chief wanted to know too. Coulon was a boss, you know? Told me what to do and when to do it."

"You wouldn't say you got to be friends, over the years you worked for him?"

"No," said Josette. She bent down and picked up a seed pod, nothing Molly recognized, and began to pick it apart. "What did the people in the mairie say? Were they his friends?"

"I haven't spoken to them yet. I came to you first, because I was really hoping you had been there that morning, and maybe seen something."

"Nope," said Josette. "Don't you think it was a robber or something?"

"Maybe," said Molly. "You have any idea who might've been mad at Coulon for some reason? Did his ex-wife ever come over?"

"He didn't talk to me about any of that. And he never had guests over. Kind of a waste, with that big house. Anyway, with me it was just 'polish this' and 'vacuum that.' That was about it."

"Did you like him? As a person?"

Josette did not know how to answer, so she just shrugged.

They did not get as far as the pond. Josette let Molly into the henhouse, hoping she did not look into the rafters and see the plastic bag stuffed between the joists. And after a cursory look around and a peek inside the barn, Molly thanked Josette, said goodbye, and got back on her scooter.

THE VASILIEVS HAD EATEN a leisurely breakfast in the pigeonnier —like all of Molly's guests, they too had discovered Pâtisserie Bujold and were addicted to almond croissants—and were preparing to go out.

"Check to see if her scooter is there," said Fedosia in Russian, styling her stiff platinum hair, and trying to make it curl around the brush.

"I already saw her leave about ten minutes ago. She went the other way, away from the village. Hopefully she'll be away for some time."

"Eh," said Fedosia, throwing the brush on the dining room table with a flourish. "Miss Sutton makes me laugh. So she is a hot-shot detective in this backwater town, so what? She is the least of our problems."

"I would like to see the two of you fight," said Vasily, with a sudden grin.

"You want to see everyone fight." Fedosia rolled her eyes. "Come on, let's get over to the lab, we've got a lot of work to do to get everything set up."

Vasily narrowed his eyes at her but said nothing. He picked up a large cardboard box and followed her through the door, banging it shut with his foot and hurrying to catch up to his wife.

"You know she left her husband. Divorced him. I know this is common, you could say it is an everyday thing nowadays, especially in America. But to me? To me it means you have no loyalty. No pride. No strength." Fedosia was walking two steps ahead of her husband and did not see his expression of approval.

About a hundred yards down rue des Chênes, past La Baraque and a little ways back from the road, stood a small stone building. It was not clear what its original purpose had been; in recent years it had been used as a tool shed and a garage, after which it stood empty for several years. It was one-story with only one room, with a small window on each wall. The orange-tiled roof was in good order, though vines had grown up and were on the verge of infiltrating the tiles if they were not trimmed soon. The Vasilievs, working through Malcolm Barstow, had been able to negotiate a very favorable rent. And considering how much income they hoped to get from the products of their lab, they expected to be making a substantial, if illegal, profit in short order.

Early that morning several trucks had arrived, one from the port of Marseille and another from Lille. Directed and paid off by Fedosia, the drivers had deposited numerous boxes inside the small building; she told Vasily to get to work unpacking them. He opened boxes containing small glass vials with blue stoppers, and placed them neatly in rows to one side. Boxes of latex gloves, labels, and plastic bottles of benzyl alcohol and benzyl benzoate. A box of glass beakers. Large plastic jugs of grapeseed oil. And in a smaller box, envelopes of yellowish powder with labels in Chinese. Meticulously and with pleasure, Vasily arranged all of his new toys on the two tables Malcolm Barstow had brought from somewhere, while Fedosia swept the floor.

When they had done all they could, Vasily took Fedosia by the shoulders and pushed her up against the wall, and growled into her neck before kissing her.

"Not now," she snapped. "We've got to get out of here before Sutton gets back."

"I thought you weren't worried about her. What happened to disloyal and weak, and I think you mentioned stupid?"

Fedosia waved him off. "Don't take everything so literally, Vasily. Just because I don't have a high opinion of her doesn't mean we should be careless. She might get lucky, you know? Keep a close eye on Molly Sutton, darling," she added, suddenly dropping her abrasive aspect and purring at her husband. "A very close eye. We've gone to far too much trouble to let the likes of her ruin everything."

A dangerous light flickered in Vasily's eyes, and he smiled a slow smile as he contemplated all the ways he could stop Molly Sutton from getting in their way.

❧ 30 ❧

Molly had given up on Frances, who found it impossible to pick a wedding date given her constant waffling on whether even to go through with the ceremony at all. Now that she and Ben had a case, she needed to know what the couple had decided, secretly hoping the wedding would be called off—but just until the killer was caught. Molly went into Chez Papa when she was sure Frances was home working on a jingle, to see if Nico would set a date.

"How about two weeks? Can you pull it together that soon?" he said, sweetly hopeful.

"Uh..."

Nico looked crestfallen, and Molly was so charmed by his fervor to wed her twice-divorced best pal that she readily agreed. "Okay, yes, of course I can pull it together. It's just a wedding, right? Not the crowning of a monarch?"

"Your mind goes to strange places," said Nico, grinning. "I'm sorry if I'm strong-arming you. But Frances..."

"I know. She's skittery about the whole thing, let's be honest. But Nico, you should know this: she is not skittery about *you*. It's simply that she's made mistakes before and doesn't want to do anything that will mess up things between the two of you. Because she's so happy."

"Right. I do realize that. I think. And I'll admit to you, Molls, that being in this position of wanting so desperately to get married? Never expected to be here. Never really gave it any thought at all, really."

"Frances..."

"Yeah," said Nico dreamily. "She's one in a million, that's for sure."

"One tiny little hitch about the date—"

Nico's eyebrows flew up and he stopped putting glasses away under the bar.

"Usually weddings are on Saturdays. But as you know, in the gîte business, Saturday is changeover day and in two weeks I'll have some guests leaving, some new ones coming in, cleaning to do...it would be awkward to be putting on a wedding at the same time. Do you think we could do it Friday night instead?"

"We can do it Monday morning at 7 a.m. for all I care."

"Excellent! All right then! I'll get going right now. If you have any particular ideas, any thoughts on the party—the food, decoration, anything—just text me. I know Frances doesn't want it all lacy and flowery so I'm just going with simple if that's all right with you."

They waved goodbye and Molly went back into the bright June day, mentally making a list—a long list—of everything she'd need to do that week to get prepared for her friends' big day. And alongside that list was another one, rather more interesting in her opinion, of what needed to be done for the investigation of Coulon's murder. Guiltily, she put the wedding aside, crossing over a few streets to rue Malbec, and knocked on the doors of the houses on either side of the mayor's. An old woman lived in the house on the right. She apologized for not being able to help, explaining that her health wasn't good and she spent most of her time asleep, and had seen or heard nothing on the day of the murder or on any other day, for that matter.

No answer at the house on the other side, and there was enough dust and dirt on the stoop that Molly correctly guessed that no one currently lived there.

The mairie was right down the street so she went to talk to some of the people who had worked for Coulon to see what they had to say about him and the people he knew.

The nineteenth-century building that held the mairie was impressive, with plenty of stately and ornate decoration on the outside. The day had heated up, but when Molly went inside, the rooms were pleasantly cool thanks to the thick walls. She went up to Annette, the receptionist, whom she had met on previous trips there for various purposes of research. She couldn't help thinking fondly of her first real case, and how the telling clue to what had happened had been found among the dusty records there at the mairie. The place was beloved to her, privately, for that reason.

"Bonjour, Annette," said Molly, hoping she wasn't too busy to chat.

"Ah, bonjour, Molly. I've been expecting you." Annette was small, compact, and alert, without a strand of hair out of place. Like a wren, thought Molly, picking a pencil out of a mug on the counter for something to fiddle with. She didn't know Annette well and wasn't sure how to encourage her to open up. Three women sat at desks, two facing each other and the third off to the side. Their eyes were glued to computer screens but Molly had the feeling they were listening as hard as they could.

"Do you have a little time to talk? Would it be better to meet after hours?"

"Oh no," laughed Annette, "we're not busy. Since the mayor... since...the last few days it's been like a tomb in here...oh, dear, I didn't mean..."

Molly reached across the counter and touched her arm lightly.

"I understand, believe me. It must be a little frightening, having that kind of violence hit so close to home. No doubt you're very interested in having the mayor's killer brought to justice. Of course I don't mean to imply anyone else is in danger, nothing like that."

Annette nodded. Her expression was entirely neutral and Molly paused, chewing on her lip, thinking of what to ask.

"Can you give me, just generally, an idea of how things were here in the mairie, in the weeks before the mayor was killed?"

Annette shrugged. "Nothing out of the ordinary, really."

"Just a lot of extra work," said one of the women behind her. "Excuse me, I couldn't help overhearing. I'm Claudine Brosset. Of course, paperwork is the lifeblood of the mairie! But last month we were absolutely swamped with permit applications. Who knew Castillac was stuffed with so many entrepreneurs looking to open businesses?"

Annette laughed, but the sound was brittle and humorless. "Thank you, Claudine," she said, implying that Claudine should sit back down and keep quiet.

Molly followed this exchange with interest, remembering her days of office work and the onerous office politics that could be harder to manage than the job itself.

"I hope Castillac doesn't get too busy," she said. "I guess it's not great for business, but I love that it's a little sleepy." She looked quickly at Annette and the others, hoping she hadn't offended them.

"Most of the people applying for permits will never make any money, even if they open their shops," said Annette.

"I do remember hearing about a high failure rate for small businesses, back in the States as well."

"Nothing wrong with trying," said Claudine, rising up from her seat again.

Annette shot her a look and she sat back down.

Molly tried to turn the conversation back toward the mayor, but her attempts did not succeed. The women at the mairie wanted to talk about the percentage of permit rejections, which had been abnormally high all year. They wanted to talk about the best place to go out for lunch. And most of all, they wanted to talk about André Lebeau and how they hoped he would be their new mayor.

All of them expressed sorrow at what had happened to Coulon, and agreed that he had been a decent man to work for, as he allowed them plenty of freedom and was not harsh when someone made an error. They appeared to be quite competent at running the mairie on their own, and more interested in their prospects for a new boss than finding out who killed Coulon, thought Molly as she headed home, the murder investigation having completely shoved Frances and Nico's wedding out of her mind.

Was that just an act, and there was more going on that they weren't admitting to?

And where was this André Lebeau, anyway? He seemed to have an intoxicating effect on the entire village, and it was time Molly found out what all the fuss was about.

31

She waited until Julien and Josette had gone off to a music festival in Bergerac, something Madame Barbeau would have enjoyed immensely in her youth but which now held little interest.

And besides, another, more powerful reason kept her home at the farm that day. Clearly Josette, lacking the most basic common sense, believed the Coulon matter was already far in the past and she had nothing to worry about. But her mother had no such confidence. She, Josette, Julien—they were all suspects, being so closely tied to the mayor, and the next days and weeks were going to be very dangerous for the entire family.

The gendarmes themselves did not especially worry her—they were a pair of bumblers, anyone could see that. But Molly Sutton was another thing entirely. And Madame Barbeau was not going to sit back and do nothing while Sutton and Dufort dug around where they were not welcome, trying to buff up their reputation with yet another arrest.

Madame Barbeau could see the whole story playing out: how Sutton would target Josette because the American was envious of her daughter's beauty, and then slowly piece together a case until she and Dufort could snap handcuffs on Josette's pretty wrists... and Madame Barbeau had no idea what she could do to stop them. They could just as easily come up with pretexts for arresting Julien, or herself...they had to be stopped.

That was all—*they had to be stopped.*

Josette had run off that morning without even doing the morning chores, as though all responsibility had magically lifted from her shoulders just because she no longer had a job at the mayor's. Grumbling, Madame Barbeau picked up a basket and went to collect the eggs. On the way to the henhouse, she stopped for a moment and looked around at the farm—dilapidated, strewn with manure from the donkey, a rooster strutting, a ragged crow coming from the woods. She pressed a hand into her lower back. The fury at her husband for bringing her to this place was always fresh, and she cursed him under her breath though he had been dead many years.

Her fingers hurt when she opened the clasp to the henhouse. The birds scurried up around her looking for grain, but she had brought nothing, no table scraps or corn, and soon they scurried away again. She breathed lightly through her mouth to avoid the sharp smell, as cleaning out the bedding was another chore Josette had put off. Eighty laying hens, give or take, a jumble of different breeds since Julien usually bought whatever they happened to have at the market when it was time to refresh the flock. Josette had been letting them out to forage, which Madame Barbeau had instructed her to do since it made for better quality eggs and lower feed costs, but she had slacked off on that job as well lately.

Slowly she moved down the row of nest-boxes, picking up still-warm eggs and gently placing them in the basket. By the end, the basket was heavy and she was on the verge of choking from inhaling stray feathers and the ammonia-laden air.

But then, slowly, as though her mind were pulling on a thread and unravelling a sweater, Madame Barbeau had an idea. Perhaps it will turn out to be lucky that Josette left the eggs to me this morning, she thought with a wide smile, moving more quickly once she had latched the henhouse door and was hobbling her way back to the farmhouse. Once inside, she carefully put the eggs down and looked underneath the kitchen sink where she kept odds and ends that weren't used often. She pulled out a narrow box and checked inside to make sure all the narrow gauge needles hadn't been used. Then, moving slowly but steadily, she went back outside to the herb garden, which was now overflowing with June bounty.

The tarragon was the size of a small bush, the chives flourishing in several healthy clumps. Behind the chervil, Madame Barbeau found what she was looking for: belladonna, which she had grown as an experiment, having heard that it can help with coughing and fever. Further research, however, in an old tome her husband had left behind, explained that the line between alleviating those conditions and killing the patient was rather thin, and Madame Barbeau had let the project fall by the wayside. She coughed, reminded of the illness that had led her to find belladonna seeds in the first place. The plants were growing nicely, the emerald leaves thick and healthy, with abundant black berries underneath. She picked a handful and brought them back into the kitchen, where she mashed the poison berries into a paste, then added a small amount of sunflower oil.

How long would it take the poison to seep into the oil, she wondered? She decided to give it until morning, the timing perfect for tomorrow's market, when she would send Julien off with a very special treat for one of his most loyal and famous customers.

$\approx$

MADAME BARBEAU WAS SO EXCITED by her plan she could hardly sleep. Just before dawn she got up and put water on for coffee, then rummaged around under the sink for a candle. There was a flurry of agitation when she could not find a match, it being June and not the season for lighting fires (and her cigarette lighter irritatingly misplaced), but eventually after much cursing under her breath she found a mildewed box of matches in a drawer, lit the candle, and waited for the wax to melt.

In less than a minute she was able to drip a single drop of wax onto an egg. She blew out the candle. She wanted the needle next, but—the box was here a minute ago, now where in the world could it have gone?

Another ten minutes evaporated as she searched the kitchen counter twenty times, finally bumping her foot against the box of needles on the floor, and realizing she must have knocked it over without noticing. She had bought the needles years ago when... was it the donkey? Or maybe that goat Josette had insisted on having? At any rate, an animal had been ill and needed regular injections of medicine, and the vet had sold her this box of needles so she could administer the shots there on the farm without his having to visit every day. The needles were eighteen gauge, very narrow, and she hoped she could get the point through an eggshell without cracking it.

Slowly she drew up several cc's of the belladonna-infused oil. She held the syringe up to the light, the sun just barely starting to glow a rosy pink through the east window. And then, with total concentration, as carefully as she had ever done anything, she held the egg in one hand and placed the tip of the needle into the drop of still-soft wax, and pushed.

She heard a tiny *pock*, and the needle was through. With her heart in her throat, Madame Barbeau pushed the plunger and then quickly pulled the needle out.

No crack.

She waited a moment, then picked off the drop of wax. Holding the egg in the light, she turned it this way and that, but to her eyes, which were still sharp, the egg looked like any other egg, with no mark, crack, or discoloration to reveal anything different about it apart from the tiny hole where the needle had gone through. Picking up the candle, she let another drop of wax fall on the egg, directly over the almost invisible hole, and without waiting for it to harden, she wiped the wax off with her finger, wanting only the faintest bit to seep into the hole to block it up.

Perfect. It was a beautiful egg, she thought, admiring its dusky brown color, its weight in her hand, its power. Molly's second crime was to come poking around the farm, sniffing after evidence that was none of her concern. Her first? Showing up in Castillac, Madame Barbeau's village, and settling there, making friends, not slaving away on a farm day in and day out but shopping for pretty dresses and going to one social event after another. (Madame Barbeau had a rather cockeyed vision of how Molly spent her days, Molly being more likely to be dressed in a pair of appalling sweatpants with dirt under her fingernails from gardening than wearing a dress and going to fancy teas.)

Josette and Julien had gotten in very late, but it was market day and time for them to get up and drive into Castillac to set up. Madame Barbeau rousted them and made them toast and coffee, reusing the coffee grounds she had used for her own cup. After they had eaten, she took Julien aside before he went to load up the truck.

"I want you to do something, Julien. It's very important that you get it right. Important for our Josette, do you understand?"

"No, Maman. What are you talking about? Let me get going, I've got to load the truck—"

"Julien! Listen to me! You love your sister, right?"

"Of course, Maman," he said impatiently.

"Take this box of eggs," she said, having packed all the eggs herself that morning, though it was usually Josette's job. "See, I have marked it with a small heart, here in the corner. Molly

Sutton is a regular customer, is she not? Or was that just a lot of talk the other day?"

"Yeah, she's a regular. Whole chicken, a dozen eggs, every week if she gets there in time."

"Excellent. All I am asking you to do is make sure this is the box of eggs she gets. Simple. Any idiot could manage that. If she's late, hold them and wait for her. Don't give them to anyone else. You understand, Julien? You won't be a fool?"

Julien had long ago steeled himself against his mother's insults and he did not flinch at that one. "Why, Maman? What's so special about this box?"

"Nothing for you to worry about," she said. "Just do it. For Josette."

She did not tell him about the belladonna because she feared he would throw the eggs in the trash. Or perhaps he was even capable of reporting her to the gendarmes. Never one to shy away from unflattering truths, Madame Barbeau understood that her son might not be trustworthy as far as his devotion to her was concerned, but she knew that he would do anything to protect his sister. Madame Barbeau was confident he would do what he was told.

But at the last minute, after Josette and Julien had rushed around getting the truck loaded, Madame Barbeau decided she would accompany them into the village and make sure Julien managed the job. She couldn't risk not knowing.

Josette rode in back so that Madame Barbeau could have the seat in the cab, where she spent the trip sulking about the ingratitude of her children, with only a little time devoted to imagining the delightful prospect of Molly Sutton writhing on the floor after ingesting one very special egg.

❧ 32 ❧

Maron had dragged his feet about letting Ben and Molly into the mayor's house for a look around, which was no surprise to Ben. He was was well aware of Maron's ambivalent feelings toward their involvement, fearing the former chief might find some clue that the gendarmes had missed. So it was Saturday before it was arranged. Monsour met the team of Dufort and Sutton at 1 rue Malbec at seven o'clock, saying he would return in an hour to lock up again.

"Thanks for coming over, we appreciate it," said Ben. "Got any tidbits you'd like to let fall?" he asked with a grin, mostly just to see Monsour stiffen with resentment, which he promptly did.

"You of all people—"

"I know, I know, just joking with you," said Ben, putting his hand on the glossy green front door and giving it a push. Monsour scuttled off down the sidewalk and Ben and Molly went inside the mayor's house for the first time.

They stopped in the foyer and looked around, taking in the feel of the place. It was sparsely decorated, and what decoration there was seemed out of date. Probably Coulon's mother had chosen the curtains and hung the pictures, and he had just left everything as it was, but the house felt a bit like stepping into a time capsule from thirty or forty years ago.

"We don't have much time. I'll take the upstairs while you do down?" said Molly.

Ben agreed and headed into the kitchen, which was neat and orderly, everything put away. The refrigerator held a minimal amount of vegetables, three bottles of local wine, and a big chunk of butter in a tub. In the door were several varieties of jam, Bonne Maman with the gingham-checked lid.

Leaving the kitchen, he checked out the living and dining rooms, which looked barely used. Not surprising for a bachelor, though perhaps odd for a mayor, who might be expected to host some social events in his house, considering how nice a house it was. Quickly Ben went outside and let himself into the small workshop, but saw nothing of interest. Going in the backdoor, he joined Molly upstairs. On the second floor were three bedrooms, one clearly belonging to Coulon, one empty, and the other a guest room with a large dark stain on the rug.

Ben stood for a long moment with his eyes on the stain. He wasn't praying exactly, but paying respects to the man who had died there. He hadn't really known Coulon (and their limited acquaintance had never suggested he would like him) but nevertheless, he was regretful about his death and fervent about catching his killer.

When he looked up and began to search the room, he felt a sort of hyper-awareness come over him, a physical sensation that caused time to slow and all his senses to ratchet up; it was almost unpleasant, and at one time had caused him a great deal of anxiety, but with a change in perspective, he now considered that sensation one of the best tools of his trade. At bottom, Ben wanted to understand people. He wanted to perceive through their choices, even careless, thoughtless ones, what they really felt and believed, and thus how they would act. And that was how he got closer and closer to the truth.

Molly, meanwhile, had been using her powers of imagination, trying to visualize the murder that had taken place in that room so recently. The bedroom was neat and clean. The coverlet looked fresh and the pile of pillows in lacy pillowcases was undisturbed. She knew it was unlikely that the murder weapon was still in the room after Maron, Monsour, and the forensics team had been through it, but nevertheless she got down on the floor and looked under the bed, and opened all the drawers in the dresser and armoire. She and Ben found no knife, no blade, nothing sharp enough to slit a throat.

They trotted up to the third floor but the rooms were mostly empty. A silver knight on a silver horse was displayed on the landing of the stairs; it was dust-free but seemed a bit lonesome there, where no one would see it but the housemaid.

Back downstairs to Coulon's bedroom. Ben stood for a long while, thinking that people probably spend more time in their bedrooms than anyplace else, and it would seem reasonable for something of interest to be found there—some expression of personality, if nothing more concrete than that. But Coulon had been orderly in his habits and there was no clutter to go through, no letters anywhere that Ben or Molly could find, not even any scribbled notes or papers or lists. Just an ugly painting on the wall over his bed, a sculpture of a swan, and clothes neatly hanging in the armoire. A novel with a tattered cover on the bedside table.

"Back in school, I thought he was kind of a nobody," said Ben. "Surprising, really, that he managed to get himself elected mayor all these years. And this house...is the house of someone who either keeps himself hidden, or has no personality at all."

"Did he glorify his parents, is that why the house feels as though everything is unchanged from the 1970s?"

"Maybe he was simply uninterested in his surroundings, and put his attention somewhere else?"

And if so, thought Molly, where?

❧

SHE HAD TO ADMIT, a Saturday with no changeover to worry about was pretty sweet. After the fruitless search of Coulon's house, Molly hopped on the scooter to head straight to Pâtisserie Bujold, but the engine coughed and died. She started it again and it caught, begrudgingly, but Molly mentally waved away any worry that her beloved might be asking in its own mechanical fashion for a spa day at the repair shop. There were almond croissants to consider and the glories thereof, and she delighted in the wind whipping through her hair as she sped through the narrow streets, stomach growling, though she quickly hit a large crowd and decided to park and walk the rest of the way.

In June, the market really got some momentum, with so much local produce on offer as well as tourists to buy it up. Castillac, on the whole, did not see many visitors otherwise. On that particular market day, Molly saw many unfamiliar faces as she made her way through the Place toward the bakery. She wondered briefly whether it was possible that the mayor might have had the terrible luck to get killed by some random stranger. She and Ben tended to dismiss that possibility in their investigations, but maybe that was a mistake. There *were* sociopaths who murdered strangers for no reason, even if it wasn't as common as most people seemed to think. Someone might have rung his doorbell and talked his or her way inside, and dispatched him before he had a chance to get suspicious. A woman most probably, she thought, remembering that the body had been found in a bedroom, and wondering how susceptible Coulon might have been to a seductive stranger.

She was so lost in thought that she walked right into a young boy who was waiting in a line to buy a comic at the Presse, the line having snaked right out the door onto the sidewalk. "Oh my, I'm so sorry!" she said. "Are you—Gilbert! It's so nice to run into you! I mean—well, I *did* run into you, literally, but I mean, it's so nice to see you! How is everything?"

Gilbert was grinning. "Bonjour, Madame Sutton," he said politely. "Are you working on the mayor's case?"

"You bet," said Molly confidentially. "I don't know if you heard that Ben Dufort and I have our own investigation business now?"

"Of course I know about that, everyone does!"

Molly was about to say that when he got a little older, they might be able to hire him to do some legwork from time to time, but his mother, the formidable Madame Renaud, appeared and clamped one hand on Gilbert's shoulder.

"Bonjour Madame Sutton," she said, her voice chilly. The two women had met during another case, and the boy's mother was not a fan of Molly's, or of anyone who got too close to her Gilbert.

"Bonjour Madame Renaud. Lovely June day! So nice to see you both."

The Renauds moved off into the crowd, Gilbert craning his neck to watch Molly as his mother marched him away.

Molly spied Manette and scurried over to say hello, just barely able to put off getting the almond croissant for a few moments longer. Manette's face was rosy and smiling as she laid a head of lettuce in a customer's straw bag after weighing it. Molly checked to see how her belly was looking and could see, with mixed feelings, the swell of her friend's unexpected pregnancy.

"How are you doing?" she asked, as they kissed cheeks.

"It doesn't get easier with age, that's for sure!" laughed Manette, and Molly nodded, thinking of her upcoming birthday. Forty. *Forty!* She knew it wasn't really old—she had friends many decades older who were very active and busy with a million things.

But for having her own baby? Forty felt *old*.

"Well, you look blooming," she said to her friend. "It must agree with you."

"You on the case?" asked Manette, leaning close so no one could eavesdrop.

"You know it," said Molly with a grin. "Listen, I'm rushing off to Pâtisserie Bujold—if I don't get some coffee in the next five minutes I might expire on the spot."

"Understood. Go, go!" said Manette, and turned to the man who was next in line.

Molly walked quickly in the direction of the bakery, and by avoiding people she knew was just about to leave the market when she spied Julien Barbeau. Might as well get that stop out of the way before he runs out of chicken, she thought.

"Julien! Glad I caught you. How are you? Is Josette holding up okay?"

"Bonjour, Molly," said Julien. He was smiling widely and a bit stupidly, having cracked open a beer as he set up first thing in the morning and continuing to drink as his customers started showing up. "She's fine. I'm the one feeling the stress, you know?" He giggled infectiously and Molly joined him. "Sorry I missed your visit the other day. Hear you're working the Coulon case."

"News does travel," she said, half under her breath.

"The usual?"

"Please," said Molly, suddenly feeling faint from lack of caffeine and sugar. Julien put a wrapped whole chicken in Molly's bag, and carefully placed a carton of eggs on top.

"Aw, you put a little heart on it," said Molly. "Nice touch." It was one of her failings as an innkeeper, she thought, not making enough small gestures like that. They could really make people feel special without much effort, and her mind just did not seem to travel in that direction. Making a vow to do better, she handed over some bills and waved goodbye. "Give my best to Josette and your mother," she called over her shoulder, walking quickly and then breaking into a trot, desperate to reach Nugent's shop and the life-giving sustenance within, and never noticing the dark figure of Madame Barbeau, who sat in the shade of a tree behind some crates, watching her very carefully.

❧ 33 ❧

B en waited for Molly in front of Chez Papa. He was not surprised that the market took longer than expected—in June, it almost always did, because the entire village was there and conversations could get long—and Ben chatted with numerous friends before he saw an over-caffeinated Molly striding along, swinging her straw bag along with a big white paper bag from Pâtisserie Bujold.

They kissed cheeks, and then lips, both smiling and happy to see the other.

"Uff, it took forever," said Molly. "I talked to about ten people, but I only got two little scraps that might be useful to the case. Wish we'd found something in the house."

"Same. Maron and the rest were thorough, I guess. What are the little scraps?"

"Well, I ran into the guy who drives the ambulance, I forget his name but I met him last year during the Desrosiers case. Anyway, he took Coulon's body to the morgue on Tuesday. And he told me he noticed a guy hanging around on the street the whole time the ambulance was there. His description matches Daniel's exactly, right down to the color of his shirt."

"Good work," said Ben. "And there's something more?"

"Yeah. This Lebeau character sure has some of the village women all stirred up, and apparently he's something of an aggressive type."

"Aggressive? Who told you that?"

"The kid who helps Manette unload the truck since she got pregnant. I think he's a cousin? Anyway, I was just leaving to come here when Manette called me over and said the cousin—Geoff—had something to tell me. Geoff works out at a gym on the south end of the village? I didn't even know we had a gym."

"I go sometimes."

"Oh, really?" said Molly, raising her eyebrows comically and squeezing his bicep.

"In fact, I was wondering…it's true I don't go that often, but I've never seen Lebeau there even once."

"Maybe he works out at home?"

"Maybe. But for someone with his physique, that's a lot of equipment to invest in. Plus, part of the point is to show off, you know? The bodybuilder types at the gym do a fair amount of preening in the mirrors."

"Right, I can picture that. I'm not really a gym sort myself, but I totally take your word for it."

"So go on, what did Manette's cousin have to say?"

"That Lebeau had come up to him on the street and started giving him a hard time, saying he needed a real trainer to show him how to work out because whatever he was doing, it wasn't working. Obviously very strange coming from some random guy Geoff had never even met but just passed on the street. Anyway, so the cousin argued back and Lebeau shoved him pretty hard. They almost got into a fight but they both had friends who pulled them apart and Lebeau took off."

Ben was shaking his head. "And this guy is running for council?"

"I know. Manette told me that she had heard him speak and

he seemed reasonable enough. She agreed with a lot of what he had to say. But his temperament...he doesn't sound like someone we want in charge of anything. I was hoping to see him at the market, try to ask him a few questions, but he wasn't there."

Ben nodded. "Okay, listen, I know we were going to have lunch together, but I think I'll take the opportunity of a crowded village to talk to some more people. So far no one that I can find saw Josette or Julien in Castillac on the day of the murder, but I'd like to hear what Rémy has to say before setting her aside. And I'd very much like to meet Lebeau as well, if he shows up."

"Do you want me to come with you?"

Ben considered. "Of course, always," he said with a quick smile. "But you've got a chicken to put in the fridge, and plenty to do at La Baraque I'm sure. Just to double-check, I'll knock on all the doors on the mayor's street, swing through the end of the market looking for Lebeau, and meet you back at your place?"

They kissed again, lingeringly, and Molly went off to find her scooter. She was thinking, for once, not about Coulon or Coulon's murderer, or about Frances and Nico's wedding, but about whether she should ask Ben if he wanted to move in at La Baraque.

But why potentially ruin something when it's going so well? she thought, echoing Frances without realizing it.

The scooter started up with no problem and she got the chicken and the carton of eggs with the small red heart safely home and refrigerated, and set about trying to figure out her next step.

❧

THE MORNING'S almond croissant already a distant memory, Molly ate an enormous salad dotted with plenty of sardines and some leftover potatoes, and with renewed energy set about attacking the weeds in the front border. She put earphones in and listened to the blues, quickly reaching that almost blissful state in which her hands were busy and productive but her mind was ranging all over the place, mostly in the direction of Coulon's murder.

Opportunity, she thought. Opportunity first, means second, motive last. Either the murderer is someone Coulon knew and invited inside the house, or someone who talked his way in. Because if the entry had been forcible, it's unlikely the murder would have taken place upstairs, especially since there wasn't any disturbance downstairs, no sign of any struggle.

Which category would Daniel Coulon be in, she wondered, reminding herself to call Daniel's mother and see what she might have to say. If it was true that Coulon had never met his son— that could be all the mayor's fault, or just as easily the mother's. Daniel's mother would by definition give a biased view, but of course, sadly for the mayor, it was the only one available. If you had never even met your father, could you be angry enough to kill him? Probably so, thought Molly, even if the way to get there was to have spent a long time blaming your absent father for everything that had gone wrong in your life. And definitely so if his death meant you would come into a significant amount of money.

Hell, people will kill for next to nothing, she thought with a resigned shrug. Daniel for sure does not lack for motive. But we can't put him in the house, at least not yet. Maybe Ben will strike gold when he interviews the neighbors.

Molly troweled down into the dirt, trying to get all the roots of that noxious weed she could never get ahead of, trying to imagine the minutes before the murder. Someone knocked on the door in the morning, before Coulon left for the mairie. Was there an argument, a dispute that turned violent, surprising them both? Molly couldn't figure out why Coulon would have invited anyone he wasn't getting along with up to the second floor, so that scenario seemed unlikely.

So, she reasoned, Coulon might not have realized what the

murderer had in mind. The two of them might have walked upstairs together, talking about any old thing, with Coulon completely unaware. Was anyone that clueless...able to overlook that the person standing next to you wanted to kill you?

Was someone staying with him, a friend from another time in his life, university in Rennes for example? And did this guest come prepared, with a knife hidden in his jacket, ready to settle some old score that Coulon had possibly forgotten about?

She tried again to see the murder unfold, but the image refused to come into focus. Eventually Molly got tired of weeding and went inside looking for a cold drink. No sign of Ben. She texted him to see when he might show up, feeling hungry and anxious to start dinner.

Another hour passed with no word, and Molly restlessly went to the refrigerator and took out the eggs, having planned a soufflé for dinner. She grated some cheese and then put an artichoke in the steamer, expecting Ben to text any minute....and then, abruptly, said to hell with it, shoved the carton of eggs back in the fridge, turned off the stove, and headed out to Chez Papa. She had spent hours alone and she craved some company, a kir with friends, and a laugh or two.

As she steered the scooter onto rue des Chênes, she did not pay attention to Bobo, who stood at the end of the driveway barking at the man who appeared out of the dusky evening on a bike, following Molly at a distance meant to prevent her from noticing he was there. Bobo had not been a fan of Vasily from the beginning, occasionally being a better judge of character than the human she lived with.

✵ 34 ✵

Chez Papa was packed and Molly could hear shrieks of laughter coming from inside as she parked the scooter out front under a twinkling string of lights hung in a scrawny tree.

"Molly!" shouted a chorus as she came inside.

"This is just what I needed," she said, grinning as she slid onto the only remaining stool next to Lawrence.

"I'm happy to see you, my dear. I don't mind saying that while I'm glad things seem to be so jolly between you and Ben, it does mean that I don't see you nearly as much as I used to. And it takes some willpower not to pout."

Molly kissed her friend on both cheeks. "Well, you know Ben *is* sort of a homebody. Though where he is now, I can't say. I expected him for dinner..."

"His loss, our gain," said Lawrence, signaling to Nico that he wanted another Negroni. "Now tell me, how's the case going?"

"Mmm, so-so. We've been hired, as I guess you've heard, but that's about it. No actual progress yet, though we've got a few weak leads to follow up on. Let me ask you something: if you were about to be murdered by someone you know, do you think you would realize you were in danger? Like, if you weren't actually arguing or anything, but the person had reasons for wanting to kill you—do you think you'd be able to sense that?"

"That depends on many things. Is the murderer a sociopath who has no feelings for other people? They can cover up their intentions quite well, or so I've heard."

"I guess it sounds like I'm blaming the victim. It's just that I can't see how this plays out any other way—the house showed no evidence of a struggle, yet the body was found on the second floor."

"And it's certain that he was killed on the second floor, not moved there later?"

"Oh yes. There would have been blood everywhere if he had been moved."

"Eww."

"Sorry. So the murderer was a guest of Coulon's, right, not someone who came in the house by force? Isn't that the only possibility?"

"Didn't he have a housemaid? Pretty Josette Barbeau, if I'm not mistaken?"

"Yes. She was home sick the day of the murder. Three people support that, and we've not been able to find anyone who saw her in Castillac that day. Nor have we found any motive for her to kill her boss, when by all appearances her job was sorely needed. Everyone at the mairie reports that he was a good man to work for."

Lawrence shrugged. "Then I've got nothing. Of course, I have the utmost confidence in you," he said, patting her knee.

"Are you being patronizing?" she flashed out.

"Molly! Of course not!"

"Sorry," Molly said, and meant it. "I'm...I guess I'm a little on edge. All we've got is a bunch of unpromising nothing. Often when I'm on a case, I get this...it's hard to describe...I get this sort of tingling feeling, when I'm on the right track. It's like...this feeling of confidence that even though I don't know what happened yet, I am going to know."

"And you're lacking it this time?"

"Yes. Mostly."

"Bonsoir, Molly," said Nico, sliding a kir in front of her. "Frites?"

"Of course," she said. "Where's Frances?"

Nico just shook his head and looked away. Uh oh, thought Molly.

"I suppose you haven't ignored the possibility that it was your client who killed him?" asked Lawrence.

"Well, of course not," said Molly, realizing with a sharp pang that deep down, she had believed Odile completely, perhaps over-identifying with her as a fellow divorcée. The deadly assumption raises its head again, she thought ruefully.

"I suppose there's no chance it was a suicide?" asked Lawrence.

"I—well, that never occurred to me. I guess we should consider it. Do people actually slit their own throats?"

"People will do *anything*, dear Molly, surely you of all people know that." Lawrence swiveled on his stool and caught a glimpse of someone outside on the sidewalk looking in, but the figure stepped back out of sight and Lawrence made nothing of it. "So, did you hear the latest? About Lapin?"

"No!"

"He and Anne-Marie eloped. Our dear friend is now a married man."

"You're kidding! Incredible! How do you know?"

"He sent me a postcard. The two of them went up to Poitiers to a big flea market, and I guess it was a spur of the moment thing. Obviously it's hard to get much from a postcard, but I gather they're blissfully happy."

Molly nodded, smiling, but inside she was starting to feel cranky.

The case felt stubbornly closed-up and all anyone ever wanted to talk about was weddings. She looked over at Nico, who was listening to some people at the other end of the bar. His expression was droopy and he looked sad; it didn't take an ace detective to guess that the cause was Frances. With a sigh she called out to him.

"Hey Nico! Come talk to me a sec."

"Yes, madame," he said, trying to sound comic and failing.

"Want to talk wedding details? I know you said anything was fine, but since Frances is, uh, less than helpful, that leaves me in the driver's seat. I would be much more comfortable following directions about what kind of celebration you want than making those decisions myself."

Nico nodded but said nothing.

"How about you help me with the menu? I thought we'd have a dinner. It's so nice to sit at a long table all together, you know? The conversations are better than when everyone is just mingling and eating appetizers."

Nico managed to raise an unconvincing smile.

"There *is* going to be a wedding, right?" Molly said, letting a little more exasperation into her voice than maybe she should have.

Nico's eyes looked glittery and he shrugged. Molly instantly felt bad. "Okay look, I'll talk to her. I'm sure whatever it is...it'll be nothing. She's...you know, most of the time the things we love about someone are the very things that drive us crazy. Frances does not walk the expected path, Nico. She colors outside the lines. And we love her for this! And so..." Molly took a big sip of her kir, feeling both sorry for her friends and like telling them off at the same time.

"I think I'll head home," she said finally.

"You haven't even gotten your frites yet!"

Molly shrugged. "I don't know, suddenly I'm not in the mood. I think I need to get to bed early with a good book." She kissed

Nico and Lawrence goodbye, and went outside. The scooter coughed, coughed again, and the engine did not catch.

"Dammit to hell," she said under her breath.

Vasily Vasiliev leaned out of the alley next to Chez Papa, his eyes on Molly. It was dark, he was hidden in shadow, and Molly had no idea she was being watched.

On the fourth try the motor started and she took off through the quiet streets of the village headed for home, with Vasily on his bike not far behind.

❦ 35 ❦

"Bonjour, Annette," Monsour said as he came into the mairie, first thing Monday morning.

"Bonjour, Paul-Henri. I hope you've got some news?"

"We'll see. People seem to think murder investigations go like that," he said, snapping his fingers. "But usually they take time and patience. It's not as though we have a long line of witnesses," he added defensively. Monsour glanced around the office for a moment, noting the two women working at desks behind Annette. They looked busy but were no doubt straining to hear every word. "I do have some more questions for you. Is there somewhere private we can talk, or would you like to come outside?"

Annette looked rattled. She glanced behind her, then took a deep breath. "Maybe we should go out," she said.

Once on the street, she asked, "Is this...is this normal? I'm not in any trouble, am I?"

"Not that I know of," said Monsour with a slight smile. "I have just a few questions for you. You probably spent more time with Coulon than anyone, so it's not unusual at all that you are the person who can clear up a few things."

Annette turned pale. "More time? I suppose technically that's correct. But Paul-Henri, it's not as though he and I were glued at the hip at the mairie. I am behind the front desk and he was in his office most of the time.

Monsour sighed. "You are not under suspicion, Annette. But your continual protests are starting to make you sound like you have something to hide." Out of the corner of his eye, he watched her blanch, and smiled to himself. "Now then. First, I wonder if anyone purporting to be Coulon's son ever came to the mairie?"

"Son? Coulon had no son, not that I ever knew about."

"Young man just showed up in the village, says his name is Daniel Coulon. Story is that they were estranged, and Daniel came to try to patch things up."

Annette thought about how excited her co-workers, a pair of inveterate gossips, would be with that bit of information. "News to me," she shrugged.

"All right, then. Next, I want to know about the process of granting business permits. Can you tell me how that works?"

Annette swallowed hard. She tucked her short hair behind her ears several times and smoothed the front of her dress. Monsour felt alert, his ears pricking up.

"Okay, listen," said Annette slowly. "I knew it wasn't right, but the mayor was explicit about how he wanted it handled and...and maybe I should have stood up to him more. I just never thought..."

Monsour was surprised to have hit on something so easily but hid it well. "Continue," he said.

"I don't know for sure. I mean, I can't give you a tape of incriminating conversations or anything to prove it. And the thing with his wife, I mean his ex-wife, well, that was just icing on the cake, if you know what I mean."

"No, madame, I don't. Can you start at the beginning?" They rounded the corner and, without intending to, started down rue Malbec.

Annette tucked her hair again and tried to keep her voice from shaking. "All right. Sorry. I'm just...this whole thing is making me really nervous. You must understand, it's not like your boss gets killed every day, right? Things at the mairie are always so...so ordinary, you know? We get a few requests for this or that, we help out people new to the area, we fill out forms. A lot of forms. We—"

"You do not need to explain the entire scope of what the mairie does. I understand that it helps Castillac run smoothly. What I want to know is—"

"Yes, yes, all right." She took another deep breath, and Maron wrestled with his impatience, jamming his hands in his pockets and chewing on his lip.

"I can't be sure, but I think the mayor was under some pressure. From the big stores outside of the village."

"You mean to the east? The Mega-Mart and all that?"

"Yes. The mayor had a number of meetings with representatives from those companies, the ones all down that road—the huge DIY store, the supermarket, and a few others. In his office with the door closed, which was not unheard of but a little unusual. It was right after one of those meetings that he told us to stop giving permits to small businesses."

"Meaning, if someone wanted to open a shop he wouldn't be able to?"

"That's right. Obviously, any successful small business is going to take profits away from the big stores. They're like ravenous sharks, those places, and they aren't happy with getting some of the local business, they want it all."

"Did you overhear anything, read any notes or reports, anything to support that claim? Or is that just your personal opinion?"

"Like I said, I can't prove there's a connection. I wasn't at the meetings so I don't know what was said. I have no idea how they got Coulon to agree, either—could have been the carrot or the stick, if you ask me. And, for the record, we issued almost no rejections of applications. Coulon didn't tell us to outright refuse anybody. Just to keep taking the applications for small businesses and putting them on the bottom of the pile. Any other work, no matter how incidental, came first. And so what happened in most cases, I believe, is that people just gave up. You understand how that would be—if you're making plans to open a shop, you can't sit there twiddling your thumbs indefinitely. The investment money is ready to go, and you need a decision. And so eventually, if they don't get one, they go on to something else."

Monsour was thinking hard. Was it possible some disgruntled prospective shop-owner had killed the mayor out of frustration and anger?

"And how did the applicants react to this treatment? Did any of them come into the mairie and confront Coulon?"

Annette looked down at her feet as they walked quickly along the sidewalk, approaching the Coulon mansion. "Odile Dupont. His ex-wife."

Monsour smiled, then suppressed it. "What exactly happened? As detailed as possible, please."

"I don't like to...I'm maybe the only person in Castillac who doesn't like to gossip. Which I've always told myself is a very lucky thing, because being in the mairie for so long, I know private things about a lot of people's business. Sometimes things they wouldn't want made public. So it makes me uncomfortable to talk about Odile, when it's not like I know—"

"Annette. I'm not asking you to gossip. A man has been killed and I am trying to gather evidence so that we can figure out who did it and bring that person to justice. It is not a straight line from your remarks today to Odile's rotting in prison. You must give me the facts and trust that I will use them honorably."

Annette looked into Monsour's eyes and uttered a soft whimper. "All right," she said softly. "Just last week—the week before... before he was killed...Odile came into the mairie, and boy, was she furious. She slammed the door, scowling, and demanded to see the mayor. When I tried to tell her he was in a meeting, she ignored me and breezed right into his office. That door slammed too, I heard shouting, a crash which later turned out to be an ashtray heaved against the wall, and then—maybe five minutes later?—she came back out, face blazing, shot me a dirty look and left.

"Was there some reason she was angry at you?"

"Not me, no. I figured she was furious at the mayor because her permit application still hadn't gone through. She's opened shops in other towns and wants one here as well. Beauty products, you know. Too expensive for me, but I have friends who swear by her face cream."

"And had the mayor said anything specifically about Odile's application?"

Annette threw Monsour a look of agony. "I really must get back. With no mayor, the office is in a bit of disarray and I don't think it's overstating to say that I'm sort of holding things together."

Monsour, showing unusual fortitude, waited without saying anything.

"Yes," Annette said finally. "He told us to make sure her permit never got to the top of the pile."

With that, she said goodbye and broke into a jog. Monsour stood listening to the sound of her heels hitting the sidewalk, thinking that he was glad he had no ex-wives, and feeling extremely pleased with the way the interview had gone.

❧ 36 ❧

Ben was following a similar path of investigation as Monsour, and had gone for a short run in the cool morning before leaving his apartment in his creaky Renault. After pulling into the vast parking lot outside Mega-Mart, he started to text Molly but called instead.

"Hope I'm not waking you," he said, his voice sounding more seductive than business-like.

"Not at all!" Molly protested, the phone having jolted her out of a deep sleep in which she had been dreaming about running down a deserted road, terrified but quiet. She shook her head quickly to banish the dream and wake herself up.

"I'm in the Mega-Mart parking lot. I'm about to go in and look for a manager or, hopefully, someone higher up," he said.

Molly propped herself up on one elbow and tried to push her curly hair out of her face. "What for?"

"Picked up a few tidbits in the village yesterday. Monsieur Clement, who lives across from that café over on rue Picasso that's usually mostly empty? He told me that Coulon and one of the bosses at Mega-Mart used to meet there regularly. Clement noticed because he thought it was strange they would go there when the mairie is so close to the Café de la Place. Said he thought there was something fishy about it."

"How did he know who the other guy was?"

"Well, he doesn't, not exactly. All he told me was that he recognized him from Mega-Mart. Apparently Monsieur Clement is a big fan. He told me I could get a garden hose for practically nothing if I hurried out here fast enough before the sale ends."

"Those stores are killing the shops in the village," said Molly, waking up fully now that she had something to sink her teeth into.

"Not news to me, chérie. France has worked quite hard to keep those big stores out of sight at least. But obviously we can't force people to shop in certain places and not others."

"Is cheaper Scotch tape worth losing village life?" she cried, jumping out of bed. Bobo barked and ran over to get in on the excitement.

Ben laughed. "Molly, I'm heading in now, trying to find the guy Clement described to me. What's your day look like?"

"I'm calling Daniel's mother."

"Excellent. See you for dinner."

Molly put her cellphone down and flopped back on the pillows, wishing for a genie to arrive at her bedside with an enormous, steaming cup of coffee. She had not had enough time to assemble her thoughts before she heard someone banging on the terrace door, and Bobo streaked out of the room barking.

"Wesley! Good morning!" she said, arriving at the French doors a few moments later, disheveled but dressed. "Did you lose your key?"

He stared at her. "Why would you think that?"

"You're banging on the door?"

"Oh, that," said Wesley, standing up straight. He was at least six foot four and he towered over Molly. "I wanted to speak with you and felt uncomfortable knocking on your bedroom door."

Molly held back a smile. There was something moving about

Wesley; his awkwardness and good intentions combined to make her quite fond of him.

"I definitely thought you should know: I've seen someone following you," he said.

"Huh?"

"Well, I'm traveling alone, as you know. I do not have a companion to distract me, and I believe this has made me much more sensitive to my surroundings. And I was already quite sensitive."

"Yes," said Molly, "that you are."

"I have been feeling a bit 'under the weather'—a maritime expression, as you probably know, taken from a seasick person going below decks on the 'weather side,' where the storm is hitting—and so have been spending more time in my room than I might otherwise, sometimes just looking out of the window and allowing my thoughts to ramble. And it was thus that several times I witnessed you, Molly. In the garden, and going into the village. And both of these times, a man was hidden, watching you."

"From where?" Molly's mind was evenly split between wanting to dismiss what Wesley was saying and feeling that spark of dread when you sense that someone warning you has good reason to do so. "Did you see who it was?"

"I'm afraid I could not, though of course since I am not a native, he is unlikely to be someone I would recognize in any case. When you were in the garden, he was standing in the shrubbery between La Baraque and your next door neighbor. Standing as still as a statue, watching. As far as I could tell—regretfully I did not pack my binoculars, they are Bushnells and I've been quite pleased with them—as I was saying, this person's eyes were pinned on you. Well, to be precise, I could not see his eyes. But his body was facing you and he stood there, not moving, for quite some time. I was quite certain he was trying to stay hidden so he could observe you."

"Why didn't you come outside and tell me?"

"I...I'm sorry to say I can't answer that. It did not occur to me. I am sorry, Molly, in retrospect that is what I should have done. I did keep watching until you came inside and I thought you were safe, since he did not follow but rather melted into the shrubbery until I could see him no more."

"Oh, don't blame yourself, I'm fine. And...you say he did it again? It's definitely a man?"

"Yes, a man. The second time—that I witnessed, of course there may have been others and I would say that is likely—was Saturday night. I happened to be looking out of my window just as it was getting dark. I saw you get on your scooter and turn onto the street toward the village. He jumped on a bicycle and followed you."

"Maybe he was just going for a ride?"

"At night? And why did he have a bicycle hidden in the bushes next to the road, as though he had planned ahead to wait there for you?"

Molly's first thought: was the stalker Daniel Coulon? She had decided during their first meeting that he was unreliable, but she only realized after hearing what Wesley had to say how much she distrusted him. "I need coffee," she said. "Can I get you anything? Some tea?" She put the pot under the faucet and filled it up. "And...thank you. This case I'm working on, I don't have much of a handle on it at this point, but I honestly don't think there's anything dangerous about it. I can't think of any reason at all that someone would want to follow me. My life really isn't all that exciting."

"I thought something similar as I watched the man watch you in the flower bed. Gardening is of course quite a healthful pursuit, but I would not characterize it as a spectator sport."

"No," said Molly, baffled, not noticing that Wesley had implied her life was a bore.

"All right then, I just thought you should be apprised. No need for tea. I plan to walk into the village and from there over to the Sallière vineyards. Even though I rarely drink alcohol, as you know, the process of making wine is a fairly interesting one. And there is a host of jargon for me to collect as well."

"Have fun, Wesley! Say hello to the owners for me, if you see them. It's a young couple, can't remember their names at the moment. I don't know them well but they seem lovely."

With his heavy-footed step Wesley disappeared to his room upstairs to prepare for his sojourn, and Molly absent-mindedly took the carton of eggs out of the refrigerator once again, this time too distracted to notice the little red heart drawn on the corner of the carton. Daniel had mentioned his mother's last name and the town where she lived, and she hoped that would be enough to go on to find out her phone number. Mentally she rehearsed the call, hoping that the woman wouldn't be angry to get a call from a stranger out of the blue asking a lot of personal questions about her past.

Bobo had curled up on Molly's feet, making breakfast a more difficult meal to prepare than it might have been. "Come on, girl," muttered Molly as she took a couple of eggs from the carton and cracked them into a bowl. "Get up, you've got me pinned!" Bobo grumbled and moved away, keeping her eyes on Molly.

Molly put the whisk down. Glancing at her watch, she decided to call Daniel's mother before cooking the omelette. It had not been a lesson she learned early in life, but at nearly forty Molly knew that if you're dreading a task, it's far better to just get it over with. She took coffee and sat on the sofa, thinking about how to find out the woman's number, then jumped up and went to her computer. In a matter of minutes, she had a list of four Clarys who lived in Laval, not far from Rennes where Coulon had gone to university.

Steeling herself, since making phone calls in French was still not her favorite thing to do, she went down the list one by one, asking whoever answered if she had a son named Daniel. The first two said no, one irritably.

After one ring, the third woman answered. "Âllo?"

"Yes, bonjour Madame Clary, this is Molly Sutton. I live in Castillac, in the Dordogne. I am wondering if you have a son named Daniel?"

A pause. "May I ask why you are calling? Is Daniel in some sort of trouble?"

Bingo, thought Molly with relief. "No, I don't think so. He hasn't called you in the last few days?"

"He has, yes. Why are *you* calling me?"

"Um, and so, I'm sorry, this is awkward, has anyone notified you about your ex-husband, Maxime Coulon?"

"What about him? We are long estranged, and do not speak."

"That's what I understand. But have you...I'm very sorry to be the one to tell you, but...it turns out that Maxime Coulon has died. He was murdered last Monday, a week ago."

Molly thought she might have heard a snicker, but wasn't sure. It sounded so out of place that she shivered.

"Well," said Molly, "I am a private investigator, and have been hired by Maxime's second wife—now an ex—to try to find out what happened. I know this is coming out of nowhere, but I'd like to ask you a few questions if that's all right with you?"

"Questions? You don't think *I* had anything to do with it? I am all the way in Brittany, for God's sake. Or are you going after Daniel, is that it?"

"Oh no," said Molly, half-lying. "It's that I'm trying to understand Maxime a little better, that's all. Daniel didn't call to tell you about the murder?"

"He did, actually. He's a good boy."

Strange to say that about a young man, thought Molly. People are weird.

"Did the news shock you?"

"Yes and no."

Molly waited but Madame Clary did not say anything further.

"Would you mind elaborating a bit? I didn't know him personally, even though Castillac is fairly small. Was he the kind of man...who people might...want to murder? Oh sorry, that's terribly vague. What I'm trying to ask is...some people really rub other people the wrong way. It's doesn't seem likely that Coulon was like that, because he was elected as mayor and served for so many years, so his personality must be..."

Molly shook her head. She should have written out a list of questions in advance. She was making a complete hash out of this phone call. "You have not been not in contact with Maxime since before Daniel was born?"

"That's correct," said Noelle. Then her voice softened. "Look, I'm sorry about what happened, but you must understand, that chapter of my life was over so long ago that I barely even remember him. Maxime and I—we thought we had fallen in love, but it was an infatuation, you understand? We were giddy at being out of our parents' houses, off at university, all grown up. It was over in a matter of months. Like a lingering cold," she added with a snort. "Annoying at the time, but soon forgotten. I raised Daniel by myself and remarried when he was still a young boy. I tried to tell Daniel that dredging up the past wasn't going to do anyone any good, and he shouldn't expect any help from Maxime."

"Does Daniel need help?"

"Oh, you know. Some people have a harder time finding their way than others."

"No doubt," said Molly.

"Look, I've got to hang up now. Someone's at the door."

"Would it be all right—" Molly started, but Madame Clary had already hung up.

I wonder what kind of help Daniel was looking for, Molly thought. Was it only money, or something else? She went back into the kitchen and whisked the eggs, then stepped into the garden to pick a bit of tarragon and chives to throw in. Instead of chopping it, she broke up the herbs with her fingers, thinking all the while about Maxime Coulon, a man in plain view who had turned out to be rather mysterious.

She needed to find out where Daniel was staying and see if he would talk to her. He had been seen near the mayor's house after the body was discovered, he had motive...altogether, quite a promising suspect, though she was curious about what Ben might be finding out at the Mega-Mart.

Molly could make an omelette with her eyes closed, she had done it so many times. She slid the glistening yellow semi-circle onto a plate, liberally dusted it with salt and pepper, and took it out to the terrace to enjoy with a glass of chilled rosé. Remembering Wesley Addison's warning, she looked around to see if anyone was hiding in any shrubbery nearby, but saw nothing but a wren hopping through the branches.

37

Vasily had watched Molly work at her computer and then make breakfast through the window at the end of her living room, which was partly covered by an overgrown viburnum that gave him some cover. He had discovered he very much liked stalking the detective, and would rather do that than any of the long list of things Fedosia had ordered him to do. He thought about how scared Molly would be if he grabbed her and twisted her arm up behind her back. Imagining her frightened and pleading expression gave him pleasure.

"Vasily!" hissed Fedosia, on her way to the pigeonnier. "Tear yourself away from Sutton and take care of business!" She went by, muttering under her breath. Vasily sighed and stepped out of the viburnum, making a wide circle as though he were going for a stroll in the meadow. When he was out of sight of the main house, he went straight for the small rental building where their operation was underway. He took the key out of his pocket and inserted it into the rusty lock, cursing when it did not open right away. After much jiggling and more cursing, he managed to open the door and go in.

Everything was ready. All of the equipment and raw materials to make the steroids, and a big box of needles since Fedosia had had the brilliant idea to sell the doses already loaded into a syringe. He had to hand it to her, she was a genius at organizing and planning. They made a good team, he thought, nodding as he picked up a beaker and then a glass vial with a rubber cap, turning them over and then setting them back down.

Malcolm Barstow was due to meet him there, and so far the kid had followed through on everything he'd been asked to do. Vasily looked at his watch, impatient. He started wondering what time Molly Sutton got undressed at night, and how he could make sure to be on surveillance then.

He heard a rustling outside the window, and peered out. Malcolm was moving through some underbrush on the side of the building and then gave the door three sharp raps.

"Get in here," said Vasily. "You're almost late."

Malcolm just shook his head, thinking that he would have to be a fool to be late for the Vasilievs. He knew if he crossed them they would get rid of him without any hesitation at all. He did not question how he knew this; even though his young life had been packed with as much criminality as possible, he had not dealt with people like the Vasilievs before. But Malcolm had an acute way of sizing other people up, and so despite his lack of experience, he was not wrong about his current business partners.

"Okay, look, I was happy to be helpful to you. But I've got another project going on that takes up most of my time," Malcolm said, not wanting to seem like a pushover.

"You think I am interested in your projects?" laughed Vasily. "Your project is going to be right here in this room, at least for the next month. Possibly after that—six weeks, maybe two months—we can talk about training someone to take your place. But for now? It is all yours, my friend. I have confidence you will do well."

"Do well at what?" said Malcolm, his spirits sinking.

"It is not complicated. There are people who want a product, and we want to sell it to them. Unfortunately for them, the product is not legal. But fortunate for us, yes?" he said, slapping Malcolm on the back. "Fedosia says the profit margin is very, very good. And compared to heroin, cocaine, any of that? Not so much risk. No worry about sniffing dogs at borders, and a long list of other headaches."

Malcolm waited, his mind racing to find a way out even though he still had no idea what he was being ordered to do.

"It's just steroids, plain and simple," said Vasily proudly. "For bodybuilders. They are safe and effective, it's silly that they're illegal, but we will profit from that, yes?" Again, he slapped Malcolm on the back, smiling when the boy lurched forward and scowled. "Believe me, you will get some of that profit. Not a big cut," he laughed, "but enough to make you happy. Your job, my friend, is to work here, assembling the product. You will be like a chef in your own kitchen! We will provide the ingredients, and you will make the cake."

"How will you distribute? Who's finding your buyers?"

"Leave that to us, little man. It's all covered."

Malcolm considered. It was ridiculous to be doing this barely two steps from Molly Sutton's house, he knew that very well. But on the other side was...Vasily. And money. Their eyes met and held for a moment. Malcolm swallowed. "All right then, mate, how do I start?"

ॐ

AFTER LUNCH, Molly went to her bedroom and read for over an hour. She was so absorbed in her book that she did not notice when Bobo sneaked up on the bed and curled up next to her. Finally, with a satisfied sigh, she put the book on her bedside table.

"Come on, Bobo, want to go for a walk?" Bobo leapt up, ecstatic at the suggestion, making Molly laugh. "It's not like you couldn't go run around in the woods by yourself anytime you wanted," she said. A good long walk nearly always helped Molly clarify her thoughts, and she wanted to go over her conversation with Daniel's mother carefully before she told Ben about it. Daniel was troubled, she didn't need to be an expert to see that— his quick shifts in mood when she talked to him at the bakery went beyond just a little eccentricity. He was hanging around rue Malbec so he clearly knew where the mayor lived. And of course, there was the little matter of a large inheritance. Though in the interest of objectivity she resisted it, Molly couldn't help feeling that the Coulon case was practically done and dusted.

She was lacing up her boots on the terrace when Wesley Addison clumped up.

"I thought you were off to the vineyard?" she said.

"Yes. Well, ah..."

Molly waited but Wesley seemed unusually tongue-tied.

"Well, it's fine to change your mind. I do it all the time!" she grinned at him.

"I just thought it was not right to leave you here alone. Do you expect Monsieur Dufort to come back at some point?"

"Oh, you're very sweet. Really. I don't know though, Wesley— don't you think this person might just be some nosy neighbor, or something like that? I mean, he wouldn't have to be anyone dangerous, right?"

"One needn't require certainty to exercise reasonable precaution," he said stiffly.

"Yes, well, perhaps you're right. I do expect Ben later this afternoon. I'm going for a walk now, and I'll be sure to lock up the house and stay vigilant once I get back. Go on to the vineyard, Wesley—I'll be careful, I promise."

"I do not think a walk alone is well-advised. That man could be right under our noses, listening to this very conversation. Just waiting to get you away from the house. Are you carrying your cell phone?"

"Yes. And Bobo—"

"You know perfectly well that your dog would likely roll over and ask for a belly rub if a stranger approached you. Enjoy your pet all you wish, Molly, but do not delude yourself—"

"Okay, okay, point taken. Now, we're off!" It was broad daylight and she couldn't be scared of every shadow. She waved and whistled. Bobo shot out from under the table and disappeared into the woods, and Molly followed along the edge of the meadow, thinking she would have a look at that tumbling down barn she had wanted the brilliant stone mason, Pierre Gault, to fix up. She walked for some minutes without thinking about anything, just listening to the sound of Bobo in the underbrush, the birds singing, and the leaves of the trees whispering in the light breeze, but with half an ear out for anyone behind her.

The sun was strong but it was not humid, and Molly gave the old barn a decent going-over, trying to decide if it was worth sinking what little remained from her windfall into it. It would give her at least six or seven more beds for the gîte business, but if Dufort/Sutton Investigations really took off, maybe that would be a hindrance more than a help. It was hard to predict the future, that's for sure, she thought, passing the border of her property and continuing to walk north, away from the village.

She did not, all this time, forget what Wesley Addison had told her, and made sure to keep looking around, turning quickly to check behind her, alert and on her guard.

Bobo gave a quick yip and streaked out of the woods and toward a small building on the side of the road, then zoomed just as quickly into the woods and out of sight again. Molly felt that little tingle of curiosity she liked so much, and approached, circling the building, and seeing a bicycle partly hidden in the bushes on the far side.

She didn't dare knock, being alone and having no idea who might be inside. But she did edge up to the window, being as quiet as possible, and take a peek inside.

A naked light bulb hung from the ceiling. A lot of cardboard boxes, a table with a bunch of things on it she could not identify at that distance, and that was it. No bed, no clothes...it was clearly not a habitation, yet something was going on in there.

Another yip from Bobo and Molly kept walking, heading out where the houses were sparse and the forest dense. But she stayed alert, keeping her promise to Wesley Addison, and whistled Bobo close several times, believing her beloved dog to have more potential as a guard than her guest did.

❦ 38 ❧

That night, the weather was perfect for a fête. The ladies on the village beautification committee were having a dinner to raise funds for the year's projects, and much of the village was expected to turn out. The entire staff of Dufort/Sutton Investigations was certainly planning to be there with bells on, eyes and ears open. Ben wanted to see Paul-Henri and sound him out about working together on some more forensic accounting, this time concerning Mega-Mart and the late mayor. Molly hoped to find Daniel. Ben had gotten back so late they had barely been able to shower and get ready before the fête, with no time to talk over the day's events and discoveries.

Ben parked on a side street and they walked over to the Place, holding hands, both lost in thought. Others, friends and strangers, were walking in the same direction. Swallows swooped overhead, and Molly breathed in the smell of roses tumbling over a back fence.

"Just quickly, before we get there—I talked to Daniel's mother today," she said, quietly enough that other fête-goers couldn't hear. "We didn't talk long. She wasn't friendly at first, but eventually opened up a little. The only interesting bit I got was that she implied Daniel had come looking for his father because he needed help."

"What kind of help?"

"She didn't say. I pressed a little but she was vague. Though... you can just look at him to see he needs money. Makes sense that he'd ask his well-off father, doesn't it? And maybe...maybe Coulon said no. And Daniel figured he could get the money, *all* the money, no matter what his father said."

Ben slipped his arm around Molly's waist and gave her a squeeze. "Might be something there. Good work. And I've got plenty to tell you about Mega-Mart," he said, "but let's enjoy our dinner first. My news will be your dessert," he said with a grin.

She knew it was foolish in the extreme, but she couldn't help wanting *her* suspect to be the guilty party, as though she and Ben were competing. And so she hoped—childishly, she was well aware—that whatever Ben had to tell her wasn't going to be much of anything. Guiltily she leaned in and kissed his cheek just as they reached the Place. Two rows of tables stretched from one end to the other, making seats for something close to three hundred villagers, all out enjoying the clear mild evening and each other's company.

"My heavens," said Molly, the long tables reminding her that Nico and Frances's wedding was in *three days*. She had put it so far on the back burner it was in danger of being forgotten entirely. Then she gasped. "Look who it is!"

Ben followed her pointing finger to see Lapin, already seated with a plate loaded with food, fork in one hand and the other holding the hand of Anne-Marie.

"Lapin!" said Molly. "I don't know whether to congratulate you or slap you!"

"Molly, my dear! I have no idea why you would want to slap me."

"Because you ran off and eloped and cheated us out of coming to your wedding!"

Anne-Marie giggled.

"I thought you told me something like 'couples need to do what's right for them,' or some such thing. Well, that's exactly what we did. Right, darling?" he said, looking at Anne-Marie with an expression Molly had never seen on Lapin's face before. It was not lascivious, not joking, not satiric, but tender and loving.

"I'm only teasing," said Molly. "And congratulations to you, Anne-Marie. I know you'll be very happy together." She felt something close up in her throat just then, and stepped back so Ben could speak to them.

Marriage. The whole subject just makes me lose my appetite, she thought.

A cheer went up near the statue and they all turned to look. "It's André Lebeau," said Lapin, rolling his eyes. "No doubt parading around showing off as he always does. I don't mind saying I've pretty much had it with that guy. If he wins a place on the council, we're all going to be sorry."

They could see the head of Lebeau sticking up out of a crowd of admirers, and hear their laughter and excited talking without being able to make out what anyone was saying.

"Shall we get plates?" Ben asked Molly.

"Yes, let's, I'm suddenly starving. What's being served?" she looked down at Lapin's plate and saw a heap of something she couldn't identify and a long sausage. "Are you drinking cider?" she asked Lapin.

"Yes, and it's very fine. Bring some mustard when you come back."

Molly nodded and followed Ben as he made his way through the crowd. "I'll go get tickets, you wait in line?"

"Sure," she said, swiveling her gaze all around looking for Daniel. I guess he might not be able to afford the meal, she thought, or maybe he's worried about not knowing anyone. It was obviously premature to confront him in any case, but she felt an irresistible pressure to clinch her suspicions about Daniel before Ben could tell her what he had found out at Mega-Mart.

"Molly!" someone shrieked.

Molly whirled around to see the grinning faces of her gîte guests, Emily and Nancy. "Oh! I'm glad to see you here. You've become fixtures of the village," she laughed. "Sure you don't want to just move here and be done with it?"

"Don't tempt me," said Nancy. "We want to really live it up these last few days. Go get us some more cider, Emily!"

"We'll need to go in the hospital to recover," said Emily, cheerfully going for the cider.

"I'm off to get in the food line. Maybe I'll see you later?"

"I hear there's going to be dancing," said Nancy, jumping up and wiggling her hips.

Molly laughed and kept moving, scanning the crowd, not giving up hope that Daniel might be in the crowd somewhere.

Behind Molly, about fifteen feet away and blending into the crowd, was Vasily Vasiliev, shadowing her as she moved slowly through the crowd. And behind Vasily loomed the large and awkward figure of Wesley Addison.

Ben got the tickets and joined Molly in line. "This is not a very good place to have a conversation," he said, as they were continually interrupted by friends wanting to talk about Frances and Nico's wedding, the latest political ridiculousness, or Leda Vidal's new cheese. "But I want to give you just the outline of what I found out—yes, bonsoir to you, Madame Gervais!" He bent to kiss her wrinkled cheeks, taking both of her hands in his and squeezing them. "How are you feeling this evening?"

"Fit as a fiddle," the old woman told him. "Bonsoir, Molly. How's the case going?"

"Quite well, actually, I think I might be—"

But Madame Gervais was swept along in the crowd by several of her friends, and Molly and Ben finally had a free moment to talk to each other.

"All right, have this as an *hors d'oeuvre*, then," said Ben. "I'm almost positive Coulon was taking kickbacks from Mega-Mart and possibly several other large stores, in return for suppressing small business in the village."

"Outrageous!"

"Yes. Corrupt, greedy, lots of things you could call it. I've got an eye out for Monsour—he can get access to Coulon's bank accounts and I think he knows some accounting. If I'm right, I don't think it will take long to prove."

"I have to admit, I'm feeling a little stupid. Annette mentioned the permit thing to me the other day, and I just didn't think... I didn't see how the murder...how did you get anything out of Mega-Mart?"

"I went in there with both guns blazing. I pretended we had them dead to rights and the only way to make things easier in terms of sentencing was to cooperate, starting that minute, no second chances."

"Wow!" Molly was impressed. "But so...is this just a side issue or do you think the kickbacks had something to do with his murder?"

Ben shot Molly a look. "I don't think uncovering criminal activity performed by a murder victim is a 'side issue'."

"Me neither! I didn't mean it like that. But listen, I really think Daniel—"

"Madame Sutton, Monsieur Dufort," said an officious voice behind them.

Molly and Ben turned to find Paul-Henri Monsour, holding a plate with an enormous sausage curled upon it. "I know this is not the best time and place, but I would like a word with both of you, if I may?"

"Yes, of course," said Ben. "I have something to discuss with you as well. How about we get our plates and join you? Can you save us seats?"

Paul-Henri nodded and Ben and Molly inched up in the line.

"It's true that Coulon's corruption doesn't automatically point to one person as his murderer," Ben said in Molly's ear. "But you must admit, it opens up a host of possibilites. Was anyone else in on it? What about Monsieur Lachance, Coulon's banker? If the sums were large enough, there would need to be some sort of money laundering involved. Maybe he or someone else thought Coulon was backing out or going to the authorities, and decided to shut him up?"

"Well," said Molly, trying not to sound grudging, "you're right, could go a lot of ways. But at this point, those possibilities are awfully vague, aren't they? Whereas with Daniel, we've got someone who was seen near the scene, has a massive motive, and who's a little off, to boot!"

"What do you mean, 'a little off'?"

"Well, like I said, he zigzagged. He would seem angry, then sort of friendly, then—talking about his father's murder—almost giddy. I'm telling you, it wasn't normal!"

Ben nodded, hearing what she was saying but also feeling some stubbornness about his own discovery and wanting Molly to be more excited by it. At long last they reached the purveyors of sausage and had their plates loaded down. Molly added a heap of frites because she could never say no to frites, and they went in search of Monsour, stopping to say hello to yet more friends and acquaintances along the way.

A small band got up on the makeshift stage and started playing Irish jigs, and children crowded around, hands in the air and legs flying. For a second Molly stood still and looked around at her beloved village, all these people she cared about sitting down to a meal together, lit up by strings of fairy lights, under the deep dark blue sky. She felt emotion bubbling up and had to choke back tears, she was so happy to be there, in that place, with Ben right behind her and her best pal Frances off somewhere causing trouble, no doubt. But as she glanced around, she did not see Daniel, and worried that he had skipped town before she had another chance to talk to him.

"How is the sausage?" Ben asked Paul-Henri, who had eaten half of his before they got settled in their chairs.

The three of them talked of grilled meat and fried potatoes for a minute or two before getting down to business.

Molly, for her part, was focused for the moment on the food. Murder was serious, and solving one crucially important. But a girl needs sustenance, she was thinking to herself as she sliced into the perfectly crisp exterior of the sausage after slathering on some mustard. If she had to travel to Brittany to interview Daniel, that's just what she would have to do. Constance could manage things while she was gone. And Frances and Nico's wedding...well, it would all come off somehow.

"I wanted to speak with you both as a matter of professional courtesy," said Monsour. "We are not quite at the moment of writing out a warrant, a few details remain to be worked out, and as you are quite aware, the collection of certain kinds of evidence can be numbingly slow—"

"Yes?" interrupted Ben. "Who do you have your sights on?"

"Your client, Odile Dupont."

"What?" said Molly, leaning forward and forgetting about her frites. "Odile is innocent! You can't just arrest people without any reason!"

Monsour smiled and sliced the last bit of his sausage in two. "The motive is multifold," he said primly. "Not only was there a great deal of rancor about the divorce, but Coulon had been actively hurting her financially. He had instructed the workers in the mairie not to review her application for a business license. Odile, you see, runs a conglomeration of beauty shops. I can tell you that in Paris, these sort of places do quite a serious busin—"

"We know, Paul-Henri, we know," said Ben. "We are aware of the situation with the permits you're talking about, but have drawn a different conclusion about who is implicated."

"Were others in Coulon's office the week before his murder, throwing ashtrays and making all sorts of threats? Because your client was," said Monsour.

Molly and Ben looked at each other. Seems Odile had left a few details out of her version of the story, and how were they going to slow down Monsour while they figured out who the real killer was?

Or for once, had the gendarmes beaten Molly to the truth?

❧ 39 ❧

The next morning Molly sped into the village early with two goals in mind: get a few wedding errands crossed off her list, and find Daniel Coulon if he was still in town. She rode through the Place, eyes peeled, but did not see him, then went down rue Malbec in case he was still hanging out around his father's house. Still no sign of him.

She and Ben had decided not to tell Odile how close the gendarmes were to arresting her, agreeing that the news might put enough pressure on her that she might do something she shouldn't—make a run for it, cause a scene, anything other than just go to work every day and not throw ashtrays at anybody. All Dufort/Sutton could do to protect their client was try to offer the gendarmes other possibilities, equally convincing, to buy some time.

Was it possible that Nico and Frances's wedding was in only two days? How was that even possible? She felt totally unready, though as she ran through the items on her list, the situation wasn't completely hopeless. The menu was simple enough, just grilled steaks and whatever vegetables looked freshest that day, sautéed in butter. Salad, of course. Edmond Nugent was bringing bread and making the cake, and she had arranged for the steaks, vegetables, and liquor to be delivered Friday morning, so that was done. She already had tables, tablecloths, cutlery, glasses, all bought for the Chef du Monde contest she'd put on in the winter. Unless she was overlooking something crucial, all she had to do that morning was see Madame Langevin about the flowers. The timing had turned out to be terrible but she could hardly blame Frances and Nico for that, or the mayor either, for that matter.

But first, *coffee*. She parked outside Pâtisserie Bujold and went in, waving to Edmond as he talked to another customer.

"Well, bonjour, Malcolm," said Molly, when the boy turned to see who was coming into the shop. "Nice to see you again."

"Hullo," he said, then turning back around. His longish hair was a bit matted and his shirt did not look fresh. Molly wondered how things were going at home, unable to imagine what family life must be like when your father is in prison.

"How's your family?" she asked, unwilling to give up on engaging him.

Malcolm turned his face towards her but not his body, and shrugged. "Fine, I guess," he said, mumbling.

Hm, she thought. He's certainly out of sorts about something.

Malcolm bought a fancy layered cup covered with crushed almonds and a red feather sticking out of the top. Molly admired it and laughed as the boy immediately dug his spoon in and ate, but could get no more response from him.

"He a regular?" she asked, when Malcolm had left.

"Hardly ever been in. Doesn't usually have the scratch," Edmond said in a low voice, leaning across the counter. "At least in here the display case keeps him from walking out with half the merchandise."

"Listen, the guy I was talking to the other day? Coulon's son? Have you seen him around since then?"

"Yes, as a matter of fact. Funny you bring him up right on the heels of Malcolm Barstow. So that guy, Daniel his name is, he comes in yesterday, maybe it was the day before, and orders a couple of caramel éclairs. I put them in a box and stepped away for just a second, had to take a delivery in the back but it wasn't more than a minute. Came back and Daniel had polished off one éclair and was making headway on the second. Gluttonous behavior," said Edmond, shaking his head. "But still worse, he hadn't the money to pay. Just smiled at me, saying he'd be back eventually with the money. Didn't say when."

"Did you call the gendarmes?"

"Over a couple of éclairs? Nah. Not worth it. I don't think he'll be coming back, though. Probably off to scam the next guy... maybe he'll go to Fillon," he added with satisfaction.

"It's obvious he's pretty hard up," Molly said, actually arguing with Ben, not Edmond.

"I fail to feel a great deal of sympathy," said Edmond with a sniff.

"He didn't happen to say where he was staying, or anything like that?"

"No. But by the look of him, I wouldn't be surprised to hear he's sleeping rough."

Molly raced off, not forgetting her small bag of pastry, wanting to get the florist over with so she could get back to La Baraque before everyone was up. The fête had gone very late and Ben and the guests were all sleeping in, so she figured she could squeeze in Madame Langevin, as long as they didn't get carried away talking.

The shop wasn't officially open yet, but Molly could see Madame Langevin inside sorting an enormous armful of roses on a stainless steel table. Molly knocked on the door and waved, her mind zinging from Daniel to Odile to Mega-Mart to the wedding, like a battered pinball game on the point of throwing sparks.

"I wondered if I was going to hear from you," Madame Langevin said with a smile, as she opened the door. "The wedding is this Friday. Cutting it a bit close, are we?"

Molly shook her head. "I know, it's completely my fault. I

should have called weeks ago. It's just that Ben and I are on the Coulon case and it's taken up every single bit of time." She paused. "And you know, just between us, Frances has been so back and forth about the whole thing that it just never actually felt real to me. I had to go see Nico to get a date. Of course, when I agreed to it, I had no idea..."

"Tell me, do you think Frances...is she not enthusiastic about the marriage? Nico has been in here multiple times to get flowers for her—you remember the bee sting episode?"

Molly nodded, her eyes wide. "Oh yeah—scary."

"Well, there's no doubt in my mind that Nico is absolutely gaga over Frances. But maybe it's a bit of a one-way kind of thing?"

"No, no, I don't think so. She's equally gaga, I'm positive of that. It's more of a resistance to the formality. Anyway, I'm sorry to be short but I am in a terrific hurry. Would you mind coming up with something simple and bringing it over on Friday, early afternoon I suppose? A small bouquet for Frances, not frilly but simple, and maybe a couple of arrangements for the table? It's not going to be a swanky affair, just a quick ceremony and small dinner with friends."

"No disco dancing this time?"

"Not this time," laughed Molly. "Just send me the bill. And thank you!"

That out of the way, on the drive home Molly thought she should probably call Odile and give her an update on their progress. They needn't tell her all the leads they were following, but she had a pretty good idea that when someone pays as much as Odile was going to be paying, they want to feel like they're in the loop. But could she do that without telling her about Monsour's suspicions?

Too many things, too many things, I need to sit down and make a list before my head spins right off into the sky, she thought, taking a sharp turn into the driveway and hoping everyone was still asleep.

Bobo greeted her with wild barking, and Molly came in through the terrace door to find Ben pouring a cup of coffee, looking bleary from the late night.

He and Molly kissed warmly, though she felt a hint of that competitive feeling still lurking about.

"Sorry to bother you," boomed Wesley from the corridor. "Good morning! I'm afraid I am unused to keeping these irregular kinds of hours. I wonder if you would mind making me a hearty breakfast, Molly? I feel rather depleted."

"I would sign up for that too," said Ben, with a sly grin.

"All right, eggs and bacon fit the bill? I'm properly caffeinated, and here are some croissants to munch on if you're feeling faint." She put the white bag from Pâtisserie Bujold on the table and got the eggs out of the refrigerator.

"Scrambled okay?"

"I do prefer a sunny-side up egg but I can go with the flow," said Wesley. "Interesting bit of slang, 'go with the flow'. It makes one wonder what sort of flow is being referenced, does it not?"

Molly was half-listening to Wesley ramble, and half-thinking about going straight back into the village after breakfast and covering every square inch until she found Daniel Coulon. So she was not paying attention when the orange cat hopped up on the kitchen counter when she went to get out the butter, and when she turned back around the cat startled her, she jumped, and it flew off the counter in a rush, knocking the carton of eggs to the floor.

"Well, dammit," Molly muttered, opening the carton of Barbeau eggs in hopes something could be salvaged. But there had been ten eggs left, and every one of them was smashed to bits and running onto the floor.

IV

❦ 40 ❦

Madame Barbeau had taken to her bed, her knees on fire. She asked Josette to bring her just a bowl of soup for lunch and spent the afternoon napping, her room pungent with the smell of the ointment she had made to soothe her joints.

After making and delivering the soup, Josette was enjoying the sunny day by wandering around the farm doing nothing. She remembered the goat she had as a child and considered spending her stash on another one. She crossed the meadow to the small pond and stood looking into it, seeing the fish rise, her mind blank.

Oh, Josie, Julien said to himself, seeing her standing there. She was so beautiful—beautiful, with an alarming deficit of common sense, he thought, walking across the meadow to join her.

"Listen, I've been thinking," he said. "We've talked about going to America before, right?"

Josette nodded.

"Why don't we just go, get the hell out of here! I know we don't have much money, but we have enough for plane tickets and living expenses for a few months. We can find work once we get there."

Josette looked at her brother gratefully.

"Can you imagine?" he continued. "No more of her Subjects? No more going on about restaurant food, or our father, or any of it?"

"You really mean a fresh start?"

"Totally fresh," said Julien with a grin. But then he looked down at his feet, realizing how many hoops there would be to jump through. "Of course, we'll have to get passports first," he said.

But they had the money. He wanted the fresh start, for both of them, so badly he could taste it.

"Listen, I'm going to get passport applications done. Maybe we can pay extra and they'll rush them. And don't worry about the hens, Maman can manage by herself better than she lets on."

"I'm a little scared of America," said Josette.

They stood without speaking, staring at the water. Julien bent down and picked up a handful of stones and began chucking them into the pond.

"But not so scared I can't go with you," she said quietly, and her brother let out a whoop.

"I'M GETTING MARRIED in two days, Molls. *Two!*"

"I know. Grab the end there and we'll lift on three. One, two, three!" Molly backed out of the storage shed holding the end of one of the tables, and Frances groaned and complained while walking her end along, until eventually, with more minor hysteria from Frances, they had three tables set up in the yard where they wanted them, in one long row.

"Am I crazy not to have dancing? All good parties have dancing."

"There's nothing stopping anyone. Impromptu dancing can

break out anytime," said Molly patiently. "I can hook up music and we can let 'er rip on the grass. Easy."

"Am I making a terrible mistake?"

"Not having a dance floor?"

"No, you knucklehead, getting married for the third time!"

Molly faced her old friend. She stood for a moment with her mouth closed tight, willing herself not to blow up. "Frances? You are making yourself crazy. If it turns out that marrying Nico is a mistake, and you liked it better not being married, then get another divorce. You guys can just go back to the way things were before, no harm done."

"But Nico really wants children."

Molly's chest felt tight and she said nothing.

"And I don't have any idea how I feel about that, and I know it's a bad subject for you but if I never talk about it then that's weird in its own right."

"I'm not telling you not to talk about it."

"Okay, well, it's just that I have this traditionalist streak in me when it comes to kids."

Molly managed to laugh. "You do? I didn't think there was a whisper of the traditionalist anywhere near you!"

Frances hung her head. "I know. It's embarrassing."

"So, just to finish up here—I've got white tablecloths ready to go, plus napkins, and Madame Langevin is doing some flowers, nothing over the top at all."

"I do love flowers."

"There, that's a good bride! I've got to make a phone call. How about you go to the closet in the new addition and pull out the box with the tablecloths? I think there are salt shakers and pepper grinders in there too."

Frances skipped off like she was ten. Molly pulled out her cell and gave Odile a call.

"Well, it's about time," Odile said, the second she realized who was calling. "Is it your usual practice to get a client and then ignore them while taking their money?"

"We should have agreed on a timetable for communication," said Molly, feeling too pressed for time to argue. "And I am sorry, I don't have a lot of time right now."

"You're putting on a wedding, that's what I hear. Very unprofessional, I have to tell you. Have you made any headway on Maxime's case at all? I'm feeling extremely anxious about it, Molly. It's very unsettling when violence hits so close."

"I'm aware," said Molly, and then tried to hide her irritation a little better. "Ben and I *are* making progress. Did you know that Maxime had a son?"

"Of course. We were married, you know."

"Not infrequently, married people keep secrets from each other."

"Well, maybe they do, but that's irrelevant, isn't it? Maxime told me about the son. He spoke about it just once. I believe it was a source of...I was going to say shame, but the truth is, he was worried that the son would show up and embarrass him, that was the main thing. He never lifted a finger to try to find him or anything, not that I know of."

Molly could not get her head around the idea of a parent not caring where his child was, not wanting to know him, or even to meet him one time. It boggled her mind completely. "His son is in the village. Or he was, I haven't been able to track him down for a couple of days."

"Is that it?"

"No," said Molly, feeling defensive. "But you must understand, Odile. I'm sure with running your own business, you're used to knowing everything about the details. But there are things Ben and I can't talk about because they are involved with the investigation out of the gendarmerie, and we are not allowed to speak about them even with you."

Molly spoke to Odile for another fifteen minutes, dodging

more questions and eventually succeeding in placating her, mostly through sounding confident. But as she put her cell on the kitchen counter, she felt like the least confident detective who ever was. She had no proof that Daniel was the murderer, only a collection of circumstantial evidence that she hoped was damning. *Hoped.* With a deep sigh, Molly lay down on the sofa and closed her eyes, trying to go over every detail of the case to see if there was anything she had missed.

A detective worthy of a good reputation has got to have more going for her than hope, she thought, as she drifted without intending to right into a nap.

❧ 41 ❧

The next day, her best friend's wedding minus one, Molly rode into the village with the idea of picking up some trinkets to put by each wedding guest's plate. Something silly, something to lighten the mood, to make Frances laugh in spite of herself. At least the weather seemed to be holding, which was a tremendous blessing since if it rained, the whole thing would have to be squeezed into Molly's living room, which would not be—

Oh! Molly realized she had forgotten to call Constance to ask her if she could clean tomorrow. Fearing she and Thomas would have some grand plan that could not be interrupted no matter what, Molly pulled the scooter over and immediately hit speed dial for Constance.

She was about half a block from the bank, so when Maron and Monsour came out holding a man's arm, she saw the whole thing. Ben came out of the bank last. Molly squinted, trying to see if she recognized the man between the gendarmes.

"Constance? Molly. Listen, could you…sorry. Bonjour. How are you?…Yes, I'm fine, too. I wanted to ask you—it's sort of an emergency, actually—can you come clean tomorrow, before the wedding? I'm going to be busy cooking and I just don't think....yes, bring Thomas with you. I can think of about ten things I could give him to do....right, right...thank you *so* much!"

Molly hurried off the phone, parked the scooter, and ran down the sidewalk. Maron, Monsour, and the banker had disappeared around the corner, but Ben had seen Molly and waited for her.

"What the heck?" she said, breathless.

"Turns out Coulon wasn't any good at all at hiding his tracks," said Ben, proudly. "Once Monsour started looking through his accounts, he found evidence of money-laundering right off the bat."

"What? What does that even look like?"

"There were regular deposits, five hundred euros apiece, going back many months, even years. Did you know that there are all kinds of people who, by law, are supposed to report anything suspicious relating to money-laundering? Legally, for example, a banker has to report incoming money with no apparent source. Monsieur Lachance, the banker you just saw being marched off by Maron—he oversaw Coulon's accounts for years. And Monsour said there were suspicious deposits even as far back as 2001, and he hasn't had time to go back further. Coulon was probably extorting from others besides Mega-Mart, ever since he managed to get elected mayor.

"And on top of all that, as mayor, Coulon sometimes acted as a sort of officer of the court, and so he could protect Lachance in case a magistrate ever got interested in the banker's affairs. Coulon was simultaneously a golden egg, a protector, and a noose around Lachance's neck."

"Nice work, detective!" said Molly. She opened her mouth to ask about the connection to the murder, but closed it again.

"Thank you," said Ben, knowing perfectly well what Molly was thinking but not holding it against her. "Given all that, I do think Lachance deserves more of our attention. All right, I'm going to catch up with Maron. See you tonight."

Molly sat on the scooter for a minute, thinking about Coulon.

He must have been paying off Lachance to keep him quiet, and it looked as though that worked both ways. Maybe Lachance pushed him for more money, and they got into a fight that turned deadly?

But in the guest room of his house, on the second floor? It didn't make sense. She ran through the rest of the suspects other than Daniel—André Lebeau, Josette, even Odile—but out of the holy trio of means, motive, and opportunity, none of them had more than one. One was barely worth bothering about, she thought irritably. Was there someone else, someone she and Ben had failed to consider? He or she would have to be right under their noses.

What other secrets did Coulon keep?

She started up the scooter and slowly rode through the streets of Castillac, looking for something with which to amuse the wedding guests. Not an easy errand when she was feeling out of sorts. Eventually she found herself outside Lapin's shop, and figured she would give that a try.

"Bonjour, Lapin," she said, coming into the agreeably cool front room. "How's married life treating you?"

"It's beyond my wildest dreams," he said, looking at her with... yes, those were actual tears in Lapin's eyes, Molly was shocked to see.

"I'm so happy for you," she said, and meant it. This new, earnest Lapin was going to take some getting used to. She glanced around, thinking that there was no way she was going to find wedding favors among the broken lamps, dusty portraits, and fusty furniture that clogged up the aisles.

But as long as she was there, Molly figured she might as well go ahead and explain what she was looking for, and Lapin not only understood completely but put his finger on just the right thing.

"I usually don't take toys, unless they're especially old or interesting," he said, pulling a medium-sized box out from under the counter. "But something about these made me smile, so I picked them up from the last estate I did. I might be able to let them go for a reasonable price."

He put down the box in front of Molly, and she looked at it. Inside was a jumble of plastic dinosaurs. She took one out and stood it up, then another. "I always did like dinosaurs," she said, laughing.

"I think they say *Frances and Nico, together always* like nothing else possibly could," said Lapin. "The whole box, thirty-five euros."

"Are you high?" said Molly. "Ten. And that's still a rip-off."

Molly was smiling to herself as she came outside and strapped the box onto the back of the scooter. She was so busy imagining the guests coming to the table and seeing place cards held by dinosaurs that she failed to see the front wheel of a bicycle poking out from the alley down the block. As she went along, she checked the side streets and looked in shop windows hoping to find Daniel, but no luck. Nor did she see, in her mirror, Vasily Vasiliev on that bike, following her as she made her way through the village and onto the empty rue des Chênes.

❧ 42 ❧

Once home, Molly got out an old calligraphy pen and got to work on the place cards. She had a much wider traditionalist streak than her friend, and if old-fashioned place cards were going to be the only way she could express it, that would have to suffice. But she was out of practice and kept leaving unsightly blotches, her lines wobbly instead of graceful, and in the end, a job that she had thought would take thirty minutes ended up taking three hours.

"Come on, Bobo," she said, capping the pen after the last one was finished. "Not half bad, even if did take forever," she said, having no compunction at all about talking to Bobo as if she were human. "Want to go for a walk?" Bobo, to Molly's never-failing delight, leapt in the air and spun in circles, thrilled with the idea.

Wesley Addison was lurking in the corridor and heard Molly. He stood still, knowing full well that his step was heavy, and waited for her to get on her walking boots and leave by the terrace door. It was dinnertime but still light out, and when he moved to look out of the window in the corridor he saw her heading across the meadow to the north. He considered following, but then contented himself with standing guard from that very spot in the corridor of La Baraque, where he could see Molly clearly and thus would be able to see a stalker too, as long as they came from the direction of the house or the village, which seemed likely.

It never failed to cheer Molly up, watching Bobo bound after rabbits which she never caught. She walked around the ruined barn and headed straight to the small building on the neighboring property, still curious about what was going on inside. As she reached it, Bobo having disappeared into the forest, she was careful to stay at an angle, so anyone inside looking out would not be able to see her easily.

Ben, meanwhile, had come home late after long discussions with Maron and Monsour in which they combed through the mayor's finances and tried to map out the web of corruption he had spun around himself and the mairie. He was tired and pleased by the work they had done.

He let himself into La Baraque and was startled to see Wesley Addison standing in the corridor, staring out of the window.

"Good evening, Wesley," said Ben, never very confident of his English. "Is everything okay?"

"*No*," said Wesley. He glanced at Ben but turned right back to the window. "Just now...I believe I saw someone, in the shadows by the woods."

Ben joined him at the window and looked out. All was serene, and he caught a quick glimpse of Molly as she disappeared behind a copse of overgrown walnut trees.

"Someone has been following Molly," said Wesley. "I was intending—in any case—I...Monsieur Dufort, go after her. Right now."

Ben cocked his head. He looked into Wesley's eyes. And then he nodded and took off through the front door and across the meadow, in the direction Molly had last been seen.

Wesley did not stir but kept watching, fretting that he should have gone after her to begin with. Perhaps what I saw was a deer, or some other sort of wild animal, he reasoned, though he did not believe it for one second.

&.

MOLLY WAS ALMOST positive she could hear someone moving around inside the building. She eased up next to the wall, careful not to step on any twigs, and slowly moved to look in the window.

She had to choke back an exclamation, for someone was indeed inside, and to her surprise it was Malcolm Barstow, sitting at a table with some pots and boxes in front of him, bent over and scowling.

Molly whipped her head back out of sight. Well, this is interesting, she thought, trying to decide on her next step. She bent down and scampered under the window, intending to open the door and confront Malcolm.

But before she could put her hand on the door-latch, Vasily Vasiliev appeared, seemingly out of nowhere, and grabbed her by the wrist.

"Not your business," he said.

"Vasily?" said Molly, utterly baffled.

He twisted her arm up behind her back and she cried out.

Inside, Malcolm heard the cry and his head jerked up. Uh oh, he thought, quickly getting to his feet.

"You're always putting your nose where it doesn't belong," said Vasily.

"You speak English!" said Molly accusingly, as though that were his worst crime.

"I am not the stupid oaf you took me for," he said with satisfaction.

"Please let me go," said Molly. "Honestly, I have no idea what this is about. I never thought you were an oaf, anyway—what are you even talking about?"

Vasily did not answer but squinted his eyes, thinking, and then held both of Molly's wrists behind her back. "Come on," he said, tugging her painfully. "If you struggle I will be forced to hurt you, so I suggest you be *docile as little lamb*," he said sneeringly, in the heavy faux-accent Fedosia had been using as a way to inhibit conversation with Molly and the villagers.

Malcolm crept to the door. He knew Vasily had got his hands on Molly and that she needed help. But Vasily terrified him, and his feet moved forward as though underwater.

Vasily was very strong. Hurriedly he pulled Molly toward the forest and she stumbled along, mind racing.

"You yell, you will be very, very sorry," he said, leaning close to speak in her ear.

She fell, and he did not allow her to get up but dragged her through the tall meadow grass. Only forty feet, now thirty, until they were swallowed up by the dark forest. Bobo barked and growled, running back to the building and barking at Malcolm.

"*Help!*" Molly screamed, thrashing her legs trying to slow him down.

"You shut up!" hissed Vasily, pulling her harder.

❧ 43 ❧

From behind the ruined barn, Ben flew out as though shot by a cannon. Malcolm saw him, though not Molly or Vasily, and paused, then raced after Ben, who reached the Russian running at breakneck speed, his body slamming into Vasily and knocking him flat on his back.

"Ben!" cried Molly, but he did not acknowledge her until he had punched Vasily in the face enough times that the other man was no longer moving. Malcolm had managed to call for help and before any of them had time to speak, they heard sirens coming from the direction of the village.

"Thank you," Molly said to Ben in a small voice. He hugged her hard, quickly turning back to make sure Vasily was still out cold.

The ambulance arrived at the scene before the gendarmes, and so after making sure Molly was all right, Ben got in back and rode to the hospital with the man he had just pummeled into unconsciousness. That left Molly and Malcolm standing in the meadow looking at each other in wonderment, neither quite able to understand what had just happened.

"Okay, then," said Molly finally, giving Malcolm an encouraging smile. "I think it's time you told someone what the hell is going on in there."

Malcolm took a deep breath. A snitch was the lowest form of life imaginable, and he had no wish to count himself among them. On the other hand, he would be overjoyed if Vasily were arrested, and could practically taste the relief that would bring.

"Well," he said, trying to make the words come out but not getting very far.

"Why don't you show me?" said Molly. She kept her tone light and friendly, trying not to spook him into silence. As they walked back to the small building, she rubbed her wrists and swiveled her hands around to ease them.

"What in the world is all this stuff?" she said, once they were inside. Boxes lined one wall, pots stood on the table filled with liquid, along with a box of syringes. Malcolm had just mixed up a batch and been filling the syringes—a slow, terribly tedious process—when Vasily grabbed Molly. "Drugs?" she said, seeing the needles.

"Kind of," said Malcolm. Yes, he involved himself in all manner of activity that strictly speaking was against the law, but he had never stooped so low as to deal or take drugs.

"Malcolm. You saw what Vasily just tried to do to me. God knows what he might have done if he'd gotten me into the woods. You've obviously been working for him and for sure you don't want to be dragged down with him. So talk! What have the two of you been up to?"

"It's not just us two," Malcolm protested. "Fedosia is in on it. Lebeau and his friend Alain are in on it. So if anything happens to me, I just want to make sure I'm not the only one doing time. It wasn't even my idea! I hate drugs, Molly. I had a friend...."

Molly waited but Malcolm decided to keep the story of his friend to himself. "And Lebeau?" she said, wonderingly.

"It's not heroin or anything. It's not even that bad, really,"

Malcolm said, edging toward the door, thinking about making a break for it.

"Well?" said Molly, getting impatient.

"It's steroids. You know, bodybuilding drugs. The whole thing is stupid, if you ask me, but some guys are really into getting the huge muscles, and they'll really pay." He stopped, screwing his face up. "At least, that's what Fedosia said anyways."

"So the Vasilievs came to Castillac just to start this up?" Molly couldn't quite believe it. Drug dealers in her pigeonnier! "And Lebeau? What does he have to do with this?"

"He's one of the distributors. And obviously, a user," said Malcolm with a contemptuous laugh.

Molly took out her phone and called the gendarmerie, looking for Monsour. Maron was meeting Ben at the hospital, but someone needed to come gather all this evidence. She was still shaky, the adrenaline having a lingering effect; she couldn't quite catch her breath and didn't feel entirely steady on her feet. But she brushed that aside, remembering with intensely mixed feelings how Ben had rocketed out of nowhere and slammed Vasily to the ground.

And then hit him more than was strictly necessary.

One on hand, it felt wonderful to know he had her back, that he would act quickly and aggressively to protect her. On the other, she felt a little prickly, as though he thought she wasn't able to take care of herself and needed him to ride in on a white charger and save the day.

She understood that in fact, she had needed saving. She just didn't especially like it.

Molly turned back to Malcolm. "How did you get mixed up with these people, anyway? Doesn't really seem your cup of tea."

"Oh, it's not," Malcolm agreed. "My mum is going to be furious with me. It was just...I met Fedosia in the village one day, and she asked me if I could help them out...."

"So out of the kindness of your heart...?"

"Yeah, exactly!" said Malcolm with a crooked grin.

"One more question. Be forthcoming, Malcolm, this one's important."

Malcolm nodded.

"Any connection with Coulon in all this?"

The boy shrugged. "I don't know anything about that. Coulon's crooked, you've probably figured that out by now. Dirty money every which way you look. So it's no shocker that someone killed him, but I haven't heard a peep about who that might have been, I swear."

Molly looked closely at him, and felt satisfied he was telling the truth. It was a funny quality for a kid who had been caught stealing and breaking and entering multiple times—but as far as Molly knew, he was not a liar.

A drug ring, in Castillac. Whoever would have thought?

🦋 44 🦋

Friday, the day of the wedding, broke cloudy with an off and on drizzle. Molly was up early. Her wrists and arms sore from being dragged through the meadow, she felt unsettled, the stress having caused her to fall asleep before Ben had gotten home, still full of far more questions than answers. Drug-dealing, multiple villagers implicated in the scheme, an attempted abduction—but was any of that pertinent to Coulon's murder? It felt as though they kept uncovering wrongdoing in every direction but the one that mattered.

Was Coulon mixed up in the Vasiliev's drug ring as well, and if so, had that gotten him killed? She had no problem imagining Vasily committing the act, not now. But she had nothing to connect him directly to Coulon, nothing but a devious and murderous nature, which did not equal much of anything in the eyes of the law.

With a sudden panic, she realized she had gone to bed the night before without finding out what had happened with Fedosia. She ran to put water on to boil and then woke Ben up.

"Sorry," she said, giving him a quick kiss. "But I just realized —the other half of the criminal enterprise is in the pigeonnier!

Did anyone tell Fedosia that her husband is in the hospital? And according to Malcolm, she was a partner in the whole thing—"

"Monsour took her in. That's probably why you couldn't reach him last night about securing the crime scene in the building up the road."

"I admire your ability to wake up and be coherent right away."

"I was dreaming about you," he said, putting his hands on her shoulders and pulling her closer.

But Molly twisted away and stood up. "I've got a million things to do," she said. "I can't quite believe it, but the wedding's *today*. I'm expecting deliveries any minute and I just realized that I forgot to get Nico's ring from the jeweler's. I'm going to sit down and drink one more cup of coffee and go through my list, see if there's anything else important that I've forgotten. And please—pray it doesn't keep raining?"

Ben watched her leave, knowing she was chattering because there was something she needed to say but was not yet ready to say it. With a sigh, he rolled over, hoping to grab just another fifteen minutes of sleep before facing the day, but as soon as Molly was gone, Bobo jumped on top of him and licked his face.

"Good dog," he said, pushing her out of face-range just as his cell buzzed.

"Bonjour, Dufort," he said, propping himself on an elbow. His hand hurt from the fight with Vasily, his knuckles bruised and tender.

"Vasiliev has made a complaint against you," said Maron, with no preamble. "Look, I understand the circumstances, believe me. But his nose is broken and he has a concussion. The doctor...the doctor said you bashed him up pretty bad."

Ben felt the same rage sweep through him that he had felt when he saw Vasily with Molly. "Are you telling me I did something wrong? That I wasn't completely within my rights to stop him—and make sure he stayed stopped—given what he was attempting to do? If I had been two minutes later, if Wesley Addison hadn't warned me—"

"I just need you to come to the gendarmerie to fill out the paperwork. Don't worry, we'll get it sorted out."

They said goodbye and Ben swung his feet to the floor, angry and sleep-deprived. *The creep had his hands on Molly*, he thought, again feeling an uncomfortable surge of adrenaline.

He came out to the kitchen looking for her. She was just putting her mug in the dishwasher and getting ready to leave.

"I have to go down to the station," he said. "Is there anything you need me to do today to help you get ready? Besides the praying," he added with a smile that Molly did not return.

"Coulon," said Molly simply. "All this drama with the wedding, and the Vasilievs, and drugs...but what we need is Coulon's killer. And correct me if I'm wrong, we have nothing but circumstantial evidence and shaky suppositions to show for our efforts."

Ben took a deep breath to fend off a flash of anger. *Why wasn't she more grateful? Hadn't he stopped her from being dragged into the woods by that thug?*

MOLLY WENT BACK INSIDE to get a slicker in case the rain got worse, then hopped on the scooter and turned the ignition. It did not cough or even sneeze, but made no sound at all. She turned the key again, then again, but it was undeniably and completely dead.

"Dammit!" she muttered under her breath. Pausing, she considered asking Ben to drive her into the village, but shook her head. She just didn't feel like being around him just then. It was not that big a deal to walk.

"Stay, Bobo!" she said, as the dog trotted hopefully with her to the end of the driveway, then turned back with an expression of woe.

I just want to be alone for a few minutes, thought Molly. I need to get my head clear and *think*.

Have I failed to look objectively at Odile, she wondered. It's true that as a fellow divorcée, I felt sympathetic. Maybe too sympathetic. She might have had keys to Coulon's house. She might have come up with any number of reasons to get him up on the second floor—something she'd forgotten to take with her when she moved out, even seducing him for some reason. Her temperament was fiery, possibly to the point of violence. How could she and Ben approach her, what questions could they ask so that she might incriminate herself without realizing it?

Walking quickly past the cemetery, the drizzle intensifying, Molly felt even more dispirited. The very last thing she felt like doing was hosting Frances and Nico's wedding, and knowing that she had volunteered for the job—not to mention the guilt she felt, knowing they were her best friends and deserved her attention and joy that day of all days—did not improve her mood either.

What had happened to Daniel Coulon, anyway? It felt as though he had loomed up out of nowhere but then disappeared, like the elusive whale in Moby Dick, she thought, laughing in spite of herself. The disappearance is somewhat incriminating behavior, thought Molly, unwilling to completely let go of him. Had he returned to his mother in Brittany? Molly did not think pursuing his inheritance would necessitate staying in Castillac; she made a mental note to ask Ben about it later.

It was not yet ten o'clock when Molly turned into the alley, taking a shortcut on the way to Pâtisserie Bujold for a rejuvenating almond croissant before going to pick up the ring at the jeweler's. The drizzle had blessedly backed off and she slowed down, her eyes drifting over the gardens and backyards as they always did when she walked this way.

Then she stopped. She clambered onto a small pile of planks to get a better view. And the realization hit her violently, as though someone had come up behind her and clapped her on the back of the head. It was just like the classic Sherlock Holmes clue: the dog that did not bark, the thing that was not there. She stood for a moment, staring and thinking hard. What she now understood—it wasn't quite enough, she didn't think, for an arrest. Molly was almost certain she was right about what had happened, but they were going to need just a little something extra to prove it. She had a few ideas of what that might be, but would Maron agree to help her find it?

And was there any way to get it done before the wedding?

❧ 45 ❧

Back at La Baraque, Ben was doing some thinking of his own. The events of the day before had clarified some things for him, and as he stood at the window looking out at the meadow, the memory of seeing Molly being dragged through the grass replaying over and over, he nodded slowly to himself.

The doorbell rang and he took the delivery for the wedding food and put it away. The wine and liquor delivery arrived soon after. He kept glancing outside, listening out for Molly, but there was no sign of her.

Wesley Addison came down and made himself tea, and Ben brought him up to date, thanking him profusely. "If you hadn't told me to go that instant..." he said, his English quite good, since he was feeling the memory so strongly he forgot to worry about grammar.

"I am only glad I could help," said Wesley. "Well, I will not keep you. I know the wedding is tonight and you and Molly no doubt have much to take care of."

"Are you..." Ben started, feeling awkward.

"No, I am not invited nor should I have been. Nancy and Emily have invited me to dinner in the village, as a sort of farewell before they leave tomorrow. I believe they have made reservations at La Métairie."

"Ah! Well, you will certainly enjoy the meal. The chef is quite accomplished." Ben was talking but his mind was all the way across town, wondering what Molly was doing and why she had not come back.

"Doubtless whatever Molly makes for the dinner will be most larruping," said Wesley. Ben nodded, not even trying to understand what he was saying.

Then Frances was at the front door, her eyes red, and Ben had no idea what to tell her. "I'm sure she'll be right back, she just mentioned one quick errand...um, is everything all right?"

"All right? Haha! Yes, everything is dandy, Ben! Oh, you mean my eyes? Yeah, I know, it's crazy, I had a little bit of a crying jag this morning when I woke up. Not sad-crying though, it was happy-crying."

Ben nodded, having no idea what she was talking about either.

It was past one. Thirty people were coming at four, the bride looked like she wanted to jump off a bridge, and still no Molly.

Constance came wheeling down the driveway on her bicycle, late for cleaning. "I'm just going to fly through here like a tornado," she said to Ben. "Where the heck is Molls?"

"We have no idea," said Frances. "But I'm not worried. She probably uncovered an international jewel thief when she went to pick up Nico's ring. Once she has him subdued and his entire network under arrest, she'll amble back here, whip up an incredible meal for a big crowd of people, and I don't know, perform a few other magic tricks along the way."

"Sometimes I don't know when you're kidding," said Ben.

"Me neither," said Frances, shrugging. "Anyway, I'm serious when I say I'm not worried. I've been friends with Molly for like twenty-five years, and she's never let me down yet."

"Where's your dress? asked Constance. "I bet it's incredible."

"Nah. Look, this is trip number three down the aisle. You start to get a little spooked by symbolic stuff like wedding dresses when things have gone horribly wrong so many times."

"Constance, how about you get the work out of the way now, so Molly has less to worry about when she gets back?" Ben suggested, trying to get preparations moving in the right direction.

Constance shot Ben a look and went off to find the vacuum cleaner.

Frances took a long, deep breath and wondered whether having a shot of whiskey would be bad luck.

A rap on the door and Madame Angevin came in holding a gorgeous bouquet of pink roses. "Congratulations, chérie," she said to Frances. "I'm going to see if this can fit in the refrigerator. You don't want to walk down the aisle with a wilted bouquet!"

Next Lawrence swept in. "Ben, can I have a word?" he said, after exchanging the necessary kisses and greetings all around. The two men stepped into the corridor. "I heard from Molly. Apparently your phone is dead?"

Ben's eyes bugged out. He took his cell out of his pocket and saw that indeed, it did not show a pulse. "Mon Dieu," he muttered.

"Happens to the best of us," said Lawrence. "Listen, Molly has been at the station talking to Maron. She's pretty sure she's figured out who killed Coulon—and she didn't go into details with me, damn her soul—but there's some piece of it Maron has to take care of. She asked me to tell you she's on her way home, and the wedding should be able to go ahead on schedule."

"No details at all?"

"Zero. I tried, my friend, believe me. But she was in a great hurry so we didn't talk long. I was already on my way over to help Madame Langevin with the flowers, and get the music set up. I offered to pick her up, but for some reason she insisted on walking back. Anyway, she should be here in ten minutes at the outside."

Constance was the picture of industry as she went over the living room rug and even, as opposed to her usual practice, vacuuming under the sofas. Thomas showed up and set up the bar outside, Lawrence and Madame Langevin took bowls of flowers out to the tables, Frances had disappeared with a bottle of Jameson's, and there was nothing for Ben to do but wait and wonder.

❦ 46 ❧

"I know, it seemed like such an extravagance," Molly was saying to Lawrence as she put four enormous bowls of salad into a second refrigerator in a utility room off the main corridor of her house. "But for moments like your best friend getting married, having a second refrigerator is an absolute must!"

"I'm going to tell you, because we're old pals, that your voice is rattling on about an octave higher than usual. Are you going to tell me what's going on?"

"Can't!" said Molly, flashing Lawrence a grin. "Would you put candles on the tables? They're in the closet of the room in the new addition. And be ready with matches or a lighter or something when it gets dark. You're the best!" she said, giving him a loud kiss. He gave her an exaggerated scowl.

"I don't know how Ben puts up with you, I really don't."

Molly shrugged. "There's just not time right now. Let me get the last of the wedding stuff done, take a shower, get dressed—and even then, it would be so rude to overshadow Nico and Frances's big day with a bunch of talk about a murder investigation. And you know it."

Lawrence laughed. "It's not like they met you yesterday, dear one. Even if you managed to get through the entire night without uttering a single word about Coulon, don't you think Nico and Frances would know very well that you're thinking about it? Just tell Ben and me, and I promise to stop harassing you. Just give us the name, chérie."

"You're relentless! Now I'm beginning to understand how you always know what's going on in the village. You hound people until blood starts pouring out of their ears!"

"What an unsavory vision," said Lawrence with a sniff. "Ben has been setting up the chairs. I'll go get him, and you can at least give us a big hint. Please?"

Molly shook her head. "I've got to get the steaks ready, there's the—"

"It will take three minutes!"

"Oh, all right. Get Ben while I season the steaks and check on the grills. But first, check to see how Nico is doing? I told him he could hide in the annex until the ceremony is ready to start. He's very sweetly superstitious about seeing Frances beforehand."

"Will do," said Lawrence, wasting not a second.

In ten minutes Ben was hustling along after Lawrence and they met Molly outside, around the corner of the building, where none of the people working to decorate, clean, and set up for the wedding could hear them.

"I can't believe I had to strong-arm you into telling your own partner," said Lawrence indignantly.

Ben looked amused. "I've learned that Molly has her own timetable, and it's best not to try to force her onto yours."

"Well, you're disgustingly understanding. Okay Molly, out with it for God's sake. What did you figure out? Who killed the mayor?"

"I don't one hundred per cent know, not yet. And I'm sort of amazed I didn't realize it sooner. It's sort of a long story which is why I wanted to wait, but here goes the short version: before I got the scooter, I walked into the village almost every day, sometimes more than once. And a lot of those times, well, most of them actually, I was on my way to Pâtisserie Bujold, and so I cut through the alley that comes out on rue des Chênes on the edge of the village."

Ben and Lawrence listened, mystified.

"And all right, I snooped a little bit, looking into people's backyards. I peered over some walls, curious about what was behind them. And I noticed, starting right when I moved to Castillac almost two years ago, that someone was hanging some very fancy lingerie on the line in the backyard of one of the houses. La Perla is the brand—it's quite expensive, quite luxurious. And you know, it made me wonder. I mean, you know I love Castillac from the bottom of my heart, but I would not say—no insult intended—that it is chock full of glamorous wealthy women who look like they might be have La Perla on underneath."

"*Molly!*" shouted a rather desperate-sounding voice.

"Oh—that's Frances. She sounds on the brink of something," said Molly. "I'll finish this story later. Just hang on, and let's see if Maron gets anywhere—"

And then she was off, leaving Lawrence and Ben standing in the corridor with bemused faces, painfully frustrated, wondering how in the world fancy underwear could possibly have anything to do with the death of Maxime Coulon.

❧ 47 ❧

Molly ran to her bedroom where Frances was getting dressed.

"You're fine, right?" she said, smiling at her friend, who looked absolutely stunning in a simple white silk sheath, lips a luscious red, jet-black hair brushing her shoulders.

Frances took a slug of Jameson's out of the bottle. "Giddy," she said. "I'm giddy, I'm nuts, I'm utterly and madly in love—"

"You're done with this," said Molly, laughing, nimbly plucking the bottle from Frances's hands.

"Oh, it's not the whiskey making me talk this way. I'm fine, I really am. But I feel like I'm one of those cliff divers, you know, from South America? The ones who sail out from an impossible height to dive into that blue, blue water? It's a wonder they aren't all killed," she added under her breath.

"Fear and love, they're connected very closely," said Molly. "Can't have one without the other."

"Oh, we're back to Molly, Zen Priestess again?"

The two friends hugged, holding back tears so that their eye makeup wasn't ruined before the ceremony.

"Ready?" asked Molly.

Frances nodded, still fighting back a sob.

Meanwhile, in a mad flurry, with newly arriving guests pitching in to get everything organized, the tables had been dried and beautifully decorated. Lawrence had a string quartet playing on his boom box. Guests were relieved to see that the bride had not absconded, and Frances began greeting her French friends with her usual warmth and sometimes mystifying humor. Nico, the long-suffering groom, waited impatiently in the annex for Lawrence to give him the signal. Alphonse, owner of Chez Papa, had been tapped to perform the ceremony, and he waited nervously, rehearsing his lines under his breath even though he had everything written down.

As Molly surveyed the yard, she couldn't help feeling satisfied. Somehow—with a lot of help, actually—she had managed to pull it off. People were munching happily on hors d'oeuvres and drinking kirs, laughing and telling stories. The place looked lovely and very suited to Frances's wishes—it wasn't fussy, but only tables with plain white tablecloths, some bowls of pink roses, and a ribbon on the tree under which they planned to say their vows. The tiny dinosaurs held or propped up place cards. Bobo sported a red ribbon on her collar, which Molly had cleared with Frances in case it was too cute, but with the ceremony only a half hour away, the bride was surprisingly calm, given the intermittent bouts of hysteria over the last few months anytime the subject of marriage came up.

Ben and Lawrence kept their distance from Molly, but they both noticed that she continually checked her phone, presumably for texts from Maron. Lapin and Anne-Marie told the story of their elopement and made everyone laugh and then cry. Manette's husband found his pregnant wife a chair, then got another for Madame Gervais, who at a hundred and four had good reason not to stay on her feet for too long at a time, and they and the rest of the villagers picked the plates of hors d'oeuvres clean.

Alphonse did a lovely job; the ceremony proceeded like most, with tears springing up all over the place and a glowing bride looking at her new husband with unadulterated joy while he appeared to be the happiest of men. Molly was of course as glad as anyone, though she acknowledged a whisper of sadness too, because no matter how happy you are for a good friend, a big event like this in someone else's life can make you feel a bit left behind.

And just like that, Frances and Nico were married. After serving champagne, Molly went to the three grills (two of which were borrowed) and threw steaks onto the perfectly timed coals. She checked her phone again, but still no word from Maron.

"Okay, it's time," Ben said, joining her by the grills.

"I know. If it hadn't been for all this," she said, gesturing to the crowd, "we'd have been able to talk it all through. So I'm sorry if it's felt like I left you out. Well, I *did* leave you out. I suppose I'm hoping that Maron will get in touch and I'll be able to present the whole thing to you with no loose threads."

"That's not how our business works. Not how a partnership works."

"You're right," she said. She should have simply paused the wedding prep and told him everything. How could he not be furious with her? She flipped a steak and gave him a sidelong glance, but Ben did not look angry. Though perhaps at the limit of his patience.

"Okay, come close so no one can eavesdrop....are you kidding, you know perfectly well everyone in this village is a master eavesdropper!"

Ben laughed and slipped his arm around her, bending his ear close.

"I was telling you about the La Perla underwear that had always been a mystery to me. Especially early on, when I'd just moved here, I would be at the Saturday market and look around, wondering who was wearing it. Okay, maybe that is not particularly normal behavior, I understand that. But here's the thing: I never thought to figure out which house that clothesline belonged to. I never once counted how many houses that backyard was from the corner, and then walked around and counted on the street-side to see whose house it was. I guess I sort of enjoyed savoring the mystery, you know?"

Ben waited, resisting the urge to push her to go more quickly.

"But so this morning I was walking through the alley, and I realized that I had not seen the La Perla hanging on the line for a while. Today I finally counted the houses and walked around the block to see whose house it was. Right, one guess—it was *Coulon's.*"

"But Molly, you know how Castillac is. If an unmarried man had women's underthings hanging on the line, people would talk."

"Right, they would. But the backyard isn't open, it's a walled garden. For me to see the lingerie in the first place, I had to climb on a rock or a stack of planks so I could see over the wall. From time to time I'd peek over, just checking to see if it was still there, but it's not like just anyone could see it as they strolled along the alley, you had to be a little snoopacious. And before you mention the neighbors—the person living to the right is in bad health, and probably not using the upper floor of her house where she could look down into Coulon's backyard. And I'm pretty sure the house on the other side has been empty for some time."

She gave Ben a look of triumph as she turned three more steaks, the grease making the flames shoot up.

"I'm sorry, you're going to have to spell it out. Coulon lived alone. Are you saying he had a mistress or a secret girlfriend living with him?"

"No! We've asked those questions all over the village and no one has said one word about any girlfriends—I'm not saying it's impossible, but we have no evidence for that at all."

"Are you saying Coulon wore the underwear himself?" he asked, eyes widening.

"No, not that either! Listen—we searched the mayor's house,

remember? If some girlfriend had been keeping things there, or Coulon had been wearing it, we'd have seen it. The underwear would have been in a bureau somewhere. But there was nothing. No lingerie in that house anywhere. I checked all the drawers in all the rooms, remember?"

"And so? Where is this taking you?"

"The only woman who regularly went into the Coulon house, as the neighbors all told us, was Josette Barbeau."

"Josette Barbeau," said Ben slowly. "You're saying she and the mayor were having an affair? The Josette with an alibi from Rémy and no apparent motive, unlike the rest of our list?"

"Yes, that Josette," said Molly. "I don't have to tell you that this business of ours is not about feelings or premonitions. But when I stood outside 1 rue Malbec and realized that the mayor's house was the La Perla house all this time, I *knew* it was Josette. I'll make any bet you want to name that she killed him. And then took the fancy underwear with her."

"So how are you going to prove it?"

"Well, I called Rémy and leaned on him. At first he was stubborn, but when I pushed harder, he admitted that on Thursdays and Mondays he does errands off the farm, sometimes including outreach with other farmers. He did go to the Barbeau farm to talk to Julien about those chickens—but he could have mistaken last Monday for the Thursday before. Just a few days apart, a mistake anyone could make."

"Okay, so her alibi is a little shakier. She still has her mother and brother standing by her."

"You know we can't trust family members in a case like this. Hell, *I'd* probably lie to protect some people really close to me."

"It's just…I don't want to slam your idea, Molly, but you're still working on supposition here."

"What if Maron finds La Perla underwear at the Barbeau farm? Would that convince you?"

"That steak is about to burn, Molly," said Ben, pointing. "And actually, no, it wouldn't convince me, not by a long shot. All that would tell us was that she took some underwear. Where is the motive, even if she was having an affair with him?"

Molly stabbed the steak and put it on a waiting platter. "I know, I know, the whole thing isn't all the way sewn up," she said. "But you have to admit, it would mean she's been lying. Which leads to the inevitable question of what else she might be lying about? All we can do now is wait to see what Maron finds," she said. "But I have to tell you, I'm feeling pretty good about our chances."

They looked around at the party, which was humming along without their help, a jubilant Nico and Frances at the center. The sun was drifting toward the horizon and the light was soft on everyone's faces. Molly saw the tail of the orange cat sticking out from underneath a table, and hoped it did not bite anyone's ankle during dinner.

"I think we've pulled it off," she said, grinning at her partner. "Life is good."

Ben tucked a wild curl behind one of Molly's ears. "Will you marry me?" he asked, before he realized what he was saying.

❧ 48 ❧

Josette had a small bag packed and was waiting in the barn for Julien to return in the truck and pick her up. She made no excuse at all to Maman, even knowing full well that Maman would be driven wild when she discovered that her children were gone—that they had left for good without a word.

Josette hummed to herself, looking forward to the journey. And then, with the force of a thunderous wave slamming down on the beach, she remembered what she had done.

She had killed a man.

Her brain formed the sentence and she knew in her conscious mind that it was true—knew even that it was the reason she was standing in the barn with a small bag at her feet—and yet it seemed absurd and unbelievable. Slowly she remembered what had happened after she had done it.

Julien had been having breakfast at the Café de la Place, and hurried over in the truck to the mayor's house when she called. As they drove away from the mayor's house for the last time, all of the La Perla lingerie stuffed into her straw bag, Josette tried at first to keep from telling him anything, but she could not come up with a reason why she had called for a ride home when she had only been at work for an hour. Not to mention that her brother noticed blood spattered on her arm and pressed her.

"Josette, you've got to tell me what happened. I can't help you if you don't tell me."

"I..."

"Did he hurt you? Is *he* hurt? Whose blood is that?" The truck sped erratically down the narrow road as Julien kept looking over at Josette.

"It's...um..."

"Look, you know I've got your back, no matter what. I just need to know what we're dealing with here."

Josette nodded and tears began to slide down her cheeks. "I didn't mean to. Well, I sort of did," she said.

"Mean to *what?*"

"He was going to get me in trouble. Like, really really *bad* trouble, with the gendarmes. But it's...it wasn't just that. He...he said he would never marry me. And after..." she drifted off, staring out of the window at the sunflowers about to bloom.

"Josette! Tell me what happened!"

"I killed him," she said simply, and then laughed because it sounded so implausible. "I slit his throat like he was a chicken."

Julien gasped. He gave his sister strict instructions to take a shower the minute they got home— no, even better, go to the pond and have a swim. He had seen a TV show once where forensics had been able to get blood samples out of a shower drain, so better safe than sorry. "If they find even a speck of his blood on you, you're sunk," he told her, knowing it would frighten her but not wanting her to be sloppy.

Josette had followed his instructions and even, for some moments, enjoyed her swim, floating on her back looking up at the cloudless sky, happy that she would never have to see Coulon ever again. She thought about Lebeau instead, about how tightly he had held her around the waist, and tossed her up on his shoulders where the other girls had looked at her enviously.

It's not like she had planned it. It was simply the way events had unfolded, almost like finding herself in a movie, swept along in a story she did not write.

The next morning she had gone to look for some lipgloss in her bag and found the balled-up La Perla, the frilly pink matching set that she'd been wearing when the surge of violence overtook her. It was grotesquely decorated with the mayor's blood, and Josette did not need Julien to tell her she had to get rid of it immediately, no matter how much she would have liked to keep all of the beautiful underwear for her own. She stood thinking, and finally decided that the pond would be a good place to put it. With a grimace she picked it up, balling it up as tight as she could, and slipped out the side door of the house before Maman could ask what she was up to or give her a chore that had to be done that second.

Walking along the dirt path along the side of the field, she wondered: was she going to end up in prison after all? Maybe she deserved it. She knew it was wrong to kill another person—not just legally wrong, but morally so. But what if the person was horrible? Was she supposed to suffer on and on forever, putting up with his horribleness into infinity?

In Josette's mind, options were very limited and always had been. All she knew how to do was try to escape whatever punishment was coming her way, however she could. All she could do was react to what was happening to her, even though this strategy had been working less and less well the older she got.

On that fateful morning, Coulon had berated her from the minute she entered his house. He criticized her coffee, said the spoons were tarnished, and mocked her for hinting about marriage. All of that, Josette was willing to endure, knowing that her family needed the money she earned at the mayor's, and being unable to find a way to stand up for herself.

But then he had followed her into the guest room where, on his direction, she was about to change the pillowcases even though no one had slept in the bed, and he had grabbed her like she was nothing but a plaything, not even human. Josette had an instant vision of her future, trapped in Coulon's house forever, never having love or even a pet goat, but only her employer's unwanted attentions and contempt.

She snatched up a curtain pin from the top of the dresser and cut him without thinking. And on the whole, she admitted only to herself, she was not sorry.

When she reached the pond, she looked around for some rocks and found them easily. She wrapped the rocks in the pink and bloody underwear, and threw the bundles out into the pond as far as she could.

For a long time she stood at the edge of the water, her shoes getting damp, listening to the cries of birds in the distance, and watching the rings in the water pulse outward until the surface was flat and it was as though nothing had ever disturbed it.

❧ 49 ❧

Molly stood by the grill, frozen, unable to believe what Ben had just asked her. "Really? Marry you?" she said, with wide eyes, and he laughed, taking the fork out of her hand and pulling her close.

At that moment they both felt her cellphone vibrate. Molly grabbed it from her pocket.

"What's Maron say?" asked Ben.

"It's not him," said Molly wonderingly. "It's Malcolm Barstow, telling me to get to the train station right away." She paused. "He doesn't say why...but I trust him."

"I'm coming with you," said Ben, and though Molly hesitated for just an instant, she quickly waved for him to follow her.

"Can we take your car?" she asked. "I'll text Lawrence and ask him to take over hosting duties. Frances and Nico will be fine. Hurry!"

Ben was an expert driver but Molly had never seen him in action before. They flew down rue des Chênes, zipped around the edge of the village to the west, and got to the train station before Molly got any answer to her text back to Malcolm, asking for details.

As they hurried out of the car with no idea what they might find in the station, Ben wished he had his pistol. "Wait," he said urgently. "Slow down. Let's try and see what the situation is before we go rushing in."

Using every bit of willpower she could muster, Molly stopped running and let Ben walk slightly ahead of her. He *was* trained, after all.

Ben slipped into the building using the door farthest to one side. A train had arrived five minutes earlier, and travelers were already streaming through the station. Molly followed, looking everywhere for Malcolm. They searched the waiting room and the small café attached to it, but saw nothing out of the ordinary and no one they recognized.

Molly ran through the doors to the platforms, and caught the barest glimpse of Josette Barbeau disappearing into a car of the waiting train.

"Ben! Hurry!" They tore down the platform and reached the door to the train just as the conductor hopped on board to prepare for departure. Ben did some quick talking and they were allowed to board.

They found Josette sitting next to Julien, three cars down.

Molly stopped for a moment, feeling a pang of sadness, knowing in her heart that Josette had committed a terrible crime, but wishing she could somehow be brought to justice without inflicting so much pain on her brother. She turned to look at Ben, and instinctively he understood what she was thinking and looked sad as well, and then nodded that it was time to act.

Molly walked to where the Barbeaus were sitting and dropped into an empty seat across from them. The train lurched twice and began to glide out of the station.

"Josette," she said, simply.

"Well bonjour, Molly!" said Julien, falsely hearty. "I'm afraid I've got nothing to sell at the moment! I'm taking Josette on a little trip, just a few nights away. It can get boring for her, stuck on the farm with Maman day after day. Where are you off to?"

Josette shrank into the seat. She pulled her feet up under her and curled her body as small as she could make it, not looking at anyone.

"Come on, Josie," said Julien, but his tone was hopeless. He could see she had no fight left in her.

"I didn't really mean to do it," said Josette, still not making eye contact. "Doesn't that count for something?"

❧ 50 ❧

The next night, the entire wedding crew—minus Nico and Frances, who were off on their honeymoon to parts unknown—plus a number of other villagers, showed up at Chez Papa to get the full story and latest news on the mayor's murder. Uncomfortably, Maron found himself the focus of everyone's attention as he related what had happened on his visit to the Barbeau farm the day before.

"I heard they were halfway to Brive, making a run for it!" said Claudine Brosset, who was drinking a beer with Annette. "And she used a curtain pin, of all things!"

"They *are* awfully sharp," said another woman who worked at the mairie.

"Come on," said a fellow who had been tirelessly working to get Lebeau elected to the council. "We deserve to know the details, the mayor was a public figure, after all."

"Hear hear!"

Maron put up his palm to quiet everyone. He couldn't help wishing he were about to tell the story of his own accomplishment, instead of Molly Sutton's. But he took a breath and soldiered on. "I was given some information by someone I'm sure most of you know, at least by reputation, Madame Sutton." He nodded in Molly's direction and she could not stop herself from blushing, though it made her feel ridiculous.

"I went to the Barbeau farm and undertook a thorough search. What you may not realize is that the investigation into Coulon's murder uncovered a number of other crimes that had taken place or were still ongoing. I'm afraid our mayor was something of a fraud. He was involved in money-laundering and taking kickbacks from various sources, and this sort of thing takes time to investigate. With only two officers, you can understand—" Maron paused and took a sip of his wine. "Anyway, it turned out that the corruption was not the central part of the case and had nothing to do with his murder. After receiving Molly's tip, I found several pieces of evidence at the farm that had not been suspected previously. That is all I am free to say at this point. The trial, obviously enough, is still a ways away."

Molly took Ben's hand and smiled. Of course she was thrilled that Maron had found a bag of La Perla underwear hidden in the barn, but by that time she and Ben had already caught up with the Barbeaus on the train and heard Josette's confession. Besides the bag in the barn, Josette told Molly and Ben, there was a pair of frilly pink panties and a camisole at the bottom of the pond. Maron had waded in and ducked under the water to get it, and though it had been underwater for many days, the bloodstains were unmistakeable.

Also included in the new evidence was a silver sugar bowl that had been stuffed under the seat of the truck.

"What about Julien?" someone called out.

"I'm afraid we had to take him in as well. He drove her home after the murder and was trying to help her get out of the country, though they had not yet managed to get passports. Allow me to interject here that I'm disappointed in all of you that not a single person saw either of the Barbeaus the day of the mayor's murder. The investigation would have gone much more smoothly if her alibi had been shaky from the beginning," he said, sending a quick dirty look in the direction of Rémy, who looked down at his shoes.

"I guess we can forget the Bresse chickens," Molly heard someone say, and she felt another stab of sadness about the young man, who seemed like the one Barbeau with a truly kind heart, and who was getting dragged under because he had tried to help his sister.

"I can't help thinking of Stendhal," said Lawrence quietly.

Molly gave him a questioning look.

"A famous quote of his, that beauty is '*la promesse de bonheur*'— the promise of happiness. I think I might say that the promise is very often not realized. Josette's loveliness was her undoing, don't you think?"

Molly shrugged. "I don't know. Lives are complicated. You can't boil things down to their essence quite like that, I don't think."

"Hm," said Lawrence, musing.

Malcolm Barstow caught Molly's eye and winked at her. She grinned and nodded. For an inveterate thief, he had turned out to be quite helpful, even if he had acted at least somewhat out of guilt for not coming to Molly's rescue when she was attacked by Vasily Vasiliev. He had been hanging out at the train station looking to pick a few pockets of the evening train travelers, and overheard Josette and Julien talking quietly about how they could get passports before Maron caught up with them—and he figured that was a conversation Molly might be very interested in.

Ben squeezed her hand, and with the case finally disposed of, Molly was lit up once again with the memory of the night before and Ben's blurted-out proposal by the grill. When they had returned to La Baraque after leaving Josette and Julien in the care of Monsour, the wedding guests had all gone home. They decided to leave the mess of the party for the morning. Ben had taken Molly in his arms and explained that when he saw Vasily holding her wrists and trying to wrestle her into the forest, he had realized with perfect clarity that he did not want to live without her. And Molly, despite (or perhaps because of) all of her moaning about being sick of the subject of marriage, did not need any persuasion.

They agreed to keep the news just between themselves, for a little while, enjoying the pleasure of a shared secret, and Molly grinned hard there in Chez Papa, knowing what a juicy tidbit of gossip they were holding back from everyone.

"But what I want to know," said Madame Tessier to Molly, "is why didn't you ever ask anyone about the La Perla underwear, if you'd been wondering about it all that time?"

Molly shrugged. "I don't know. I guess…Castillac is my home now, and I feel like I've been given a very warm welcome. But maybe if I started asking what kind of underwear everyone's wearing, that might be going a little far, even for an American?"

Madame Tessier laughed. She admired Molly's investigative skills, and always felt a little envious that she herself had never pulled off the solution to a crime.

"What about all the rest of it?" an older man asked from the bar, his tone on the unfriendly side. "Why has Castillac suddenly become the center of all this corruption and drug-dealing? We used to be a quiet, peaceful community."

Others murmured agreement.

"It will help when we have a mayor who is not involved in these sorts of things," said Monsour, happy to pipe up about his own contribution. "He was blocking business permits both for his own vendettas and for kickbacks. We've opened an investigation into his connection to the black market as well. Is it any wonder that a pair of thugs like the Vasilievs—and Lebeau too, let's be honest here—would choose such a village to start up their business? They probably believed the mayor could be bought off and they could skate along doing whatever they wanted. And they nearly got away with it, too." He was about to add that

Dufort/Sutton Investigations had helped to crack that case as well, but decided they'd gotten enough credit for one evening.

Lawrence watched Molly with Ben. He noticed that she looked pleased when Maron gave her credit for catching Josette, but also that she looked a little distracted, as though her mind was somewhere else. She leaned back into Ben and he wrapped his arms around her.

Something's going on, Lawrence thought. And somehow, I'm going to find a way to get to the bottom of it. But first, another Negroni to celebrate the end of a *very* long week.

THE END

ALSO BY NELL GODDIN

The Third Girl (Molly Sutton Mysteries 1)

The Luckiest Woman Ever (Molly Sutton Mysteries 2)

The Prisoner of Castillac (Molly Sutton Mysteries 3)

Murder for Love (Molly Sutton Mysteries 4)

The Château Murder (Molly Sutton Mysteries 5)

Murder on Vacation (Molly Sutton Mysteries 6)

An Official Killing (Molly Sutton Mysteries 7)

Death in Darkness (Molly Sutton Mysteries 8)

No Honor Among Thieves (Molly Sutton Mysteries 9)

GLOSSARY

Chapter 1: gîte...rental unit, usually by the week

Chapter 2: mairie...city hall
    VAT... Value-Added Tax

Chapter 5: chérie...dear

Chapter 7: pâtisserie...pastry shop

Chapter 10: épicerie...small neighborhood grocery

Chapter 11: au revoir...goodbye

Chapter 12: brébis...sheep's cheese

Chapter 13: les femmes...women

Chapter 15: apéro...cocktail

Chapter 18: terroir...territory, specifically a region where a particular product is grown or produced

ma beauté...my beauty

Chapter 23: centime...cent

Chapter 25: comme ci comme ça...so-so (literally, like this like that)

ACKNOWLEDGMENTS

Once again, truckloads of thanks to Tommy Glass and Nancy Kelley. You are the *best*.

ABOUT THE AUTHOR

Nell Goddin has worked as a radio reporter, SAT tutor, short-order omelet chef, and baker. She tried waitressing but was fired twice.

Nell grew up in Richmond, Virginia and has lived in New England, New York City, and France. Currently she's back in Virginia with teenagers and far too many pets. She has degrees from Dartmouth College and Columbia University.

www.nellgoddin.com
nell@nellgoddin.com

Made in the USA
Las Vegas, NV
19 March 2022

45905812R00184